A SONG OF SALVATION

Books by Alechia Dow
available from Inkyard Press

The Sound of Stars
The Kindred
A Song of Salvation

A SONG OF SALVATION

ALECHIA DOW

ISBN-13: 978-1-335-45372-3

A Song of Salvation

For questions and comments about the quality of this book, please contact us at CustomerService@Harlequin.com.

Inkyard Press
22 Adelaide St. West, 41st Floor
Toronto, Ontario M5H 4E3, Canada
www.InkyardPress.com

Printed in U.S.A.

To the stars that shine and the black holes that devour.

A PROLOGUE

Written and Performed by Rubin Rima

Everyone has a different story of how our universe began.

I've heard several myths from elders I've met on my many journeys over the years. What can I say? I'm a curious being. The most persistent theory is that bacteria collided with particles floating aimlessly in space. That collision created interstellar creatures that could see and shape the future. These creatures, called the Jadu, were in a constant and painful state of forming and reforming. They were hungry, alone, afraid.

Until, by chance, the Jadu found something magical: stardust. Fragments of life, death, and everything in between.

Stardust gave them solidity and satisfied their hunger. And with stardust, they could do anything... Trouble was, the universe needed stars to have a constant source of stardust—and in turn, stars could never foster life without stardust. So the Jadu made gods who could create stars, create life, and keep the Jadu fed.

Sounds ridiculous, right?

Yet, it's the one story told in every culture from Minor Sidarra to Maru Monchuri still being told.

Regardless, I think we can all agree, where once there was silence, now there is a symphony.

Some believe all of this is because of gods that the Jadu created, and others don't. There is no right and wrong. But I hope—I *need* you to exercise compassion and keep an open mind. Because otherwise, this story will mean nothing to you. And that'd be a real shame.

So let's start with The First Chaos, and let's do it in a not boring way.

Once upon a time, there was a god named Indigo.

They could create life through songs.

They created whole solar systems with a movement, an aria, a melody... Yet, the more they created, the more the universe needed balance.

Thus began the chaos. Stars began to disappear. Some will tell you that Indigo forgot their notes, but that's not true. Indigo did too much, too fast, and the universe reacted accordingly.

Ozvios, the god of Destruction, was born.

Ozvios was like a black hole—his sole purpose was to devour worlds. His power was immense and growing stronger with each life he destroyed. And as Ozvios thrived, Indigo became weak.

These two opposing gods could not exist simultaneously

or peacefully on principle. Worlds fell into nothingness, until finally, Indigo and Ozvios faced off in a final battle.

Indigo, determined to save the last of their worlds, relied on all their creations. If they joined together in unity, they could defeat Ozvios. And they did. They sang a song so harmonious Ozvios vanished. Peace came to the universe at last and Indigo faded away, no longer needed.

The gods, it seemed, were gone.

But that's not where this story ends. No, I already called this the prologue, so keep up! This is where I beg you to posit: What if the gods, who may or may not even exist, never perished?

What if they were biding their time, waiting for the right opportunity to clash again?

And what if Ozvios chose a new path of destruction, one through colonization and manipulation?

And what if Indigo no longer wanted to save us all?

That's where this story begins.

PART I

WELCOME TO THE UNIVERSE

CHAPTER ONE

Zaira

"Every line in every love song is about her. She's the stars in my eyes and we've never even met."

—Allister Daniels, unfinished songs

Tomorrow night I will die and yet my hands remain as still as stone.

Since I was born, I've been told that I'll hold the universe in my grasp and I must never shake. Even when the world around me is unsteady.

Never shake. Never falter.

Nevertheless, my insides are currently flipping and fluttering at the alarm wailing in my mind. I've barely lived and I'm doomed to die tomorrow. Acid rises up my throat and I stare down at my lunch sitting untouched in front of me. I should eat. I'm ravenous. And yet I can't.

"Zaira." My grandmother's voice cuts through my thoughts. "Your emotions are loud."

I chuckle mirthlessly, my bracelet thudding against the table as I pick up the fork beside my plate. "The curse of being an Andarran, I would imagine."

Her bright gray eyes pierce mine as she smiles. Her light brown skin shimmers against the white dress—a style we both wear for her upcoming period of mourning. "Do you know, that's my favorite part of being an Andarran?"

"Really? Not the fact that you see the future and past simultaneously?" I cock an eyebrow. "If I could see the future—"

"You would be less morose," she says quickly, glancing at my food and then back at me. "Eat. We have plans, my darling, and they will require energy."

"Yes, *Arja*." The Mal Aresian title of grandmother leaves my lips with all the respect she deserves. As an Andarran, she's eternal, and the only living family I have left. Though we aren't related by blood or race, we're related by choice. By need.

Despite the knots in the pit of my gut, I shovel the flavorless prota mash into my mouth. Unlike her, I may not know what lies ahead, but I do know I need to be strong for it.

"I must tend to the Ilori," she admits with a grimace. "We cannot afford to alienate them yet."

"Why? It's not going to stop them from killing me like they killed my people." My voice cracks, and I swallow the rising anger. The Ilori colonizers have long controlled Mal Ares, my home planet. They slowly starved its inhabitants to death, and those who didn't die naturally met their end in ways I'd rather not think about. Ways that were unfair and unjustified. Punishable, if anyone in the universe cared.

"Behave, Zaira." She rises from her seat, holding my gaze. "Trust me."

I dip my head at her command and wait until her footsteps retreat down the hall before sneaking off.

Under the constant night sky and in a tattered jumpsuit that doesn't cover my long legs, I leave the crumbling palace on the hill and head for the thicket of dead, dry trees. They're remnants of a time long ago when Indigo made this planet to be lush and full of life. When Indigo was a god bursting with power and a desire to create beauty.

Indigo could save this world, but instead they died and were reborn into a Mal Aresian body.

Mine.

Indigo's black constellations swirl upon my skin, so faint one might easily overlook the markings, unless they knew what they meant. That I am power enclosed in the body of a teenager, with the universe Indigo created printed upon it as a reminder of whose name I bear.

Sadly, that's all the god gave me. I haven't acquired Indigo's power or memory—anything that would be helpful in saving my planet and its people. And unless I manage not to die tomorrow, I never will. But I doubt the Ilori will suddenly change their minds, finding a way for me to be useful to them after all—not when my existence poses a threat to their god, Ozvios, remaining in power.

A cool breeze nips at my cheeks and I hurry up toward the mausoleum, careful as I tread through the dirt. The Ilori always have their eyes on me wherever I go, but once I'm inside the mausoleum, I'll be hidden in the crushing darkness. My eyes can adjust to the lack of light here, but the Ilori can't. They may be powerful, but their power could never touch nightweaving.

The door squeals open and I dart through, letting it whoosh shut behind me. There are so few intact structures left on this world, and this one has endured out of sheer will.

And magic.

"Zaira," the shadows whisper my name.

"Family," I say, bowing to the floor. "I have come to you on my last day to beg your forgiveness." My knees sink into the cold earth and I keep my eyes cast downward. "I have failed you. I have not lived up to the god within me."

"Shh," one shadow cries out, and I instantly recognize the voice. A chill creeps up my spine and I gasp. Her presence circles me in an embrace. The woman who gave me life. Halsiba. Not a mother, no, a carrier. My eyes close and the world around me drifts away, replaced by the time before. When this world was vibrant and beautiful instead of dead and dusty. When it was full of people and houses and...*life*.

The time before the Ilori.

The vision settles into place and I let out a long exhale as the magic washes over me.

Halsiba's frigid finger lifts my chin. "See me." I slowly open my eyes, meeting her gaze. She smiles down at me. Dark brown skin, gold eyes, thick body, and voluminous curls tucked into a bun. I look like her daughter. Her skin glimmers in the light of the flickering nano chandeliers hovering above us. The room is all yellows, oranges, and reds of tapestries covering the walls that match the traditional garb worn by Mal Aresians. Children chase each other giggling, and my people sit in beautiful, ornate gold chairs playing games and drinking sweet drinks. Eating foods that no longer exist here. The delicious scent fills my nostrils. It smells so much better than the prota mash from my lunch.

But it's not real for me. It's only real for them. They are trapped in time. Trapped in the magic. Trapped on a crumbling world with a dying core.

"Come, child." Halsiba steps back, her long ocher caftan billowing in the warm wind. I follow her through the hall and stop in a square of starlight. Back when the stars shone brightly here, when there were more stars than ever. "You are our greatest dreams come true. You are the last of the nightweavers—of our kind—gifted with the power of Indigo. Your existence could never be a failure."

I shake my head. "The Ilori will kill me tomorrow for their god—"

"Ozvios will never be as strong as you. That is why he hides behind the Ilori, commanding them to kill all who pose a threat to his power. He is a coward. Look what they have done." She gestures to the world that no longer exists in reality. All of these people, my people, are dead. The children running and laughing, the mothers, fathers, parents, grandparents… Murdered by the Ilori.

The nightweavers were the magical inhabitants of Mal Ares, the first world in the universe, and favored by Indigo. And like Indigo, my people could use song to move things with a magic unlocked with desire and emotion. It was—is—beautiful.

But the Ilori called the nightweavers evil creatures. Ene-

mies. Monsters. Witches. First, they stripped the nightweavers'
magic. Then the Ilori stood by as the world crumbled before
our eyes; the rivers dried and the land decayed. Our home
became the ashes of toppled buildings and piles of debris, a
pit of nothingness, rotting on the cusp of space.

Colonized.

But the Ilori did not know the shadows they created. They
did not know that nightweavers cannot die. Although we
may shed our forms, the magic lingers. That is how I can see
them now. Be with them now.

Yet, this world is falling apart. The core is dying. If it breaks
apart…even the shadows will be lost.

And without the ability to unlock Indigo's magic within
me, I'm powerless to stop it.

That's not to say I haven't tried. I prayed to the universe,
screamed into the void, and *tried and tried and tried.* I even let
the Ilori experiment on me in the hopes they could unlock
something I couldn't. But I failed, and soon I'll join my people in this ghost of a world. Which…wouldn't be so bad. At
least I won't be alone when my body is gone.

There's a tug on my side and I twist around to find a little
girl holding a doll. Her face brightens. "Zaira, will you play
with me?"

Halsiba tuts. "Zaira will join you soon, Sola. She is very
busy now—"

I squat down to give Sola my full attention. She is so small,
maybe six or seven when she died. And they called *us* monsters. "Can I play with you tomorrow? We will have all the
time in the world then."

"Really?" She beams up at me. "Do you mean it?"

I nod once, strangely calm despite the reality I'm facing: my death. And maybe that is for the best. This universe is cruel, unjust, and it has taken everything away from me and my people. Why should we not live in this little peace we've created? In this gift Indigo gave us?

Sola giggles and bolts off, her little footsteps echoing on the hard floor. When she's out of sight, Halsiba takes my hand, giving it a squeeze.

"I…" My voice cracks. "I should've fixed this world. I have all of this power somewhere within me and I failed to use it. Why?" I ask her for the millionth time, my eyes downcast. "Why couldn't I have succeeded for you?"

Halsiba sighs. "You could never fix this world, child. We are already dead, and the universe has forgotten about us. I cannot know what will happen when Mal Ares is fully destroyed. Perhaps we will be free, among the stars. We can begin again. Begin better." She's quiet a few beats and I'm not sure what to make of her words. All I can think is that I can't let this happen. I can't lose them among the stars. My people deserve this magic. Deserve this home. Deserve to exist. But after tomorrow, I won't be able to do anything about it.

Halsiba startles me out of my thoughts by asking, "Do you still dream of him?" I swivel to regard her and she laughs. "You did not think you could hide your thoughts from me here, did you?"

I take a few moments to push the images out of my mind. Halsiba cocks a sharp eyebrow and I sigh. "Every night."

"I've seen him in your mind… The one who makes your heart sing." She closes her eyes. "He is kind, gentle. Your match."

"They're only dreams. I will never know him. I'll never get the chance." I shift my feet and avoid her gaze so she can't read my feelings on my face. Sometimes I try to sleep longer to be in his presence. He serenades me. His smile makes me feel warm on this cold planet.

He's just another thing I'll lose after tomorrow.

"Dreams for nightweavers are often realities not yet come to pass." She squeezes my hand once more. "Your place is among the living. With him, with—" Her whole body stiffens. "Someone is coming."

The magic pulls away too quickly and I'm left gasping in the center of the tomb, in the dark, in the dirt. My people linger in the shadows. Forgotten. Trapped in their own world.

The door swings open across the distance and I stand on high alert. When he steps inside, my shoulders sag in relief. Ciaran. A friend. His orange eyes meet mine as the violet aura of power clings to his skin. Not too bright, but then he's not very old for an Ilori.

"Zaira." He bows slightly and his black tunic crinkles in the orb that circles him, lighting his path. "I was looking for you."

"You found me," I say breathlessly. I bow deeply and he sucks in a breath.

"Don't bow to me." He strides closer and smiles before pulling me into a hug. "We are equals here."

"We are not equals anywhere, Ciaran." He doesn't let me go, instead embracing me tighter. I let out a laugh. "You're going to crush me."

He sniffs. "It's better than losing you."

"It's another way of losing me," I whisper, leaning into his embrace. The warmth is nice, and he has always been ready for a hug when I need one. If ever there was a time to need one, this would be it.

"We can't let them sacrifice you." His breath tickles my earlobe. His voice is filled with sorrow. "We can—"

"You make it sound so easy, as if I have a choice in the matter. You're an Ilori, you know this." I pull away from him, meeting his gaze. There's a sadness deep in his eyes that I wish I could erase. "They never stop until they get what they want."

"Then give them what they want." His words turn angry, wholly unlike the Ciaran I know. He is usually mild-mannered, always calm and polished. His light blond hair sits perfectly on his head, not a strand out of place. His body is toned but slim. He's a true Ilori. They aren't meant to feel, but he does. All the time. And he feels a great deal for me. Maybe too much. But…he's not the one I dream about. "Prove to them that you are more than a nightweaver on a dying world. Prove you can be loyal to the Emperor. He will spare your planet, leave the ghosts in peace."

"I could never be loyal to an emperor who killed my people." I take another step away from him. "Besides, if I could unlock Indigo, you would be the first to know."

Ciaran's great uncle is Emperor 1lv, the ruler of the Ilori. Ciaran came here as a child to watch me grow up once the Ilori had seen the constellations on my skin and learned the truth about me. He was my age so we played together—I shared details about my people with him, although we both knew he was there to keep an eye on me.

Despite this, we became close—as close as we could grow with the knowledge that his people killed mine and destroyed my world. I know that he is not personally responsible, but a bigger part of me can't forgive him for it either. And never will. No matter how hard he tries. No matter how hard he wishes for more time, more of me. I can only be a friend.

"There must be another way. There must be—"

"There isn't." He wraps his arms around himself as if it were my chilly tone that made the temperature drop, not the fact that the core of Mal Ares no longer warms this world. "Tomorrow I will die and you will go back to your home. The universe will never know or care." My eyes get misty suddenly, and I blink away the tears before they can fall. "If there is one thing I must beg you, it's this: don't let him destroy this world. Let it crumble away naturally. Give my people time to move on."

"I will try. For you." He rushes toward me and takes my head in his hands, his fingers caressing my cheeks. The violet aura around his body pulses and pings against my skin. "I love you, Zaira. I cannot imagine my life without you in it."

And I know I'm supposed to reciprocate. I know I'm somehow supposed to make him feel that I am worthy of his love by saying I won't give in… I can't. He's not my match. He may not have killed my people like his emperor ordered, but he's complicit. He lives a life of privilege because of his proximity to colonization and death.

Still he stares down at me, waiting, hoping. I choose my next words carefully.

"I…care about you too." I lean into his touch. I hear him release a breath when he realizes I have nothing more to say.

He holds me anyway, and for a moment, I let myself be held by someone who cares about me. I let myself feel love for Mal Ares, for my people, for my grandmother. I let myself feel anger at how unfair it all is that we are dead and doomed while the rest of the universe carries on without a care.

They forgot about us. They abandoned us.

Perhaps it is good then, that I depart this world of the living. For if I stayed, all the songs of power I have churning within me, demanding to be sung...I'd use them to get revenge.

I'd destroy the Ilori. And I'd let the universe be destroyed too. I would not be Indigo, an altruistic creator, or Ozvios, a calculated destructor.

I would be the last nightweaver, unleashed from her prison.

I would be vengeance and wrath, the end of all things.

CHAPTER TWO

Wesley

"Fists clenched tight, he writhed and screamed with all his little might,
and I knew, right then, that I was fated for something better,
A new life I'd get to share, but he would never know how much I care."

—The Starry Eyed demos, "Fated Family"

There's a foul stench wafting through the cabin's vents, and I'm pretty sure it means my cargo died. Or more accurately, I killed it.

I slump in the pilot seat, trying to will the smell from my nostrils as the radio blares on.

"Now that Andarra has declared war, major planets are considering if they too should pick a side in the growing conflict," the newscaster says.

"To not choose a side would present another conflict. During times like these, we must look to the stars, look to the history of Indigo's great battle and defeat of Ozvios, and decide if we want to choose creation and liberty, or death. It seems an easy answer," the cohost concludes.

I switch the radio off. Everything is *war this, war that.* Who cares? We can talk about morality all we want but, in the end…everyone's out for themselves.

The smell wafts from the cabin again and I groan. I knew this would happen.

In my defense, I told the client my ship wasn't equipped for tentacled species and they assured me it wouldn't be an issue. But then I picked up the cargo and what do I see? A small gray tentacled blob with a million beady eyes all staring at me—sizing me up—a strange yellow disc, and a few bones scattered around its carrier. It smelled like blood and rage.

I instantly hated it. It instantly wanted to eat me.

When I put my foot down—arguing that one bad jump in my racing skipper could disintegrate the furious devil, they shook their heads. In just a few rotations, they purred, you'd finish the job and your wallet would be considerably thicker. Easy money, they said. No one would pass that up, they laughed. Especially not the fastest runner this side of the galaxy.

Flattery has always been my downfall.

But I, being one-track minded, remembered that: money equals freedom from a family that doesn't want you, from a world you don't belong to, from a destiny you chose not to accept, and schools that don't teach you.

And speaking of, I had forgotten to turn in one little school project and next thing you know, the counselor called my mother, saying I need to spend less time in my skipper and more time at a desk.

Which is promptly when I jumped in my skipper and took off. This doomed mission is without a doubt better than whatever torture I'd be enduring at that school right now.

Now, as I flick my gaze to the screen, I only see the empty case with its door flapping open. When I saw the blob had wiggled out of its box, I thought, *fine, I'll just lock it in the carrier compartment.* What could it do? Everything's sealed and ventilated. Surely, the little bugger couldn't get out of a steel-coated room.

With the stench of a rotting corpse polluting the air, I can only conclude that the blob's tentacles found a way through the teeny, tiny vent, then it died when I planet jumped toward the hyperspace bridge. Tentacled species often react poorly to planet jumping. Though I missed that lesson in school, I think it's because when you leap through space too fast (which is probably why it's illegal), sometimes matter gets rearranged. I guess having tentacles rearranged causes death or something?

Now I kinda wish I hadn't skipped that class. Although nah, school's the worst.

Anyway, it's definitely dead. No living thing can make that smell.

I sniff, my lips curling. Right, just gotta close all the vents to the central hub. My fingers inch toward the switch when a deep growl reverberates through the cabin. Instinctively, I draw back and turn in my seat.

Little bugger's not dead.

Holy ferk.

Indecision swirls around my brain. Do I go check it out

and maybe die? Or do I just lock myself in here and wait for that thing to somehow reach me through the locked vents and then die? Huge questions, no good answers.

My feet tap against the spotless tiled floor. So shiny and clean. The ship's barely a week old and already I'm about to destroy it.

Just like the last one.

All these melios saved up from several successful runs to buy the best of the best down the drain because I decided to take a tentacled monster delivery.

It's not the first time my greed has got the best of me, and it won't be the last sadly, but I hoped I'd have more time till the consequences of my actions caught up to me.

I cringe as I flick on autopilot. We'll be at Outerim 32 in a third of a rotation, and that's all the time I need. That's all the time I have before my favorite radio show comes on too, but I'm not going to think about that now. The little blob is not going to make me miss it.

My trainers don't make a peep as I stand and give myself a quick pep talk: *Listen, Wes, you're not gonna die.* With a quick, careful dash across the central hub to shove a heavy-duty stunner in my pocket, I'm ready to go. Have I used it before? Nope. Not a fan of violence. But am I sure it'll save me from getting eaten alive by some galactic monster?

Also nope.

With purposeful steps, I leave the central hub and flip the switch behind me, locking it. That way, I'll have a safe space to retreat to if needed. Unless whatever-that-thing-is finds a way through the central vents.

Nah, it can't do that…right?

I stalk down the glimmering hallway, the deep mauve carpeting inhaling the sounds of my body and racing heart. Displays on the wall flash and I glance over just as one of the cameras go down. My feet stop and my mind whirs. Without the cameras, I'm going to have to use the AI, which costs a few melios per question—which is why I wanted the thing disabled. Maybe it'll be useful though.

"AI, signs of life outside of me?"

The AI, Jimbo, as I've named him, grumbles. "One Andarran, and one…" The sounds his voice makes don't compute in my ears.

"Am I to take it that's the tentacled monster?"

"It is not a monster, it is a…" The AI makes the weird sound again. You'd think this fancy tech could translate but it doesn't perform simple tasks. "I notice your emotions are oscillating between fear and frustration, is that correct, Wesley? Would you like me to use a calming chemicallent to soothe your senses?"

"Yes, I'm frustrated but wait, I mean, no. Please don't—" I shout just as the air fills with a floral, citrus scent that automatically circulates through my body and loosens my muscles.

"Where is the whatever-it's-called?" My voice sounds like I've been wading through a pool of delicious sticky honey when I can finally speak.

Nothing is going to plan.

The AI is quiet for a moment and I inwardly groan, knowing exactly why he's hesitant. The frustration I so keenly want to experience right now is nowhere to be found. Already my mind is subsiding to the effects of the chemicallent.

This is literally the worst time to be chemically calmed.

"To access that information, you will need to upgrade your services for full AI usage or pay a fee for three more assistances. Proceed?"

I let out another groan that sounds like a sigh of relief, which is not what I want to be feeling, and which may or may not have drawn the attention of the monster currently making a mess of my brand new skipper. "Three assistances. Charge my account."

The AI beeps once. "Payment declined."

I try to clench my fists but they hang limply by my sides. It's okay. It's all okay. I don't need the AI right now because... What was I doing again?

Pictures flash in my brain of a little tentacled pet that I desperately want to cuddle. I need to find it and make sure it's not hurt. The owner would be devastated without it. Just like I would be.

Right, so all I have to do is find the cutie-pet and bring it home to its best friend. How nice is that? My fingers tap the edge of my pocket where the stunner's stuffed inside. Why do I have this? The blob won't hurt me. Although maybe I'll find something else that could hurt the poor thing. I am its protector after all.

My eyes blink slowly and I pick up my heavy feet, one after the other. After a century, I make it down the hall into the carrier compartment and flip the switch. The metal door whooshes open and disappears into the wall. And there in front of me is the empty case and...bones. Lots of little strange bones like I'd seen when I agreed to do this run, only there are much more of them now.

The odor whiffs around and I realize it reminds me of

freshly picked biallolilies on Maru Monchuri. How beautiful! What a wonderful ship this is and wonderful life I'm living! What was I doing?

Ah, yes, the cuddliest, cutest pet in existence is lost. Right. I must find it and keep it safe.

Gingerly, I walk around the cage, wondering how it got out of there. I stop in front of the vents, but they don't seem to be bent or dented in any way. What a clever creature! It must've squeaked through somehow.

As I stand beneath the flowing air where the lovely odor is strongest, there's a blur of movement in the corner.

That's when I understand I'm not alone in this room.

If the pet is emoting, I can't sense it under the overwhelming scent filling the space. Something pings in the back of my head that I'm being watched, maybe hunted. A growl pierces through the cold compartment and I know, without a doubt, I'm in danger.

A smile stretches my cheeks. Danger is good because it makes you feel more alive while you confront your everpresent mortality. I'm very lucky! And I'm thinking as such when I'm struck by an invisible hard tentacle in the pit of my stomach.

I'm whipped across the room by the force of it. Air bursts from my lungs and between my teeth. My back strikes the metal wall and I let out an *oof*. I stay there briefly, letting my mind acknowledge the situation. Besides, pain is good, because it too allows you to confront your ever-present mortality and appreciate the fragility of your body.

All of that doesn't matter right now. What matters is that the pet isn't dead. Or rotting. No, it's a smart little treasure.

Apparently it can remove its bones and shift its visibility. Doing so must cause it to secrete that special smell. Doing so is what allowed it to survive the jump.

Some of the chemical fog suddenly clears from my mind, allowing me to put the pieces of the puzzle together as quick as I can. It's not a cute pet; it's dangerous. And right now, I need to make sure that very tentacled, very scared blob isn't attacking me.

I need to get the creature back in its cage and hurry this run up. All while fighting off the effects of the chemical calm—easy, right?

"Hey, little blobby..." I say in the most cheerful tone I can muster. "Who wants to go back in its little cage? Who's a good little blobby that wants to be nice and safe within its metal walls?"

Its breathing picks up as if it's excited by my question, like every other domesticated creature that just wants pets and snacks. But what does this thing eat besides *me*?

"Come here, little blob..." I stare at the corner of the room, giving a welcoming grin, which is easy at the moment.

The creature shifts out of chameleon mode, its body turning gray with little black dots across it. Eyes, I realize. Its many, many—way too many—eyes look at me and a tongue flops out of its mouth. Its tentacles loosen their hold on the walls. It's rather small still, thank goodness.

The perfect companion size really. A perfect creature.

This chemicallent is killing me.

"Come here, blobby." I pick up one of its slippery, jelly-like bones from the floor and the creature perks up, coming closer. This is all pretty normal, right? I throw the bone into the cage and shout merrily, "Go get it!"

Blobby's tongue wags and it slides quickly into the cage. We make eye contact as I slowly close the latch.

"Who's a good blob? You are. That's who!"

The creature bounces around its cage once before swallowing the entire bone whole. I watch in mild horror as one of the tentacles solidifies slightly into a curved shape. Blobby looks at me and I know what I have to do but I don't really want to do it.

The chemicallent is telling me this is going to be pleasant and everything's perfectly fine, though there are teeny patches where my brain is screaming the contrary. With a deep breath, I throw another bone in the cage and the same process happens again, over and over until all the bones are gone and my hands are caked in goo. Just a few minutes until the radio show starts. *Come on.*

Blobby eventually settles down and falls into a cute little nap and I hate myself for calling it cute but it's the perfect way to describe it. When the creature is finally snoring, I speedily shuffle out of the room back to my central hub, where I learn we'll arrive in Outerim 32 in a matter of minutes and that I haven't missed the one thing I look forward to every single week.

Thank the gods. I slouch into my seat and close my eyes. The odor's still wafting around, though it doesn't quite bother me anymore. No, now I'm just a bit numb. This entire exchange has exhausted me body and soul and I never ever want to do anything like this again.

Unless the pay is better.

Honestly, I'll probably do this a million times if it means I'm a few steps closer to complete freedom. Because the alternative is not an option.

My mother shipped me to a boarding school three systems away when I was only seven. And the school itself is a hellscape where I always have to watch my back. As an Andarran on Fer Asta, I'm just too different. Too colorful. Too…much.

Andarrans feel *everything*. We read emotions like words on a page. Sometimes, for those bitten by the mysterious and magical fish called the Jadu, we can even see the future as clearly as we see our past. We, along with the Ilori, are the oldest civilizations in the universe. Instead of colonizing half the galaxies and creating an empire like the Ilori, we kept to ourselves. Well, as far as everyone knows, that's what we did, because we're *good*. We're righteous and intelligent and always fall on the right side—the winning side—of conflicts. Until war was declared and we chose to align ourselves against the Ilori.

But *we* are not *me*. I may have been born an Andarran, yet that life isn't mine. The Jadu never gave me a destiny. Well, more accurately, I never gave them the chance. And because of that, my own mother threw me out. Being an empath is cost enough for the lineage I bear.

Therefore, I feel justified in saying I don't owe Andarra or my family a single thing. My life is mine, and to keep it that way, I need to be flush with melios in my very fine, very beautiful ship.

I'm going to see everywhere and be beholden to no one. It wasn't just my mother that sent me away in shame; it was my home. Now I have none. All I can rely on is me, myself, and… I flip the switch on the radio and cringe when the voice of Allister Daniels croons out a melody with his band The Starry Eyed.

A memory flashes in my mind.

"Wesley, please. I don't want to leave you. Please forgive me. Please don't let me go without embracing me," he'd said. "Please."

I took one look at him, scrunched up my face, and ran away. My big brother who I admired and aspired to be like was leaving me to our monstrous mother who loathed my lack of ambition. My "cowardice" for not facing my destiny. I didn't want to say goodbye. I didn't want to be without him. I watched from our backyard as his ship took off and decided I would never see or speak to him again.

Shaking my head, I quickly change the channel, not needing to be reminded of another person who abandoned me as I wait for my favorite broadcast. Thankfully, I don't miss a single beat.

"Hey, spacers, it's Rubin Rima, coming to you live from my ship, The Star Chaser! We just left Major Sidarra, and boy do I have a story for all of you! You ready?"

Finally, no more talk about the war. No more The Starry Eyed or thoughts about people who didn't want me. I've never been readier in my life.

CHAPTER THREE

Zaira

I don't want to disappoint my grandmother, I really don't—but I'm shaking, and I will very likely falter. I'm unprepared for my death that looms before me now.

Tonight, I'm meant to stand in this ugly lacy dress and listen to speeches praising the necessity of my death. The announcer is telling everyone how two gods are not meant to exist at the same time and I must be the one to die, since I never materialized Indigo's power in a way that could be channeled by the Ilori. That's what they originally wanted. My power, stripped away and given to Ozvios as a gift. Yet, I've proven myself to be both useless and a threat to Ozvios just by existing.

I wish I could move this along faster. Speed through the ceremony and the death and begin living on the other side. With my people.

"Mal Ares was the first creation of Indigo, and the first Ilori colony," the unbearable man blathers on. I shift on my silk slippers, trying to keep my feet warm despite the incessant cold seeping through. "It is only fitting that in this world, we would find Indigo reborn."

He and the audience of Ilori turn to face me. Their gazes scan me, taking in my ill-fitted caftan, the headdress of dead leaves from my ancestors, and the black constellations on my brown skin marking me as a god.

I take a deep breath, force a neutral expression on my face, and clench my grandmother's hand tighter.

"Though she hasn't displayed the abilities of the god, we must assume Indigo lives within her. Therefore, she remains a threat to our beliefs." He pivots back to the audience and his words turn solemn. "Ozvios demands our strength and worship. War has come to our universe. For victory, we must use every advantage our beneficent god has bestowed on us to help our empire grow. We must kill all who oppose him and oppose us by extension."

The crowd murmurs their agreement. Though I see their faces—the ten or twenty Ilori, they mean nothing to me. They *are* nothing to me. Just high-ranking Ilori bent on power and profit as they are wont to have. They stand in their beautiful warm suits, violet hazes hovering around their forms, gawking at the world they broke. They undoubtedly complain to one another through Il-0CoM, their collective hive mind, about the frigid breeze that whiffs of rot and death. They don't want to be here for this ceremony, but they have no choice. Like me.

"Mal Ares once was the home to nightweavers, our natural

enemy. Emperor 1lv saw it fit to eradicate their magic from this universe, deeming it too powerful and the people too volatile to be loyal to our empire. This girl is the very last of her kind. There can only be one solution. Death and destruction." The audience titters at that. No one, even people who believe themselves above all creatures, wants to be reminded of the genocide their emperor committed.

Rage festers inside me and must twist my face because a few in the crowd step back and my grandmother slides me the side-eye, telling me to keep calm. I give her a slight nod.

The speaker wags a finger at me. "See the bracelet she wears around her wrist? The Emperor himself had this commissioned to keep them docile. Only an Ilori can unlock it. She is harmless." He continues on but I zone out. I am powerless, and that anger will only make my death worse.

Across the platform, Ciaran stares at me, regret swimming in his bold orange eyes. His white-blond hair billows in the wind. His tunic, white embossed with gold thread, washes him out, making him appear paler than he already is.

He swipes a tear rolling down his cheek. He cares so much about me and I… I don't know what I feel about him. Not enemy. A friend.

Never lover.

Resolve hardens his expression, and he tilts his head to the side, calculating something. My own feet edge forward, wondering if he found a solution, when my grandmother taps my hand, a warning. I can't leave. This is it.

Ciaran shakes his head. Losing isn't something he does. Misery isn't something he experiences. He stalks around the crowd, maneuvering through them and onto the shabby platform. He loops his arm through mine, yanking me from my grandmother's grasp.

When the announcer stops to view the commotion, Ciaran holds up a hand. He bows slightly to Ciaran, his tone shifting in acquiescence. "Let's take a momentary pause. I hope to see you all for the sacrifice after dinner. Please do wear white to honor our Emperor."

The audience steps back into the shadows, muttering their assent. Once they're gone, the announcer cocks his brow to Ciaran, saying "Your grace," before stalking off the platform, leaving just the three of us. Ciaran holds my grandmother's gaze until she too reluctantly bows and saunters off. When he and I are alone, he puts his hands on my arms, gasping.

"You're so cold. They shouldn't have left you out like this." He pushes me back into the stone performance hall, erected recently around the Indigo monument. A perfect place to die if there ever was one.

When we're inside, where it's warmer though not warm, I meet his gaze. "Ciaran, you need to let me go. The sooner this is over, the sooner—"

"I can't. I won't." A smile lifts his cheeks. He closes the distance between us. "There's still time. You just have to show them that you can be loyal. That this world need not be destroyed. Please, Zaira."

"There's nothing to show. They know I'm powerless and they don't care." I cringe as his scent wafts around me. He smells like every other Ilori; the ashes of broken dreams and fallen civilizations. "I'm going to die, but it will be okay. Do you understand? I will still be here. I will be on the world I love, surrounded by people who love me."

"Surrounded by ghosts on a dying world," he mutters angrily before looking down at me with pity. "If the Emperor saw you as more than a nightweaving Mal Aresian bearing the marks of Indigo, he'd have to let you live… Especially if you offered your power in the Ilori expansion."

I hold up my wrist to him, despair dripping from my words. "How could I even try if your people never let me take this off?" Truthfully, the bracelet may inhibit my nightweaving abilities, but the Ilori took it off to experiment before, and Indigo's power never unlocked. There's no reason to believe it will now. Still, I'd rather die with the magic thrumming through my veins than incomplete and ordinary.

Ciaran regards me carefully. I've given him no reason not to trust me. For years, we've known each other and I've never lied. Never hurt him.

He takes my wrist carefully. I hold my breath as he presses down on the small pad and the bracelet disengages, falling from my arm onto the floor.

"Now?"

"Yes," I say, relief and magic flooding my senses. "I feel free. Thank you, Ciaran. Even if it's just for a few moments, I can hear the songs in my head."

He leans in, his arms resting against the wall beside me. "I care about you, Zaira." My lips wobble as he presses closer to me, and my arms wrap around his neck. He has always been kind to me, and yet…his nearness makes my stomach churn. "I can't lose you before we…before we ever had a chance to see what we could mean to each other."

This isn't what *I* want. He's not the boy who graces my dreams—the Andarran with long black-blue hair, beautiful purple eyes, and a smile that makes my heart leap. That boy most likely doesn't even exist.

Everything feels wrong. Power surges within me and whispers echo through my mind.

Get away, get away, get away.

My back presses into the cold stone. Ciaran's eyes close and his forehead rests against mine. He doesn't ask anything of me, but he lets his guard down. A song vibrates to life in the back of my throat. My lips part and before I can tell him that we could only ever be friends, that I could never care for him the way he does for me, a melody escapes.

The nightweavers whisper in the corners of my mind and their song leaves my lips in a blur. And I don't mean to hurt Ciaran, I don't, but something in me needs to get him away from me.

His eyes widen. He has no time to react, no time to understand. Neither do I. My song throws him across the room into the wall. It cracks on impact and he slumps to the floor. Knocked out. Mal Aresian magic will do that. I scamper over in a panic, checking to see I didn't somehow kill him.

"I'm so sorry, Ciaran. I'm sorry—"

There's a sudden flurry of footsteps in the hall and I twist around, fists clenched. This looks bad. Really bad. But then again…they are going to kill me anyway. And Ciaran's alive. He'll know it was an accident. He'll tell them that. They will still make my death quick and painless. Right? The words leave my mouth in a rush. "It was an—"

"Zaira." My grandmother comes to stand in the doorway, staring me down. My shoulders unhunch. "I don't have time to explain. The less you knew the better. The Ilori are everywhere, watching, listening."

"Grandmother, I—"

"There's no time for doubt now. The die has been cast, the roles assigned. The pieces are moving and now you must too. I'll keep them back a few moments, but it won't be enough if you don't hurry." When she notices my brows threading together, she shakes her head. "You need to run, Zaira. There's a pod on the edge of the clearing beyond the graveyard. Get inside. I will tell you everything there."

"I don't—" My entire body's shaking. I've been so resigned to my fate that I can hardly believe what she's saying. "You'll meet me there?"

"You won't be alone," she says, stepping closer to me. "Zaira, you need to go now."

Uncertainty still manages to creep into my voice. "My people—"

"—are dead. You can't save them, but you can save everyone else. You can save this world and all others. The universe depends on you." She shakes her head, looking back down the hall. "We've cleared the path for you, my darling. You must take it and take it now."

With a nod, my beaded slippers slide on the polished floor of the performance house as I step toward the exit. I'll be leaving my world and people behind. And for what? Why now? But I know I can't question her. She's Andarran. She sees the future. She wouldn't tell me to go if she didn't think I was meant to.

I sweep a glance back at Ciaran's crumpled form. His blond hair flops over his face, the haze of his power pulses faintly around him, and momentarily he's at peace. I *could* still stay. I could disappoint my grandmother. Give up my power. Allow myself to die for the Ilori. Let my world die in the darkness that has been consuming it slowly for too long.

All because I'm afraid of what lies beyond the door. I'm less afraid of death than I am of the unknown.

"Go," my grandmother says one more time. She crosses the room in a few strides and touches her forehead against mine. It's smooth and soft and makes me feel safe and loved. "Please, Zaira. Time is running out."

I reluctantly break our contact, worried it might be the last time I'll be held by her. The last time I'll see her. But no, she said she'll be there on the pod. She said I won't be alone.

She said I can save Mal Ares, the first Ilori colony, abandoned by the rest of the universe. It deserves saving.

"I will go. I will wait for you." I give her one more glance as I wipe my sweaty palms down the side of my tatty gown. She holds my gaze for a long moment, and in it, there are so many words left unsaid. But we can speak freely when we're off Mal Ares. Together.

"Zaira," Ciaran groans from the floor. *"Go."*

Right.

I run.

THE RUBIN RIMA PODCAST

Broadcasting live

Rubin Rima (RR): Good evening, spacers! It's Rubin, coming to you live from The Star Chaser outside a very secret location. Now, as you might've heard, I've been issued a formal warning *cough, cough, threat* from the Ilori Empirical Offices of Media to cease and desist my radio show. In fact, here's the clip...

Ilori Empirical Officer of Media: It has come to our attention that the latest podcast from performer Rubin Rima slanders our great empire, specifically Emperor 1lv. Therefore, it would behoove Mr. Rima to not only delete this episode but issue a public apology. Failure to comply will result in a formal ban and pursuit of criminal charges, including but not limited to forfeiture of life.

RR: So there you have it, the Ilori Empire wants me to delete my episode calling out Emperor 1lv on not only the colonization of Terra, but his many crimes against species. Here's what I said, in case you need a refresher.

RR (*seven rotations prior*): It's ya boy, Rubin, coming to you live from XiGRa prime where King AnYeck zumBuden aka King Yecki and Queen LaTanya just gave a massive press conference. Before I get into the fashion—and believe me, Queen La didn't miss—we'll talk about their declaration of war. It was epic with a capital E. War is never good, but if you must go to war, it should be for an absolute necessary, absolute righteous reason and holy ferk is it. The Ilori

Empire is accused of colonization, assassination, and crimes against species. Whoa, right? For real, for real though, I have no doubt the Ilori, especially evil incarnate Emperor 1lv, are guilty. That sucker is millions of years old, hasn't been seen in public for a couple millennia, and last I heard, likes to bathe in calef juice with a few drops of sacred Jadu blood he had smuggled off Andarra. What I'm saying is, the man's gross and he deserves to get locked up in interstellar prison for *at least* eternity. Cuz someone that evil most likely can't die.

RR *(present)*: See, it wasn't *that* bad. Though probably broadcasting the snippet again today means they're definitely not going to be happy with me. Therefore, let me make a shout-out to the Ilori listening: I don't care about your threats. I'm a journalist, first and foremost, and it's my duty to report what's happening, whether you like it or not. Yes, I was being a bit flippant with how I stated the facts, but they are facts. You and your empire are at war because of all your wrongdoings. None of us are perfect, but can you honestly look at your past and say you did good things for the universe? That your legacy will be one that is respected and remembered fondly? No. So take your threats and shove them up your—

CHAPTER FOUR

Wesley

I roll off the bed and land on the bright orange shag carpet with an *oof*.

"Wesley, get up. You've got class in ten." The house director pounds one last time on the door and then shimmies over to the next room to do the same. Even from the floor, I feel my classmate's annoyance in their room through the walls. This place is a pit of negativity and I'm pretty sure being here all day everyday would be the death of me.

I groan and suck in shag, nearly choking on the strange fluff. That's the problem with living in an elite boarding school—you can't decorate your own space, you must be in your bed by midnight, and they know all your comings and goings around campus. I hate it, but I've got nowhere else to go. I can't just jump in my ship and take off, never to return; I can't afford it. Sure, I'm allowed to gallivant around the universe, but you need money to afford living in a ship.

Also, my ship isn't even paid off yet, doesn't have a bed, and the special license that lets you sleep aboard costs too much.

I roll onto my back and stare up at the ceiling until Blobby snores beside me. He adjusts himself in his little cage, all of his many eyes closed in slumber. I can't believe I'm stuck with the thing. Once I delivered him, the owner took one look and didn't want it anymore. Apparently the creature had formed a bond with me—and once the whatever-it's-called forms a bond, it will only ever follow my commands or something. So it's mine until I can manage to sell him, since he cost me half the commission.

Gods know it's illegal to have him here. But then again, almost everything I do is illegal, why should this be any different?

With a deep heave, I push myself to my feet and stretch. The room smells dank, a combination of Blobby's natural odor and stale prota bars that have been left in simulation too long. I grab my least dirty clothes—a solid black tunic that hides the stains and matching silk pants—and shuffle into them. My foot gets caught on the edge of the bed and I catch myself from toppling over onto Blobby's cage. As I stand, I peek out the window at the false sun.

Fer Asta shimmers outside as if it's completely natural. Truthfully, it's a species-made planet. The Juxto warlords made this homeworld using the very best tech available at the time; we're talking nano buildings, simulated grass, water, and sun… Unfortunately, that was at least a century ago and the entire place is dilapidated. Then the Juxto warlords caved to the Ilori, and it all went to hell.

Though, according to the news, this might be one of the safest places to be now with the impending war...if you're not Andarran. I'll never know what possessed my mother to send me here, but I do know, deep within my bones, I have to get out. Fast.

I hit a button on Blobby's cage, and water pours into a dish. Despite hating the thing, that doesn't mean I want it to die, so I bought him food last night and made a mental note to set up a feeding system today.

I throw my backpack over my shoulder as I step into the hallway. I push my hand against the closed door onto a silver square and wait for the click of the lock. Say what you will about Fer Asta being outdated, but the dorms at least have state-of-the-art locking mechanisms. The only people in and out are me and the grand hall master.

And...the kid I sometimes pay to use my simu face and pretend to be me in class.

With a deep breath, I tread carefully through the hall, head down. I've found being invisible is a double-edged sword. If they don't see me, they can't harass me. But if they don't see me, no one knows if I'm in class, which'll land me in trouble.

"Hey, did you hear the new Rubin podcast last night?" one of my fellow classmates asks another. I slow down to hear the response, gagging on the manufactured sterile air. Is this a school or a hospital?

"Yeah, about the weird threat he got? Freaky, right? Heard he has to up his personal security and cancel his tour." They huff and I stop myself from busting into their conversation. I want to know their opinions on it and what they think that possibly entails and if it'll impact the podcast, yet I don't want to actually talk to them.

They both glance at me and their lips curl into snarls. Loathing swirls around them, whiffing into my nostrils and making the hair on my arms rise.

"What are you looking at, Andarran?" One of them steps closer to me, a sneer etched onto their face. His name's Baddri, and his friend is… I want to say, something like Unkaru… or Liev. One of those.

Unkaru or Liev smirks. "What, you got stars in your eyes like the rest of your freaky family?" This sets them both off cackling and I grimace, their emotions rolling off them in waves. "The Starry Eyed sucks. No one here likes them." A hint of violence combines with the loathing and washes over me. My stomach curdles. "And nobody wants you here."

"It's all good." I throw up my hands and back away. "Believe me, I know."

"Nah, starboy…" Baddri's hand plops down on my shoulder. "We'll make sure you know." Before I can respond or break out of his grasp, he rocks a punch into the center of my gut. The air vacates my lungs and I double over, clutching my stomach. "You can't even fight back. Andarrans are so weak."

He kicks at my legs, trying to knock me over, but I stand my ground. The moment you fall is the moment you're completely at their mercy. Andarrans have historically been pacifists. That is the only part of me that identifies with my homeworld and culture. But they aren't weak. The moment they're born, they pursue their destiny by letting the Jadu bite them. They glimpse the future, adjusting to shape it for the best possible outcome, not for themselves. For the universe. They are strong, willing to serve their divine purpose.

I'm not. *I'm* weak. I'm not a real Andarran. And that is why my mother is ashamed of me. Why I belong out in the stars. Why I can never have a home or a family.

Baddri lifts his fist and I brace for impact. Closing my eyes tight and…the punch never lands. Instead, I peek an eye open to find Dax holding Baddri's arm twisted behind him. Dax, the janitor's son who sometimes sneaks into school to learn.

Dax, the Fer Astan kid who's not supposed to be seen, lest entitled jerks like Baddri complain about his presence. Which they usually don't since I tend to keep Dax preoccupied.

"Leave him alone," Dax says in a low deep voice. Baddri and his friend stiffen, giving each other a glance, and then bolt off. Everyone else in the hallway seems to go back to their own business.

Dax glances at me. "You okay?"

"Yep, yup." I slowly stand, rubbing the bruise forming near my ribs. "Dax, you shouldn't have—"

"I'm not keen on wearing your bruised face to class," he says with a smile. "Come on."

We walk down the polished faux-stone hallway in silence. Though I just got my ass kicked, my mind's still on Rubin Rima. Pathetic, I know, but he's got the voice of an angel. Loves all the same things I do. He's just a few weeks younger than me and already a mega superstar. I have a poster of him in my ship's cubby.

The fact that he's been threatened by the Ilori and will likely be under the radar for a while is the ferking worst. Like, don't the Ilori have a war going on? Do they have so much time on their hands that they can threaten podcasters for their dissent?

Dax and I take a sharp corner into the courtyard. The simu grass sparkles a little less than normal, as if it's low on power. The sky flickers once overhead. Fer Asta's giving so much of their resources to the Ilori they can't even keep their planet running. How can this be the safest place in the galaxy when their simu sun can't even shine?

I've never really voiced my opinions on the Ilori. It seems like a waste of time, since I'll never be able to change anything. They've been around since the beginning of time, colonizing the universe, and destroying anyone who stands in their way. It's hopeless.

But Rubin Rima isn't hopeless. He makes me want to be brave.

Rubin is also the reason I'm still here.

When you're shipped from home at seven, told to live in another world away from everyone you know, and then you find out that your new home doesn't want you either, or the peace your homeworld represents—you feel lost. You feel displaced and unwelcome.

Then, one day, when I turned fifteen, Rubin started his podcast. He spoke about the space between the worlds and the adventures waiting for all of us in the stars. He made me feel like I had a purpose even when I never wanted one.

He got in his ship, and I got into mine. I taught myself how to fly. I wanted to see everything, be everywhere. I wanted to be someone wholly new, who didn't belong to Fer Asta or Andarra, but the stars. Rubin gave that to me.

He's still giving that to me every time I think I can't do this.

Dax and I trudge through the busy campus. When we enter the main dormitory, we carefully slip into the second door on the right. Dax backs into the wall, lips pulled into a frown. Emotions fill the space between us, most of them connected to impatience.

"Look, I'm sorry about all that conflict." I shift on my feet before meeting his glare.

He's exactly my height, my build, with the same hue of dark brown skin poking out of our black uniform. That's where the similarities end. He's Fer Astan, with solid black eyes, perfectly gleaming white teeth, and zero hair. No eyebrows, no nappy curls that stick up all over his head like mine do.

He exhales slowly. "I've been waiting a quarter rotation for you, and when you didn't show, I had to track you down. You know better than to catch their attention."

"Sorry, man," is all I can offer. I pull a wad of melios out of my pocket and I try to hand it to him, but he bats it away.

"I keep telling you, I'm not interested in your money. I just want to go to school. You only have four weeks left, and I need to learn as much as I can."

On Fer Asta, education is a privilege for the few. Everyone else works or takes uploads on pertinent info they might need at some point. I'm incredibly aware of how good I have it. The Astan Academy of Excellence took one look at my mother's name, our race and homeworld, and said yes, please. That's also the reason they haven't kicked me out despite my many infractions. Our money's too good.

Good money or not though, the school admin has never done much to protect me. They made sure I got a single room with an impenetrable lock after the first few beatings, but they've never put me in smaller classes where the empath energy is bearable. Because although they want me to stay here, they don't want to be inconvenienced. I could've contacted my mother, but what would have been the point? She wants me gone, and I'm someone else's problem now. Everyone else's problem.

Just having bright cerulean eyes creates an aura of hostility among my peers. And I'm lucky enough to also feel their emotions, have a pop star for a brother, and rich homeworld, so that hostility turns to action. And because I'm against violence, which I believe is the death of compassion, I make an easy target.

But Dax is a real lifesaver, in more ways than one. He puts on my simu face, goes to class because he genuinely loves learning, and when people give him a hard time, he has no problem taking them outside. He doesn't feel a million things. He can focus his energy where it needs to be.

He wants to be an engineer. He wants to fix Fer Asta and bring it up to date, out of Ilori rule. I'm glad he has the ambition, which is why I push my melios into his hand despite his protests.

"You need this money more than I do. Your sister's tuition is due in a few rotations, isn't it? And I know your dad isn't making much." I cock an eyebrow, and he hastily shoves the melios into his pocket.

"She's getting solid grades and she wouldn't even have been able to attend if you hadn't forged your mom's signature." Dax looks down at the floor. A flush creeps up his neck.

I turn away, not wanting to make him more embarrassed

as his feelings swirl around the pit of my stomach. There's anger too, although not directed at me, and... I close my eyes. Fear. "None of this is fair, you know that, right? The least I can do is help bring a little balance."

"I know," he mutters before standing tall. "But try to show up on time and not get into fights. A few minutes late means I miss something and I don't want to miss *anything*. Right now, we're learning about the Ilori Empire and the ascension of the god Ozvios. It's riveting."

"Gods aren't real," I mutter more to myself than to him. "Be careful not to fall for their propaganda. You know what the Ilori have done to the universe, what they've done to Fer Asta."

"Of course I know. How could I not?" His lips twitch and his hands curl into fists. "I am loyal to my country and to the Juxto warlords. If they say I must trust the Ilori and believe in their greatness, then I must."

A long time ago, the Juxto warlords lived within the Monchuri system and provided the royal soldiers called The Soleil. They grew powerful, the most favored among the Qadin royal line.

But then there was the uprising. The Second Chaos, they called it. Peasants rebelled against nobility. Monchuri created some weird program called The Kindred: all citizens got a chip inserted into their head at birth, which mentally connected them to someone from a different class. It was a new way to combat loneliness but also helped all voices, from the poorest to the most rural, be heard, or so they say. Unsurprisingly, the Juxto warlords refused to share their minds, their thoughts, with anyone else. Too much power, they said, cannot be shared with commoners.

I wave my arms around, unable to keep my frustration inside. "Loyalty is not in your best interests. Loyalty won't keep you fed, clean, warm, and educated. Money does. Don't be an idealist."

Dax huffs, stepping closer to me. But it's not aggression; it's a desire for me to see his perspective. "Because of my warlords, Fer Asta remains safe from colonization. Yes, we have to share our riches with the Ilori Empire, but it's still our home. Not theirs."

I don't know how to get through to him that the Ilori saying, *"Oh, we won't colonize you, we just expect you to pay us and starve your people,"* isn't fair. Yet, who am I to tell that to Dax? Who am I to this world or any world? It's a waste of time to argue. I need to go. Get off this crumbling rock and out into the universe.

"I'm sure you're right. You should go to class. Oh! And can you feed this creature-thing in my room? The food is beside its cage." I dip my head once and watch through my eyelashes as he hits the tab just below his left ear. His face quickly transforms into mine. My eyebrows poke through his skin, his lips fill out, his eyes shift from black to blue, and his bald head fills with my curls.

I inwardly cringe. Weird how I can see myself in the mirror and hate the image staring back, but when it's on someone else, I think, *Wow. It's not so bad.* I hand him my backpack and step aside to let him go live my life.

When there's complete silence around us, I flee the quiet campus, using all the back hallways and service entrances. It's not until I'm far away that I breathe easier. It's not until I hit the tab on my keys and my skipper reveals itself among the debris of the old science building that I feel right. And it's not until I stalk onto my ship's ramp that excitement builds in my stomach despite the throbbing pain of Baddri's blow.

I sit down at my pilot seat and give myself a moment to take it all in. The smell of rot is gone, replaced by citrus cleaning solution. The floors are glistening and bright. The cushion massages the tension from my body. With a quick push of a button, the ship turns on and I speak the coordinates to the Outerim.

This is my home. This is where I belong.

This is where I can be me.

CHAPTER FIVE

Zaira

My headdress wobbles on my head as I dash through the door. The world outside the performance hall is fresh and chilly, and for the first time in years, I'm well and truly alone.

I stop for a moment—just a moment to ground myself. My fingers instinctively clutch my grandmother's necklace—my good luck charm—running the bulb along the chain to steady my nerves. In the center hangs a glass bauble containing the star Citlali, my family's namesake. If I peer closer, I'll see it suspended in the black mist of the night sky. Plucked from the tapestry of space where it would have faded and placed inside a bauble where it can stay till the end of time.

My grandmother gave it to me on my eighth birthday. I remember her kissing me on my cheek and staring down at me warmly. I felt precious in her presence as she turned me around and clasped it at the nape of my neck.

Carry this as a reminder, my love, that a star can shine even in the darkest and smallest of places. One day, she said quietly, *this star will fizzle into oblivion when it chooses. When it's ready. Either as a flicker of light or a roar of flames.*

She told me, I imagine, so I could draw a parallel to my own situation. I'm the metaphorical star with the memories and power of the god Indigo inside me and I'm going to fizzle someday soon...if the Ilori have their way. And it looks like now they won't.

Not today. Not tomorrow either. That's the thought that lingers in my mind as I continue bolting into the dark.

There's no one out here. A sign from the universe that I have no choice but to follow my grandmother's instructions. *There's a pod on the edge of the clearing beyond the graveyard. Get inside, I will tell you everything there.*

And here I am, having burst through my prison doors, and I have no time to cherish it. No time to understand why my grandmother chose now for me to exist and escape. To live long enough to probably die at the right time.

I can't help but feel that I don't deserve to escape. I never unlocked Indigo. Never deserved the birthright. Never lived up to my potential. Never avenged my people.

No, no more of that now. I will be worthy of the time given to me. Worthy of the nightweavers and their magic living within me.

Escape.

Little sharp stones cut through my silky shoes, poking me in the tender parts of my feet. I wince but I won't stop. Can't stop. Just keep running. Don't look back.

The twilights twinkle above me, lighting my path. I steer

away from the shadows. There's an escape jumper on the edge of the elder graveyard ahead. I need to take it before anyone sees me. Escape from the everlasting night before the Emperor knows I'm gone.

Though my feet ache, I run till I come to the clearing, stopping just on the outskirt of it. Unseen. It's crowded with soldiers. Ilori soldiers of a different uniform—purple with gold thread—than the former imperialist line. Soldiers I don't recognize. Did my grandmother know they'd be here?

Ferk.

Despite their sheer numbers, it's eerily quiet.

They stand over the graves of my people. The soldiers laugh and let their drinks splash on the dirt.

"Ciaran said to dig them up, see if any still have the dust…" one of them says. Ciaran… *My* Ciaran?

"Why does he want dust from corpses?" another wonders aloud, taking a large swig from their cup. "We should've already left this forsaken world. He's taking too long killing her."

"He desires her, though I can't see why. She's a round, dirty thing."

I ease forward slowly so as to not draw attention. The jumper must lie on the other side of them. It will only take a moment to get there, but I hadn't anticipated soldiers.

My once-white slippers are brown and slide on mud. Mud? I scramble back, over the lip of a deep hole. A grave. Once I get a glimpse inside, just a small one, I gasp.

There's a…corpse. I can't make out their face—they've been disfigured, possibly drained of their blood when they were alive. There's a silver strand around their neck with the crest of Indigo. Of me. They were an elder in life and didn't deserve to be disrupted in death. They were one of the last Mal Aresians. Buried, not to be forgotten, but to be left in peace.

Anger fills my lungs and leaves in a scream that echoes through the field and beyond. The soldiers stir, pointing their weapons at me. Their eyes widen.

"The singer!"

Nightweavers slither from their shadows where they've been waiting, watching. They climb, crawl, crave...

"The god!"

"You shouldn't be here."

"Stand down, nightweaver!"

"Vengeance," a voice says into the black of night. The formless nightweavers circle, snuffing out the brightness of the twilights. My hands fly up in acquiescence just as the anger twists inside me. The soldiers are right, I am a nightweaver—not a god. I am the last of my kind because of them. Because the Ilori chose death over life. A decision I'll make too.

My power, Mal Aresian through and through, unleashes in a haze.

Darkness travels from the edge of my tongue into the night, spiraling in the air like shadowy wisps. A song escapes me, one I don't know the words of, but sounds so beautiful. So beautiful and so deadly.

The soldiers stand transfixed. One by one, their weapons swerve and aim at each other. Something drops in the pit of my stomach. Guilt? No. Rage.

"I can't stop." They shout to one another as their weapons train on their comrades. And I can't stop either. Not yet.

"No!"

"It's her. Make her—"

They fire. The echo of their weapons executing reverberates through my mind, and the soldiers fall into the muddy, bloody ground.

They die.

Justice. Vengeance.

They were the monsters, not us—not my people.

"I'm sorry," I say to the corpse of the elder, to myself, to everyone.

Cold swirls around me and I know I should leave. That I should say something, anything, to absolve me of these sins, but I've already gone off schedule. The pod is waiting for me. Yet, I slump momentarily into the muck and the dirt and the blood. My knees shake from the onslaught of cold.

I'm exhausted. I've never used my abilities like that before. Mal Aresians certainly never have; if they could, they'd be alive. My people never believed in violence—they agreed to wear the bracelets if it meant peace with the Ilori, if it meant they could live. Yet, it hadn't mattered. Without the magic to protect them, they became easier to kill.

But I'm different. Though Indigo's power still eludes me, the bracelet is off. My ancestral magic is free. I will use it against them.

With song, I can send shadows through the minds of bad people and make them do bad things. There's too much pain, too many ghosts who deserve blood. And if I think closely... I know I wanted those soldiers dead.

My stomach churns. A monster? Yes, perhaps, I am one too.

All of my bravado, innocence and anger, justification, and righteousness shrivel within me at the truth. I'm a murderer.

A murderer who must escape her world and become who she was meant to be. Make the universe a better place.

Am I the right person for this? Am I worthy of it? Can I continue with the plan I've already deviated from?

I was supposed to let them think I was weak enough to be controlled. Destined to die. And though I have known from the very beginning that I am so much more than a girl whose magic could barely knock a boy into a wall only moments before, I was expected to remain nothing of consequence. That is how I survived. Until now.

My feet stumble as I attempt to stand.

Until a hand clamps on my shoulder.

I must've missed his footsteps. Must've forgotten what I've done and where I was running and planning and doing.

Never shake. Never falter.

I am faltering over and over.

"Zaira...you shouldn't still be here." Ciaran's low-timbred voice trails off as he stops to stare at the dead bodies gathered around me on the dirt field. The twilights persist with their constant flickering. His gaze lingers on my tear-streaked face. He clicks his tongue as if I'm a small child needing coddling. "What...what have you done?"

"They're dead," I whisper, more to myself than to him.

"Everyone's dead here. This world no longer matters." Ciaran rubs his hand along my spine in a way I'm sure he thinks I find comforting. His eyes dart around the clearing, taking in every minute detail. "You need to go. You need to get out of here, get off this world. Reclaim who you truly are." His eyebrows furrow suddenly. "You really did this?"

His thin hair billows in the wind as his head turns.

"I... I..." My heart pounds as I craft an answer. I shouldn't have killed them. I wasn't meant to be here. I was supposed to be gone. And Ciaran should have never seen me again. Instead, I might've ruined everything my grandmother planned for me.

He sucks in a breath, his back stiffening. "They are watching from the skies and they will come for you. You have to go. The pod is just on the other side."

The words leave me in a breathless ramble. "Why...why are you helping me?"

"Because I need you." Ciaran suddenly stands a breath away from my face as he leans in. "Because I need you to become Indigo so you can free us from the Ilori."

The thoughts flee my head. "But you're Ilori."

"I can be both Ilori and against Ilori." Ciaran regards me carefully. Sweat trickles down my back. "The universe needs balance, and you will be that balance. Once you unlock the memories and power and become Indigo."

"Ciaran, I—" I try to disguise the dread in my voice. Fury unravels in the pit of my stomach. If I haven't been able to before, what makes him think I can now? What if I never become Indigo? I've already let my people down, my planet down, now I'm supposed to let the universe down too?

His eyebrows lift. "You have to." His head whips around as twigs crackle in the distance. "You have to go." Disappointment threads his tone as he pulls me toward him into a hug, and my power surges forward again, wanting violence. Hating his nearness. Hating him when he has been nothing but kind. I know that I carry my people within my blood and can never forgive him or the Ilori for what they have done.

But I can still call him a friend. "When you are who you're meant to be, please remember that I've always been here for you. Please find me, Zaira. Please."

A cool breeze pierces the heat on my cheeks, and I eventually nod, my stomach churning. I glance up at the crumbling palace on the hill, our silver stone home not fit to house anyone. A prison made for me and Grandmother. My heart quickens as fire erupts within its walls. The nightweavers have chosen now to fight, to direct the attention away from me. They want me to go.

I flinch. This is it. If I don't unlock Indigo's powers, I can't save Mal Ares before it crumbles and the spirits are lost forever. This is the only world worth saving. My home. My people.

Never flinch. Never falter.

"Stand down—" Ciaran follows my gaze and his eyes widen as he holds up a hand to a flurry of soldiers pouring into the clearing. "Zaira. Hurt me. That's the only way."

I stand tall, understanding. His orange eyes bore into mine, begging me to run. Begging me to leave. Begging me to be more than I ever was.

"You thought you could control me. *Us,*" I shout with an edge in my tone, wishing I could thank him for all that he has done. "We have been shrouded in darkness so long, we became one with it. But we will shine bright again. You may think us your lesser, but make no mistake, we were never your lesser. It was you who came here, you who clasped our wrists in iron. By the end of all this, it is you who will cower in fear. It is you who will swear fealty."

His face transforms as he puts on a show for the Ilori. "Zaira, your sacrifice is necessary for Ozvios. You can't—"

Power unravels from my lips as a melody circles around us. With the last shreds of energy I have left, my song lifts him into the air and I let him fly into a dead tree. I don't hear him land, I don't want to look, but he calls out just the same.

"Stay back." His voice echoes across the graves to his soldiers. "She's too powerful, her bracelet's off."

I don't get to say thank you. I don't have time to say goodbye to the nightweavers. My feet carry me across the rest of the clearing toward the old pod sitting beneath branches and rubble.

The hatch is open and I duck inside, hoping to find my grandmother but she's not there. I'm barely into the pod when the hatch closes and the controls come to life.

"Wait a minute," I say to the ship, as if it can hear me. "I can't leave yet—"

The ground lifts beneath me and I stumble back. My grandmother's voice streams from the console.

"Zaira, I can't come with you but you are never alone, my love. Your people are always with you, flowing in your veins just as magic."

"No, no, no," I sob. "I'm not leaving without you. I can't do this without you."

But it's just a recording and she can't reply.

"Ciaran and I have left you a note of instructions, melios, and new clothes—use them," she continues. "The ship is programmed to bring you to Outerim 32. Be in the central hall at exactly 14:37. There you will find Wesley Daniels. He's tall and Andarran, with cerulean blue eyes and dark brown skin. Together, you can free our people from their prison. Together, you can defeat the Ilori." Her voice wobbles just once to tell me that she doesn't want to say goodbye either. "Save him and you'll save us all."

The pod rockets through the air and I scramble into the pilot seat, tears streaming down my face. I want to turn around, to go back home where everything is on fire and dying. I don't know this universe. I don't know these worlds. I don't know how to fly.

Who is Wesley Daniels? Why him? If I'm to leave my home, my people, to save a boy in a far-off world…it has to be worth it. *He* has to be worth it.

I sniff back another sob that threatens to tear itself from my throat. Maybe, with this Wesley's help, I can finally unlock Indigo. Please let that be the reason I'm meant to find him. Please let that power allow me to sing my people back to life. I can make Mal Ares alive and beautiful again. I can change the rules of creation. That was what Indigo could do; with their power, I could too.

All I have to do is find him, this Wesley, surely the most important being in the universe, and everything will be okay. It has to be. It has to be worth killing those soldiers, hurting Ciaran, and abandoning the nightweavers. Abandoning my grandmother.

It has to be worth living a little longer.

A DECLARATION OF WAR

Newly crowned Monchuran King Felix and Queen Joy, First of Their Names, have declared war on the Ilori Empire citing: assassination of the royal Qadins, illegal and unconscionable colonization of several planets, and crimes against species. They will join the systems of XiGRa, Andarra, Dosani, and Major Sidarra, with more expected to pledge their armies in the upcoming rotations.

Queen Joy stated, "Violence is not our intention, though we are prepared to face the might of the Ilori Empire with a might of our own. If we don't stand for the freedom of all, we don't deserve to lead."

King Felix agreed, "The Ilori should never have been able to go this far without checks and balances from other governances. I believe it was our culture of staying out of interstellar politics that has led to this, and it is now our responsibility to our people and to creatures across the universe to stand against them. We only hope it's not too late."

Though young, the Monchuran royals have shown immense courage and willingness to change the structure that has allowed the Ilorin illegality to thrive. It has been inferred from interviews that an interstellar republic will be formed following the war. The power, it seems, will be with the people.

And as polling suggests, people across the universe wholly support a war, even if it means chaos.

CHAPTER SIX

Zaira

The planet skipper is old, one small room with a washroom attached, and it smells like dirt. But the autopilot and stealth work—otherwise I never would've made it off Mal Ares alive.

I have no excuse to complain. Especially not with this view.

Bright stars shimmer beyond the glass and I lean closer, eyes wide. It's so alive. Some worlds have magnificent rings around them, others have so many vibrant colors, and my gaze can't take them all in. I know these places… I have seen them on my skin in black ink since I could remember. The universe is vast; no one can know where it ends and we begin, even with a map. Seeing it now though, it's bigger than me and my imagination.

Vast though it may be, it is not empty. There is dust between the stars. This space, a mixture of nothing and everything, is the glue of the universe. No world is truly alone; no, they are suspended together, spiraling for eternity.

Or until destruction takes hold and gobbles them all up.

Zaira, save him and you'll save us all, my grandmother's voice whispers in my mind.

My fingers twitch at the thought of her, and the thought of destruction. Why, with the closeness of stars, was Mal Ares left alone in that darkness? Why were we forgotten? Did we not deserve the brilliance of the universe?

A sadness builds in the pit of my stomach. My grandmother. My home.

If the Ilori knew I was Indigo reborn, surely others must've heard. Why then has no one come to rescue me or my planet? Grandmother said I had to find Wesley to save the universe, but why must I spend the rest of my dwindling life serving those who abandoned my home? Indigo created them, gave them life, and they have done nothing while my world crumbled.

The planet XiGRa spins closest to the glass window. Lush green blocks of land with blue patches of oceans, and in the center, a black stone core that gives electrical heat to the entire planet. It is beautiful.

I used to study this planet and all the stars in the books that sat on dusty shelves in the once-grand palace library. They were my constant companions. I learned everything I could about them, and what I couldn't learn from a book, nightweaver elders whispered to me.

After a quick glance at the clock—half a rotation until I'm supposed to find Wesley—I set my hand against the thrusters, enjoying briefly how my dark brown skin shimmers against its white metal. Thrusters are simple; ships are complicated. After a while, I feel comfortable sitting at the console, but I wouldn't trust myself to fly without autopilot.

My grandmother was a pilot once—well, she flew herself from Andarra to Mal Ares long ago. She taught me the basics, but I never thought I'd use them. The only thing I can recall is her saying ships, even little pods like these, are intuitive, made to be flown. All of you have to do is know where you're going and point yourself in the right direction. The ship will do the rest.

It sounds easy, but Grandmother didn't prepare me for the math and coordinates. Or, more likely, this ship is just old. I know where the stars should be, but their actual locations? Not a chance. The only constant thing in this life is inconsistency.

And the Outerim? I thought it was an overall location outside a ringed star. But now I see, staring at a map on the comms system, that it includes hundreds of stations between large stars. I'm meant to go to the thirty-second one, between XiGRa and Hali Monchuri. Two worlds belonging to two different kingdoms. All created by Indigo.

I run a hand over my fuzzy scalp. I've input the coordinates, so all I can do now is glide past these worlds and hope that this boy will be, by fate, in the same place at the same time. That he will be our salvation. As long as I didn't make a mistake somewhere along the way.

My eyes blink a little slower and my lungs expand as I yawn. The seat squeals as my back settles into the cushion. It's quiet. Almost calm, if only my blood didn't feel like it was on fire.

Aboard this tiny ship shrouded from the rest of the universe, I may finally have a moment to myself. For the first time in my life, I'm safe. No one can find me. My death isn't looming over my head, shadowing every minute from waking to slumber.

All my emotions and overwhelming thoughts fall away. The rage and disappointment shrink within me. I smile. I'm alive.

Warmth trickles down my cheeks and slides to the edge of my chin. I touch the silky tears on my face. How long has it been since I cried? Better question, how long has it been since I've cried happy tears? Happy, despite abandoning my home and grandmother. Happy, because I'm alive and free.

Free.

A bark of laughter erupts from between my teeth and my entire body cringes from the unexpected movement. I throw my wet hand over my chest as more laughter pierces the quiet bubble I've gotten myself inside.

I close my eyes, relishing this truth…when the ship pings. Loudly. Like a siren in my ears.

"Destination in three hundred seconds," the ship communicator says. "Destination in three hundred seconds."

"Okay, okay," I reply frantically to no one. My back straightens. This is where I'm supposed to go. This is what I'm supposed to do. The moment is gone; my fate remains. "Can we… Do we dock there? Request to land? What am I…?"

The comms system crackles. An unknown voice comes through. "Request to dock, approved. Zone 103A-4 is all yours, skipper."

"Oh, yes, okay, well… I'll just, uh…"

The ship communicator beeps once. "Coordinates prepared."

"Oh, thank the gods," I say belatedly and then laugh again. What a silly thing to say. Who am I thanking, the god I apparently carry within me? Ozvios the Destructor who wants me dead? All the other deities, big and small, who stood in the shadows of time, being worshipped and adored by their masses? I shake my head of the thought as the ship glides toward the dock.

I run my hands down the black tunic that awaited me in the ship. It's old, musty, like it had been waiting too long for someone to wear it. And worse, it's tight.

My body is thick, strong, and sturdy. It's powerful, made from the same stuff swirling within me. Unfortunately, this outfit wasn't made for a body like mine.

One wrong move and—

The ship rocks to the side and I'm thrown against the edge of the seat. My dress tears over my stomach and I yelp. A melody comes to my lips but I press my mouth shut before it does anything I can't take back.

"Incoming ship alert, evasive measures taken," the ship's comms tells me. My pod—skipper, the communicator called it—swivels to the side as another ship, or more accurately, a floating palace, speeds past. The Star Chaser, it says in garish red letters. Smoke erupts from its tail, lights flashing from within.

As my little skipper corrects itself, I watch as The Star Chaser smashes into the dock and a small fire lights up the runway. People rush toward it in yellow protective gear, helping the passengers out and spraying some chemical solution in the air.

"Warning, dock relocation needed. Warning!" The comms

crackles again. I'm guessing this is air traffic control. Grandmother told me that there are people who have detailed pro-
cesses for coming and going so there aren't crashes. It does
make me wonder how big this Outerim is…

"You'll need to go to Zone 203-C. Thank you for understanding," comms chirps and my skipper pulls back from
the scene.

I lean into the window, staring as a hooded figure in an
animal print leotard runs toward the entrance of the hall.
There are others behind them, limping, trudging along, but
soon I'm too far to see.

My ship swoops around to the other side of the station,
where it's pleasantly uneventful and fire free. We set down
and the ship's door opens, letting in an odor that's wholly new
and different than anything I've smelled. It's sharp, chemical,
like fuel mixed with… I don't know. I don't have the words
or experiences. I suppose, if I had to guess, I would say that
it smells like life out in the open.

Out in the brightness of stars.

I step down the short ramp and throw an arm across my exposed stomach, grateful my pants weren't the casualty. I'm sure
walking into a station without pants would get me banned
right away. My ship creaks as the door shuts and a number
appears over the roof. Three hours, one rotation. Already the
numbers tick off.

A voice swirls around me as I take my first step. "One
complimentary rotation parking with proof of purchase of
twenty melios or more."

"Okay," I say again to no one. My grandmother packed
this ship with ninety-eight melios in a small silver sack. She

left a long note of instructions saying not to spend it unless necessary.

One more step forward and bright holo orange arrows appear above the spongy flooring. I trace their path with my eyes till they reach the building's entrance. Grandmother was right; it's all very intuitive. I carefully follow the arrows as ships come and go around me.

My grandmother's other instructions on the note begin to circle my mind:

Never act surprised.

Don't make eye contact with strangers.

If someone tells you to come with them, run away.

If someone offers you food, don't take it.

And most importantly, do not tell anyone you are Indigo reborn or that you're from Mal Ares. If you must lie, tell people you are an Andarran; they're consistently odd and tend to never draw questions as their answers are usually terrifying.

Right, this shouldn't be too hard... But then the doors open and I'm standing on the edge of a crowd of species from all over the universe. There are colors everywhere, neon lights buzzing from stalls selling food and wares. Voices rise one over the other, and there are smells that cause me to salivate and others that make my stomach squirm. My feet freeze to the middle of the doorway, and I think I'll be sick.

I have to go. I have to leave. I can't do this.

Why couldn't my grandmother have come with me? Why did she leave me to do this alone?

Strangers stare. People maneuver around me as if I'm a burden. Someone shouts at me to move.

My heart hammers in my chest.

My teeth chitter and fists clench.

My blood feels electric, zinging through my body on an endless current that makes my muscles sore. The air empties from my lungs. Over and over, my brain shouts: *get out, get out, get out.*

Nothing prepared me for this. No amount of reading books and listening to my grandmother's travel tales would've given me guidance for this moment.

Someone or something connects with my shoulder and I stumble into a wall. I'm at once grateful and horrified. It's loud. Just…so loud. I rub my arms and I… I slump against the wall. This is too much.

I don't belong here. I'm not made for this, for any of this. I've only ever been in a group of maybe thirty nightweavers with some true Ilori mixed in for a funeral. Otherwise, I was always with my grandmother or guardians, teachers, trainers. Never too many, never too much.

"Hey, you," an elder says to me, carrying a tray of something…interesting. There's a name tag on her shoulder that says *Ethel, she/her.* "Fresh calef meat, two melios a leg."

"No…no, thank you." My lips curl and if I could hide inside this wall, I would.

"Understood… Maybe you prefer something sweet? Starberry tartlets with precious stardust? Five melios a slice." Her eyes sparkle up at me. She takes me for a sheltered novice. A quick profit. But she's right—stardust *is* precious. Though we are all made of stardust, it's hard to get the real thing. Impossible almost. There's no way a person would extract it from the core of a star and sprinkle it on a cake.

"No, thank you, *Afraema*," I say, cringing as the Mal Aresian word for elder slips out. The woman's eyes flash.

"Arshuba," she says clumsily in my native tongue, using the word for young one. "Why does one so young speak an old language, I wonder?" She looks down at my torn tunic, and the patch of skin across my stomach that reveals just a glimpse of my black constellation tattoos. The universe that lives on me. Though it is quite difficult to see, I know Mal Ares sits on my right shoulder. The Outerim was species-made; it and other stations don't exist on my skin. "Come with me, I will feed you. You cannot trust this world. I know who you are."

"No, you do not," I reply quickly, quietly, but loud enough for her to hear me. "I am no one, from nowhere."

She nods, the wrinkles at the corners of her eyes deepening. "Yes." She speaks again in the universal tongue. "No one from nowhere, this is no place for you." She reaches out and yanks my arm toward her with alarming strength. "They will come for you. You paint a target on all of us."

Already I have exposed myself. Already I have made mistakes. I acted surprised. I spoke to and engaged with a stranger.

At least I didn't take the food.

I pull back my arm and stand tall. "If they come for me, *Afraema*, I will be ready." Darkness edges into my words and leaves my lips in little black wisps. She gasps. "Speak of this to no one and...you shall live." I try to sound threatening.

She cocks an eyebrow but scuttles away into the crowd. It's not until she's out of sight that I let go of the breath I'd been holding in. My whole body shakes. Threatening an elder, sticking out, being disrespectful—this is not who I am.

But, says a voice in the back of my mind, *you cannot be who you are here. You must find the boy and go. Before the Ilori come for you.*

I run my clammy hand over my mouth. Yes. I must find Wesley Daniels. He will know what to do and how to fix all of this. That's why Grandmother sent me to get him.

With my back straight, my stomach exposed and arms wound tight, ready for a fight, I step into the crowd.

These people are alive because Indigo made it so. And Indigo lives within me. They cannot—will not—hurt me. I will not let them. My words carry power and so do my fists. The time for fear is over, only determination can remain.

And with that, I begin my search.

CHAPTER SEVEN

Wesley

Outerim 32 is alive today. Sandwiched between the two king-doms of Monchuri and XiGRa, it's the place to go and be seen. Everyone's welcome here, from the kids looking for a concert to the criminals looking for a score.

Personally, I love it. I love being surrounded by people and species and still being alone. There's a tension, an excitement in the air, and a myriad of smells: calef meat drizzled with honey, the young and the old, cakes of every flavor, the ten-tacled and the loose-limbed, stolen ship parts and mechanics who don't really care how fast you need a fix...

It's perfect.

Last time I was here, I caught a Monchoos concert and just missed Duke Felix (now King Felix) bomb on the stage. The guy made such a huge entrance, got the crowd wild, and then took off without a peep—and that wasn't the first time either. It happened so often that it became a meme. Better, it became an honor to have seen one of his failures. The whole we-knew-you-before-you-were-a-royal joke.

I move through the crowds that seem a little thicker than usual. A hand dips into my pocket and I clasp the owner's wrist. They drop my stray coins and take off with nary a look. Pickpockets are bold here under the neon lights and open glass ceiling that shows the stars in all their brilliance. This place is a great distraction that could ruin you if you let it.

After a few more strides through the front hall, I move toward the cafés and bakeries where the spacers loiter, past the fancy clothing shops, casino halls, and jewelers, where the rich play. My destination is a small diner at the back of the station called Sky High Pies, known for offering the most private booths for the most clandestine meetings, and also truly extraordinary pie. It's Leera's base of operations; she keeps a table at the back and doles out assignments for the willing smugglers.

The bouncer at the door grunts at me. In my head, he's named Fredo, and he loves knitting and romantic comedies. In reality, he calls himself NoName, probably spends his time winning in the fighting pits and here, waiting for someone to grant him any reason to deliver a beating. That won't be me.

I set the knife I nicked from a classmate months ago on the counter and offer my wrist, which has my nano-tattoo. Fredo scans it lazily, grunting again as my name and runner-status pops up on a holo. He hands me a ticket for my knife and nods toward the open doors.

One step inside and the aroma makes my stomach grumble. Berries, citrus, sappy tree bark, and sweet oceanic cream mix together in my senses. I want it all, but that's not why I'm here. I have to stay on task and meet Leera before all the good jobs are gone.

The place has an old-school vibe. Black-and-white-checkered floors, a stone counter with floating cases filled with colorful pies, and twenty-odd booths that have privacy bubbles; little opaque walls that slide over the table, making it impossible for the customers to be heard or seen. Though I don't see Leera, I know she's in the back booth, undoubtedly tapping her fingers.

I pass by the owner, Maeve, and give her a finger wave. She smiles up at me while she slices into her blue moon pie, their best-selling product. People travel from all over the universe for it. It's a combination of strange berries topped with meringue. It's also their most coveted secret recipe. I've heard there've been many attempts on Maeve's life for it. And more than a few blackmailers tried and failed as well.

"Your usual, baby?" Maeve's head is bent down as she sets the pie on a plate.

I can't help my smile. She's the family I wish I had. But I know I'm better off on my own. I can't disappoint anyone if I never get close. "Yes, ma'am."

"Be right over," she says.

I stride to the last booth on the right and slide through the wall, onto the squishy red seat. Two faces stare at me as I adjust myself.

Leera sports her usual bored expression, though the way her fingers *tap-tap-tap* against the table tells me she's not. She's in her mid-twenties, navy-skinned with emerald somewhat-luminescent scales, blue eyes, and a head full of vibrant yellow braids. Frustration rolls off her in waves only I can detect with my Andarran senses. But beneath that... My heartbeat slows, I relax my muscles and I breathe deep. Beneath that... there's an edge of something...something I can't quite place that's unusual for her. I want to investigate, but there's not enough time and Leera loathes me using my skills against her.

I turn to her seatmate, an unknown white man. He has fluffy orange hair and a fake smile that stretches his pale cheeks. He's in a business suit. Unlike Leera, his emotions are easy to read. Smug. Confident. Self-focused.

I instantly hate him.

Leera says, "I knew you'd come after that pet delivery didn't work out. I did say maybe you should pass..." She shrugs. "At least you got half pay. And knowing you'd be here, desperate for the work right about now, I lined up the perfect score for you."

Suit takes that as his intro. "Hello, Mr. Daniels. My name is Codrec Talon and I'm the manager of Universal Enterprises Media and Entertainment." His smile expands and he offers his hand to shake. I don't take it and he doesn't seem to mind, setting it down on the table instead. "I'm here because—"

"Because..." Leera throws him a look that speaks volumes, but mostly annoyance. "Because you're the best runner I know and the only one who could pull this off."

Suit doesn't say anything to that, so I let myself sit with the praise. Usually Leera's compliments have a tinge of sarcasm to them. But not this time. This time there's no shoe about to drop.

Or maybe the job is the shoe.

My head swivels between the two of them. "What do you want from me?"

Leera takes a long inhale while fiddling with one of her braids. Suit—Codrec—runs a hand through his perfectly coiffed hair. The emotions in this booth have shifted at that one question. But right as he's about to say something, my food rises through a slit in the table and all conversation halts.

As I wait for them to say something, anything really, I scoop myself a whopping spoonful of blue moon pie. It's silky smooth and the flavors burst on my tongue. Sweet, tart, homey. The thin salty crust combined with the berries create a symphony for my senses and I have to stop eating before I truly lose myself in the experience.

Leera's not meeting my gaze. Codrec watches me, but his mind is elsewhere. I wonder where he is right now, what he's thinking about. Whatever it is, I can't sense it beneath the scent of my pie. Which, honestly, I prefer.

I repeat the question, though I really just want to eat in peace. "What do you want from me?"

This time, they both straighten. They're going to put their best feet forward and try to sell whatever mission they think I'll do after a bit of flattery and misplaced confidence.

Codrec smiles again. "We need you to deliver a client to Terra."

"Terra." My back falls against the squishy diner booth. That's the absolute last place I want to go for several reasons. "The baby planet the Ilori just colonized? The one that made the new royals declare war?"

"The very one." Codrec laughs, though it's strained. "My client has become a target of the Ilori and needs to be out of the public eye to complete his work. Terra has been colonized, sure, but their species—humans, I believe—are fighting back. It will be the stage for the rebellion soon."

That means nothing to me. I'm not wasting fuel because of some righteous cause. Terra—I remember reading it's called Earth—is dangerous, and though Andarrans were once awarded safe passage there, those days are over.

Also, I just really don't want to go. I already have a familial connection there that I'm not excited to be in the same vicinity of if I can help it.

Leera eyes me carefully. "Fifty thousand melios upfront, another hundred thousand upon delivery."

Suddenly, I'm the one sitting straighter. All my reasons for blowing off this job no longer matter. I want that money. Even if it means hard work. Even if there's a lot to this mission I'm not being told. "What's the catch?"

"No catch," Codrec begins while Leera shakes her head.

"I'm going to tell it to you straight, as always," she says, her jaw jutted out. "No planet jumping. Stay off the galactic bridges and flyways. You can't have a run-in with the Ilori. That's death."

I exhale slowly. No Ilori, sure. But no jumping, bridges, or flyways? "That'd take me almost twenty-one rotations, over a week. I have school, I have—"

"We know about your arrangement at the academy. We'll fix it up." That's Leera's way of saying they'll bribe anyone who tries to make a fuss. "As for the wardens, we can get you a right of passage for twenty rotations. You'll have to use your time wisely."

There's no way in the galaxy I can get to Earth in a week

with those restrictions. I mean, a few months ago, no one had even heard of the planet. Now it's big news. We downloaded human movies, listened to their music, started using their slang in our own languages. Everyone wants to plot an adventure there…when things settle down. And there's not a war.

Maybe I'm overthinking this. Maybe it'll be an easy feat. "Who's the client?"

Now Leera smiles, and that's altogether alarming. Before she can answer, Codrec slaps his hand down on the table. "I'm afraid I'm not permitted to share until you've accepted the terms and signed a nondisclosure. Leera has vouched for your ship and your work, yet we need special assurances."

My lips purse. This job is sounding more and more difficult by the second. But with this much money, I could be set for a long time. Blobby's delivery was supposed to net me five thousand, and I only got half of that.

More money equals more freedom. I'm going to shoot my shot here and hope I walk away with enough to change my life completely.

I keep my tone even and professional. "Make it two hundred thousand, and we're good to go."

Codrec glances over at Leera with an expression that reads, *You sure about this kid?* Leera nods, because she's a real one. "Two hundred thousand it is. But you'll lose a thousand for every day late."

A question nags at me. This is all too easy. "Will you need continual proof of life?"

This time, Codrec doesn't hesitate. "Oh, we'll get it." He takes a holo pad from his suit pocket and slides it over to me. It's loads of legal jargon saying I'll uphold the deal, blah, blah, blah.

I take another bite as I flip through the pages, scanning. It's not until I get to the last page that I nearly choke on my blue moon pie. "Your client is…"

"That's right," Codrec smirks, and for the first time since we've met, it's a genuine emotion.

"I knew you couldn't pass this up," Leera all but laughs.

My insides jumble and cheeks heat. This can't be real. I'm about to be in the company of the one and only Rubin Rima… Correction, I'm about to spend a week trying to keep Rubin Rima alive.

Holy ferk.

Codrec's eyes flash. "I take it you're a fan?"

"You could say that…" is all I can manage. There's another nagging sensation in the back of my brain telling me I should think this through more, that something's not adding up. That I'm being fleeced, manipulated. But the rest of my brain is screaming, *YOU NEED TO DO THIS!!* How many other chances will I get to help my idol? My dream boy? And this is the job of a lifetime. It's got everything: danger, war, stealth, fast ships, and even faster deadlines. This is exactly the kind of adventure I need.

So yeah, that's that on that. I place my hand on the holo and the translucent screen lights up, taking my fingerprints as a signature.

I plonk my spoon on the table. "Where is he?"

Codrec takes the holo away from me and shoves it back in his pocket. Relief sags his shoulders and brightens his gaze.

"He's waiting in his private lounge at the concert hall. I'll walk you over… Oh, and by the way—"

Leera cuts in. "He'll be taking one or two of his entourage with him. I hope you have the space."

"Well, I mean, it's a small jumper but I can—" My words cut off as the lights above us flicker. Everything's suddenly quiet, like the heart of the Outerim has stopped beating. Leera grabs a stunner from her hip holster while the color drains from Codrec's face.

A boom rips through the entire station. The bubbles collapse around us and we all scurry from our seats. Outside the doors, people run past, screaming. The floor shakes. Maeve's got the biggest stunner I've ever seen aimed at the back door, as if she's expecting some nefarious force to burst through any moment.

I yelp as another boom nearly rocks me off my feet. "What the—"

"Go get Rubin, he's not safe!" Codrec pushes me forward with a strong hand. "Maeve?"

She lifts her stunner and makes eye contact with me. "I'll cover you, babe."

There's a siren blasting in my brain. A moment ago, I wanted the danger, the adventure, but…this is already a lot.

"The money?" I ask through gritted teeth as the floor rumbles beneath my feet.

Codrec shouts behind Leera's shoulder. "One hundred has been transferred. The deal holds. You start now."

"Got it." And with those words, possibly my last, I run.

CHAPTER EIGHT

Zaira

The ground shifts and people scream, running for the exits. Cracks bulge from the station's ceiling. Booths fall over. The air smells of sweat and fear. Glass shatters on the floor, threatening to tear my tender feet apart. This is mayhem. This is an attack.

And though my instinct is to get back in my ship and go home, I can't follow it. I need Wesley Daniels. Together, we will save my world, unlock Indigo's power to create within me. With a song, I can fix Mal Ares. Keep it from destruction. Keep the nightweavers alive in their bubble of magic. I can hug my grandmother again. For them—all of them—I'd do anything. They deserve everything.

Now I just have to find Wesley. I'm in the right place at the right time, but where is he? I've memorized Grandma's description of him: Andarran, tall, cerulean blue eyes, dark brown skin. I've seen some fitting that description, but none have that shade of blue eyes.

I stalk forward, through the melee and noise. My purpose carries me onward, my fear keeps my heart beating. Never shake, never falter.

The back rooms—busy restaurants and expensive stores— spew more people into the fray. I dart around them, trying to peek inside. Trying to find salvation. Our salvation. But it's all too fast and frantic. Booms sound all around us. War has reached the Outerim.

The screams amplify to the left and I turn toward the sound. Black-suited and masked soldiers march through the station doors in sync. Not bots—we had those back home once, and those are too inhuman to march imperfectly. No, these are living beings. Powerful ones. They raise their arms and people get thrown into walls and into each other. Electrical charges thrum through the soldiers, as if they are a combination of natural and augmented species.

The true Ilori.

I stand my ground, finding a rage deep within me. Strange they are here now, bold and dangerous, when they've always liked to hide in the shadows and have others do their dirty work. They've taken everything from me. They disrupt this place. They kill indiscriminately. Indigo's creations die for simply being in their way.

They must be here for me. A melody rises in my throat and I stamp it down. They don't need to know who I am just yet. I can beat them without it. My nightweaver abilities aren't the only trick up my sleeve.

In the chaos of the true Ilori forcefully rounding up Outerimmers who attempt to run away, I move my arm to my side, exposing my constellation-covered skin, while planting my feet on the floor. If it's a fight they want, it's a fight they'll get. The nightweavers made sure to teach me to protect myself. I have trained for this my entire life.

I may have the ability to create life somewhere inside me; I also shoulder a heavy desire to destroy it close to the surface. Although I'm haunted by the faces of the Ilori I killed back home, I will do what I must to protect these innocent people. The Ilori take and take until there's only pain and suffering left. I can't let anyone else meet the same fate my people endured.

A faceless Ilori attempts to bat me aside with a swing of their hand, but it doesn't work. They try again and I smile something wicked. My blood is on fire with urgency. *Move. Break. Hurt.* The Ilori stops dead in its tracks, letting its mask fall away. Vibrant yellow eyes bore into mine. Their pale white hair sits in a knot atop their head but a few loose strands dangle by their cheeks. A violet exo-skin hovers around them, vibrating with energy.

"What are you?" they ask in the numerical language of beeps and sounds. On Mal Ares, the Ilori forced us to learn their language. So I answer in their native tongue.

"An enemy."

They lunge at me and I twirl around, my tunic tearing in several places. If this world happens to see more of me, they are the ones who must look away. The Ilori's eyes flash at the faint galaxies on my skin. They don't know who I am yet or what I can do. But they know there is power within me. They know I'll use it.

Their posture tightens as they take a stunner from its holster. I huff. They bolt forward, arm extended, ready to pull
the trigger. I ram myself at them, knocking the stunner to
the ground where it belongs. They stagger back.

There's a wildness about them now. Their hands shake.
Their hair unravels from the bun. They seem uncertain, suddenly unsure they can win this fight. They see that I'm big,
but they couldn't tell that I'm strong. This time, I move first. I
run at them, and their indecision makes their body soft. Easy. I
shove them across the slowly emptying hallway and into a wall.

More Ilori turn around toward me. Their attention allows
the people to break free and run away, out onto the landing
ports. That's when I see him. And time seems to slow down.

I've found him. Wesley Daniels.

He's just as I pictured: tall with brown skin and arresting
blue eyes. Only, instead of running toward me, understanding the mission we're fated to go on together, he glances at
me for a moment before darting toward a door to my side.
He yanks at the handle and the Ilori who were once watching me turn on him.

They are here for him? But…why?

I dash over to Wesley, only he throws his hands up as if
to protect himself from me. A song builds in the pit of my
stomach. Little black wisps leave my lips in preparation. I pay
it no mind; he doesn't know me yet, but he will. Soon. I tug
the knob open to him.

"Go, I'll protect you," I say through clenched teeth.

He doesn't hesitate. He bounds through the door, down
a dark hallway and out of sight. While I…stand there. Sur-

rounded by Ilori with stunners. I can't see their faces, but I can sense their interest. Their questions.

They aim at me but don't shoot. I don't give them a choice—my voice halts their movements and I close my eyes.

My song flows from my lips along with thick black cords of smoke. The words are ancient Mal Aresian. A song from a time long before this body was born. It is beautiful and filled with rage. I close my eyes and see flashes of my grandmother and the nightweavers, feel tendrils of their love and kindness, their hope and desires. As the darkness unfurls, I suddenly glimpse beyond my memories to a time long ago. When the universe was smaller and less bright. When everything was possible and simple.

I see people born from dust and dirt and song. I hear melodies in my own voice—but also not my voice. Deeper then, stronger too. The songs are sparkly and bright. Creations, new and beautiful sprout from the notes. They grow, they love. They, too, create. Worlds expand. Life is bountiful… and then they begin to disappear.

Too fast. Too much, the universe says. There must be balance. Chaos unfolds. The very First Chaos marked by the arrival of Ozvios, Indigo's greatest enemy. He preys upon the weak. He took advantage. He's a black hole, gnawing on Indigo's stars, destroying all their beauty. Balance has been reached and yet he does not stop. He is powerful now, too powerful, even for Indigo.

And then there is song… Their song. *Our* song. No, not mine. The creations and Indigo, they sing together. They defeat Ozvios, send him scattering into the nothingness of space. The First Chaos is over, and Indigo chooses to hide themself away in the stars, to slowly fade away. Indigo goes to Mal Ares, their first creation, and vanishes. The Ilori come. They worship Ozvios, who has found a home within their empire. They begin their destruction of Mal Ares. The trees die. The soil no longer fosters life. The sun ceases to shine. As the darkness surrounds Indigo, Indigo inhales it. Makes it part of them. Makes it a part of their power. Their spirit.

With hope, Indigo chooses to be born again.

But I am not Indigo. With anger, I choose to live.

My eyes open just as the bodies slump to the floor. Alive, yet only just. They will sleep for a long time. I may be vengeance, but I do not wish to be a murderer—no matter how justified. Something has shifted within me and my heart beats steadily. There's no time for guilt or second-guessing. Only time to move forward and do what I came here to do.

A group of unconscious Ilori lay at my feet and I feel fine. I peer down at that patch of skin along my stomach and gasp. The constellations are darker now, moving and swirling as if alive. Indigo lives within me and lets me see what needed to be seen. We are connected, though not one. Not yet.

Wesley, I remember. He's here. I need to find him. I need him to save my home.

I turn away from all bodies on the ground. The door's closed but with a wisp of power, it flies off the hinges into the abandoned station. After a deep breath, I bolt through it and down the hallway. What's left of my tunic groans and rends. The floor is sticky and the walls are dingy, covered in advertisements and posters for musical guests.

It seems to go on endlessly until it doesn't, and there's a new hallway to the right. Light sconces dot the walls, and it's substantially cleaner. There are bright red curtained rooms on each side. I consider pulling them back, looking for Wesley, but my feet plod forward. Following my senses.

Whispers pierce the quiet from a curtain I had already passed. I stop and twist around. Listening. Waiting.

"But *who* are you?" one voice says. "I mean seriously. Who?"

"I told you, I'm your escort… I'm supposed to deliver you to Terra," a deep voice answers.

There's a huff, and a small cacophony of murmurs. When the first person speaks, they whine. "But you're a child!"

"I'm literally your age."

"Which is a baby!"

This time there's an edge to the deeper voice. "Codrec paid me to get you on a ship to Ter—Earth. Do you want to go or wait here for the Ilori to find you and probably kill you on live holovision?"

This time there's silence…which is exactly when I yank the curtain open.

There, in front of me, stands Wesley Daniels, a small group of what appears to be XiGRans, and one very angry someone in a very tight, very eye-catching silver bodysuit. They stare at me with deep brown eyes and hands on their hips. Their hair, beautiful locs twisted into a crown upon their head, stands regally.

Perhaps this is a royal? Do I bow? Do I say something?

"Who are you?" They steal the question from my lips.

"I… Um… Wesley Daniels—"

They shake their head. "You're not Wesley Daniels. He's Wesley Daniels. Unless there's two Wesley Daniels, though I can't imagine why they'd name two people that extremely boring name."

Wesley Daniels exhales loudly. "She saved my life so I can save yours. Any moment now—"

Heavy footsteps sound in the hallway. Right, the Ilori. More of them.

I grab Wesley's hand. "We have to go, Wesley Daniels."

He bunches his lips together. "Who's *we*?"

"Are those the Ilori coming to kill me? Ferking ferk, it was just a little podcast. Well, two podcasts. And then my graphic illustration of 1lv swimming in a pool of blood with bodies weighed down at the bottom. But it was very tasteful." The sparkly person gives me a piercing glare. "I'm *the* Rubin Rima, he/him, fabulous podcaster icon by the way. You've probably heard of me."

I thrust my head in the direction of the noise. "I don't know you…but we have to leave."

Wesley grunts. "Again, who is *we*?"

The walls shake and the numerical, robotic sound of the Ilori language goes from quiet murmurs to clear. Wesley throws his arm around Rubin and pushes him into the hallway, causing Rubin to let out a very high-pitched squeak. His friends clamber after him, saying his name over and over again, reaching out for his embrace.

"We can't leave them here," Rubin says to Wesley, his lips drooped into a frown.

Wesley rolls his eyes and meets my gaze. "Come on, all of you. We'll figure this out as we go."

There's a commotion as everyone runs into the hallway, and I'm knocked into the wall. One of Rubin's friends shoves past me while gawking at my constellations.

The Ilori round the corner and I plant my feet on the floor. I turn to the others. "Run. I'll find you."

They don't wait to see how I'll save them, but they run just the same. Wesley lingers behind, tossing me a look, then takes off.

The Ilori halt in their tracks. There are twelve of them in neat rows of four. All in black with masks. Some attempt to use their electrical charges, but when there's no effect, they get into a new formation.

The second row holds out batons, while the first row crouches down. They advance slowly, their movements methodical, curious. I stand there, watching. A voice whispers in the back of my head to end this. There's no time to play; I need to stick with Wesley.

Now as they approach, thinking I'm awestruck and afraid, I allow the song to surge within me. A melody of anger... A melody of hope too. I found Wesley Daniels. With a quick twist, I see that he and Rubin are gone. Good, they need not watch this. They don't know what I am just yet.

I breathe deeply and let my power out in a rush of darkness. The Ilori adversaries are thrown into the walls, scattered like feathers on the wind. The silence embraces me as they lie flat on the ground, unmoving. Not dead though.

No, I will not kill anymore. My rage will not take more lives. I cannot live with that shame or guilt. Indigo created life and Indigo lives within me.

I found Wesley Daniels and he's going to save my world. My heels turn on the floor and I race down the hall, following after him.

There is hope now.

THE RUBIN RIMA PODCAST

Broadcasting live

Rubin Rima (RR): Hey, spacers, sorry for the lack of formal greeting and all the panting, but I'm in danger! I'm running down a back hallway on a station that's being attacked by the Ilori. The monsters have come for me and so far, I've only narrowly missed them. First, they hit my ship, causing us to nearly crash and—

Unknown: Are you seriously making a podcast right now? You are seconds away from death.

RR: Yes, Wesley. I'm letting my fans know I'm still alive. No thanks to you. Will you...will you stop pushing me? Friends, Wesley is pushing me out of the hallway toward the landing strip—

Wesley: Are you kidding me? Do not tell people where you are! The Ilori could be listening.

RR: That tall girl with those constellation tattoos handled them. My manager probably hired her as my bodyguard. Spacers, let me paint a picture for you. This girl showed up out of nowhere in a tattered dress, big-boned with the prettiest hue of dark brown skin I've ever seen. She's got a teeny tiny afro and a very...good energy about her. I want to get to know her, I think there's a story there. But instead, I'm stuck with Wesley, who is cute but increasingly annoying. Wesley, is that your ship?

Wesley: I'm not talking on your podcast. I can't believe I was a fan of yours—

RR: Rude. Oh, wait, there she is right now. Babe, come speak into the orbiphone.

Unknown: Um...what is this?

RR: I can't place your accent. What's your name?

Unknown: It is... What is this thing? I need to speak to Wesley—

Wesley: No, you don't.

Unknown: Wesley Daniels, you have been fated to save my home, Mal Ares. Please, I need your help. We need you.

Wesley: I think you're confused. You're looking for the other Daniels brother. You know the singer—

Unknown: Please, Wesley Daniels. It is only you who I'm meant to seek. Help us. I saved your life twice now, please save my people.

Wesley: No. Nah. I have a job, thank you.

Rubin: Don't be cruel, Wesley. We can hop on over to Mal Ares... Where even is that? I mean, the way I see it, you're being paid to escort me, so I think you have to do what I say, right?

Wesley: No.

Unknown: Do you... Do you see that? I think that's a... I think that's a ship up there. I think they're aiming, I think we might need to—

Wesley: Stop saying we. I don't know you and *we* aren't doing anything together. You can—

An explosion crackles the line. There are shouts. Loud breathing ensues.

Wesley: They blew up my ship! I just bought that ship. What the f—

RR, out of breath: Not again! What are we going to do now? Where are we going to go?

Unknown: Come with me, my ship's not far away. It's too small to hold everyone though.

Wesley: We don't know you. I don't—

RR: I'm not hiding around here while you fashion another ship from scraps and the Ilori blow the station up. We're going with her. I don't even know her name, but I trust her more than I trust you. You're a knobheaded calef if I ever met one.

Unknown: My name's Zaira. I will keep you safe. I will keep you both safe.

RR: Gotta go, spacers, me and Zaira got to get off this rock before it becomes dust. Catch you soon.

CHAPTER NINE

Wesley

The jumper's so small it's a blip of a thing sitting between two normal-sized skippers on the far side of the landing strips. It'll only fit two of us comfortably but I can't seem to shake Zaira or her beliefs that I'm somehow going to save her people, so the three of us will have to squish in together. Thankfully, Rubin's friends realized that he is a major target right now and decided they had better chances elsewhere.

Elsewhere being a backup hopper they conveniently failed to mention before I settled into the pilot seat. By the time I've got our engine going, they've already zoomed off.

Rubin's bereft. He was all calm and collected when the ship blew up, yet his friends leaving seemingly broke him. Zaira's sitting on the floor beside him, rubbing his shoulder. Meanwhile, I'm flipping switches on this ancient ship that looks like it might fall apart before we even get the chance to be shot down by the Ilori.

"I can't believe they left me. They've been with me since my second series… I thought they were friends with me for *me*, and not my fame. I can't do this alone. I'm not my best alone." Rubin sniffs and Zaira says something that sounds a lot like, "You aren't alone."

I groan, hitting a few more buttons that do absolutely nothing. "Can you both shut up so I can get us off the station being blown up?"

Zaira's suddenly at my side, hitting the weirdly numbered buttons. "It's in Mal Aresian. Your fancy translator tech—" she points to my ear where a tiny implant, a heargo, sits "—probably doesn't understand it." Nearly everyone has a heargo, and nearly every mother tongue is translated without issue. Except this one.

I shake my head. "Ah, a language absolutely no one speaks, super helpful."

She sighs. "*I* speak it. You might want to move aside, I co-piloted the ship here, and it might be too difficult for you."

I shake my head. "I'm the best pilot this side of the universe— and probably the other side too. Get this going and I'll fly us out of here." Rubin sniffles once more and Zaira nods, something like disappointment marring her face. She doesn't like me, I can tell. Or I'm not what she expected of me, I guess. I don't know. But I don't care either.

She hits another tab and the engine revs up, ready to go. "You can fly it now. I had it on autopilot, but I'm sure you can disconnect that since you're the *best pilot* and all." I ignore the sarcasm in her words. Before she can turn away and go back to a now-wailing Rubin, her gaze focuses on the small window between us and the stars. "There's a ship waiting for us behind the rim. Hidden."

My eyes widen. That's how they must have hit my ship. "How…how do you see that?"

She shrugs, keeping her secrets to herself. "Back out of here and take the bridge as fast as you can." She says it like I'm a complete novice.

I grip the thrusters. "No bridges."

She stares at me now. Her eyes are so dark they're nearly black. Her arms fold over her chest, her legs entwine with Rubin's. The swirls on her skin shimmer and twinkle. "That's the only way…"

"Don't worry, I got this." I smirk, hopefully emitting confidence. She stands there another second and then settles down on the floor next to Rubin. He puts his head on her shoulder and mumbles about how unfair it all is.

Meanwhile, I'm about to do something reckless. Something I've always done when confronted with Ilori ships. I don't need evasive tactics or a projectile. They are always so serious, so sensible… I just have to use that against them. A plan, half ridiculous, half wishful thinking forms in my head. This better work.

The ship bolts forward. Zaira and Rubin roll behind the seat, and I try not to laugh at their gasps of surprise. While I don't know much about Zaira, I do know she's a badass who took out two small legions of true Ilori—which I didn't think was even possible. Ilori, not ones to fight their own battles, created armies in labs that serve them and feed them energy through their mental connecting system, Il-0CoM. With that much energy pumping through a true Ilori's veins, they can do terrible things. Which means Zaira must be able to do terrible things as well.

And though I know Rubin, I believed he was the greatest adventurer in the galaxy—traversing through dangerous locations to get a story that would showcase his insightful and kind demeanor, not this high-maintenance and entitled superstar. I guess this is why people tell you to never meet your heroes. Or—I sneak a peek at Zaira—your (possible) enemies.

"Hold on," I say, praying this old ship can actually do what I need it to. When I push the thrusters full throttle, the walls groan and creak, but its small size and lightness gets it going. We fly straight until I catch the Ilori ship on the screen. The comms flash, alerting to close proximity—I think. "Got ya," I mutter to myself.

I aim for the ship and head toward it fast as lightning. Though my passengers grumble, I'm happily surprised this Mal Aresian hunk of junk has the power for all of this. The Ilori cruiser swerves wide and rocks to the side. I swoop back around and do it again, circling them. Confusing their targeting systems.

Before they can realign, I tap the screen to see our location. Three planets stand between us, all three of which are within the Monchuri system. The Ilori can't follow me past the system line. They're at war and one solo cruiser against Monchuri is a death wish.

I punch it, shooting us fast and forward. The Ilori recover quickly behind us, undoubtedly weighing their options between shooting us or engaging with the Monchuran army. I take the risk that they'll value their own lives over ending ours. Our teeny rusty jumper strains under the speed, threatening to shred itself in pieces around us. But there's no time for us to stop now.

Either we die in a blaze of glory because our ship couldn't handle it or because the Ilori determined it. None of this is in our control. I can only do so much.

The screen flashes again. *"Arske malere."*

"Close proximity," Zaira shouts from the floor. "Wesley, I hope you know what—"

"What I'm doing? Yeah, me too." The thrusters shake in my grip. The border between Outerim 32 and Monchuri looms closer. We're almost there. Almost...

A strange siren begins to wail, filling the space. It's so loud I can't even hear my own pounding heart. The screen's red. Though I want to clasp my hands over my ears, I can't let go of the thrusters. Not yet.

"Farschka!"

"We're being shot at!" Zaira confirms in a high-pitched squeal. She stumbles to her feet and toward me. "Turn the ship around."

"The Monchurans will save us!" Rubin declares with a calm confidence. "It's going to be fine. They're probably already on their way."

"No," Zaira says, her tone cool with a hint of sadness. "No one is coming to save us. We can only ever save ourselves. Turn the ship around. I need to see the missile."

"What?" is the only word that slips from my lips. What is she going to do? Stare at it until it hits us? I don't need to see the instrument of my death. The missile registers on the screen as the Ilori advance on us. It's a tiny consistent blip gaining on us. We have seconds before we're ferked. You can't outrun a missile, even if you planet hop or take a bridge.

"Do it," she demands, suddenly beside me. "Do it or we die."

"It's your ship," is all I manage to say, twisting the hopper around into the path of the Ilori cruiser and the atom missile that'll dust us before we can even pray to the gods. Zaira focuses on the scene before us, her eyes glued to our impending doom.

"What are you doing?" Rubin screeches, lying flat on the floor. "Zaira—"

"I'm going to save us…" she says, closing her eyes and opening her fisted hands. Her lips pull at the sides, and her brows furrow. "I've never… It's too much…" Her voice trails off. The lights in the cabin flicker and the screen reboots itself. The air shifts from filled with fear to…anger. Rage. And disappointment—not, I think, aimed at me.

Something beautiful happens then. Something a lot like magic. A simple melody pierces through the ship's siren. Everything goes quiet but for that sound. It rattles around my consciousness. My blood knows this song, knows something huge is happening. Like my body has heard it before.

Time seems to slow down.

Black smoke wisps into the cabin. Rubin mutters incoherently, while all I can do is watch. I can't see beyond the darkness between the stars outside the window, but…then… but then it moves.

The darkness moves like little slivers, like reptiles made of smoke. It yanks the missile from its path, twists it around and around as if the energy, the force of it, is nothing. The missile changes course and time speeds up again.

It darts straight at the Ilori cruiser faster than ever. They have no time to respond, no time to save themselves. The ship explodes. Hues of orange and red and blue mar the galaxy. It's massive and soundless, as if space itself swallowed the agony of it. Debris scatters and then there's nothing left. No life left.

I turn back to Zaira to see her fall to her knees, her head in her hands. "I killed them. I didn't want to... I said I wouldn't," she murmurs, lifting her face long enough for me to spot a tear slipping down her cheek.

"What are you?" I ask, shocked still. "What have you done?" She catches my gaze, her eyes black pits of nothingness. A chill creeps down my spine and I automatically shift away from her. That was her. She controlled the darkness. She's made from the stuff. In all my life, I've never seen power like that.

Her voice sounds different, deeper. "I am a nightweaver. Indigo lives inside of me. You will take me home now." Before I can ask what the hell that means, her eyes shut and she stiffly falls back. Rubin rolls around to catch her from hitting her head on the wall.

He lays her down gently, quietly. When she's settled, he tiptoes up to me. For a moment, he's silent, pensive. Nodding his head as if he's having a conversation with someone somewhere else.

When he speaks, his tone is calm, though panic lingers on his surface. "What was that? Is she a god or something?"

No. No, that's not possible. I can't go down that line of thinking. "She's not."

"How do you explain what she just did?"

A sensible response pops into my head. "Maybe former

Ilori tech... You know they loved to experiment." I exhale slowly. Yes, that must be it.

"No," he replies, wagging his finger at me. "She's not an Ilori. I'd know if she was Ilori."

The seat squelches as I shift on the creaky cushion. Too many thoughts circulate through my mind, most of them grasping for a truth I cannot know. "The Ilori have been creating their empire for centuries. We don't know all that they've done. All their weapons they made to look and act like us, to tug at our emotions and gain our trust."

"Nah," he says again. "I don't buy it. She's my friend. I trust her."

"You literally just met her," I add, though Rubin doesn't listen. I'm beginning to think all he does is talk and be generally annoying. Meanwhile, I'm trying to collect my own feelings and thoughts. What is a nightweaver? Are they like gods? She can't be a god. The gods never existed and if they did, they died. A long time ago. That's the only way the universe could become what it is now: a hell.

No, Zaira...she's just another misfit in space. Even if her emotions seem genuine. Even if her power is beyond imagination. Because she's a liar. She can't be Indigo, who created life and light. Not darkness, like whatever Zaira did. "Nightweaver" must be the name of whatever the Ilori made her into. She's something extraordinary, no doubt, but not a god. Not good.

"I *need* to make a recording of this. Get all the details down now while they're fresh." Rubin takes a deep breath and for a millisecond, there's a welcome silence. "Don't worry, I know we can't stream live even though I really need to tell people what's going on. We just stared down death, we're traveling with a nightweaver—that's what she said she is, right?—and…I also want to talk about my so-called friends abandoning me with a stranger—"

"Who was hired to escort you across the universe."

"And the fakeness, the duplicity of it all—within a creative world that threatens to self-cannibalize if left unattended and unspoken. Staying silent rewards this behavior and it's disgusting and honestly…" Rubin trails off, looking once more at Zaira sprawled out on the floor in the extremely small, extremely uncomfortable Mal Aresian hopper we find ourselves stuffed inside. His entire tone shifts as if he just realized something. "What are we going to do? How are we going to protect her?"

My brows nearly rise into my scalp. My voice stammers when I can finally manage to speak. "Protect *her*? We should be protecting ourselves. And if she's a *nightweaver* or whatever," my words drip with incredulity, "she doesn't need our protection."

"Yes," he says, staring intently at her, "she does. She came here for you. She saved you, and me, by extension. She wants you to take her home—a place, I might add, we were all told doesn't even exist anymore. She needs us and we need her."

I shake my head. "You know, before I met you, I thought I liked you."

Rubin smiles. "Everyone likes me. I'm smart and adorable."

"You're obnoxious." My lips purse. "Inflated by your own sense of talent and worth."

He laughs, a big smile stretching his perfectly round cheeks.

"Oh, just you wait and get to know me. By the end of all this, you'll be in love with me."

"Or we'll be dead."

"Or that." Rubin's face pales. "The Ilori won't quit."

"Neither will I," I say, exuding as much confidence as I can in the face of so many unknown variables. What exactly did I sign up for here? "Let's set our course for Earth."

"No." Rubin puts his hands on his hips and juts out his chin. "We go to Mal Ares. The way I see it, we can't use flyways or bridges, because they're monitored by the Ilori, right? But I'm willing to bet no one is monitoring anything near there. Though I may not be a pilot like you, I know how to get around this universe. If that's where she wanted you to go, that's where we're going."

I let out a grumble. "I've been paid to escort you to Earth. No detours. Not for some unknown entity."

"We're going." Rubin's got that edge in his voice, the one he uses when he's interviewing some politician who's been lying. The voice that made me crush on him. "Codrec works for me, and now so do you. Let's go to Mal Ares. Either there'll be a planet there waiting for you to save...or there'll be a story worth telling."

I huff but pull a map onto the screen. This ship is ancient and formatted in a different language, but at least it's intuitive to physical gestures. Planets and systems and galaxies pop up. "Where even is it?"

Rubin crouches down beside me. "You don't know geography huh?"

"I'm skipping school to be here. Where do people think you are?"

Rubin's lips cock into a grin. "I take uploads. I don't have to do tedious things like school. We learn by dissolving the info beneath our tongue and reforming it in our brain." Of course, he can afford to take uploads. My mom could've chosen that option for me too, but she just wanted me out of her house, not free. Rubin leans toward the holosimulator. "There." He points toward a teeny black dot in the middle of nowhere. "That's Mal Ares."

I examine it. The planet is the smallest I've ever seen. No tech, no docks. Nothing. Instantly, I don't want to go anywhere near it.

Rubin taps the planet once and the screen updates the coordinates. "Let's go save a world."

I shake my head. This is a waste of time. Zaira's been misinformed. All my life, my mother raised us with one belief: the Danielses will be the salvation of the universe. A prophecy bestowed upon our family by the Jadu. By the time I was six years old, everyone knew I was the wrong Daniels. Weak. A coward. No destiny that would bring my family honor.

Now Zaira and Rubin are going to find out too.

CHAPTER TEN

Zaira

The battle rages around me between the stars.

I'm weak now. Too weak and Ozvios is strong. Unstoppable.

No...not unstoppable. There is help. There is song. The voices rise up around us. It isn't perfect, this melody, and not all sing it in harmony. But it unites us, brings hope. Proves that even divided and separated by space, there is compassion in this universe. There is creation.

There is love. *We* are love.

I'm not me, not Zaira. I am Indigo.

Ozvios cannot destroy that which is not physical. He succeeds when we are torn apart, when the desire to hate is strongest. He succeeds even when there is no desire to hate, but there is no desire to love either.

We have found a way. We have given him love. We have given him unity.

And he screams at me. His voice is all hard edges and rage. "You may destroy me, but you'll see… You'll see the very thing you hate will become a part of you. They will disappoint you. They will break your heart and you will become like me. You will choose me. You will join me."

My eyes fly open and I shoot up from the floor, knocking my head right into Rubin's.

"Ow! Damn, your head is hard, girl." He rubs the spot where we collided. "I mean, can I call you a girl? Or nightweaver plus Indigo? Are you Indigo?"

"Sorry," I mutter as the realization slams into me. I told them, didn't I? I shouldn't have done that. Knowing the truth could doom them… Being in their presence, I suppose, could doom them too. The Ilori will kill me for their god, and until I'm dead, they'll chase after me across the universe—putting anyone with me in danger too. But there's no taking it back now. "Yes. I am… Well, I believe I might be Indigo. It's complicated. I have fragments of their memories in my mind."

My body aches as I sit up slowly, this time careful of Rubin's nearness. This hopper is so tiny we're basically on top of each other. My arm shakes as I put my palm flat on the hard floor. I used my abilities too much, too fast, and in a far too challenging way. I didn't even know I could do that, but I'm paying for it now.

"Are you okay?" Rubin pats my back, though I feel the hesitation in his movements. He's afraid of me. Of course he is. I'm afraid of myself. In the span of one day, I've killed and hurt Ilori.

I chance a glance at Wesley. His hands tighten on the thrusters as if he feels me regard him. He's afraid of me too.

With Rubin, there's something about his spirit that makes me feel safe, like I could be understood…but Wesley, he's closed off. He has his own motives and directives. Saving my world isn't one of them.

"Where are we going?" I wonder, staring out at the universe passing us by. We're on a flyway, which I thought he wouldn't take. There are no other ships passing by at the moment, no multicolored stars… Nothing but black space. It feels familiar, although my body is a map to all of these places, so it should feel familiar.

"We're going to Mal Ares." Rubin's hand plops warmly on my back, settling my urge to jump up and ask what changed. "We're going to save your world. Because we believe in you and we thank you for saving our lives. Even if you dress poorly and might be a god."

I turn to look at him. For some reason, I can't help but smile. "I didn't choose this outfit."

"Oh, that's for certain. It does nothing for your complexion and also just—" he swoops his arm around me "—yikes. Thankfully for you, I always keep a few spare necessities in my bag." He holds up a finger and darts into a little jeweled clutch that's strapped across his waist. There's absolutely no way there could be anything in there but a snack, maybe, and his orbiphone.

Still, he pulls out a small dark purple bundle and shoves it in my hand.

"Built in undies and everything. Just open it, and insta-jumpsuit, baby. This one has these little stardust pearls that'll just do wonders on your skin tone." When I don't immediately move, his gaze narrows on me. "We're going to your home. Personally, I think you looking clean will give a good impression to your people. Besides, not everyone can survive multiple murder attempts and look this amazing."

I can't tell him that my people are dead—that would be a long conversation—so instead I just chuckle weakly.

Rubin is as thick and wide as I am, but he dresses and exudes confidence in a way I never have. His locs are twisted up into a flawless elegant bun on his head, not a bit of frizz at all. His gold and black leotard doesn't have a single rip or smudge. He does look pretty good, considering.

"I never cared for fashion before I got into showbiz, but now I love it. Now I understand that fashion is armor," he says as if reading my thoughts. "You need armor when it seems the universe is constantly trying to tear you down and stop you from exposing truth." He smiles wistfully. "Who knew this ethically-made number would hold up after all this chaos and running for our lives? I could walk a white carpet later. In fact, I should give the designer a shout-out on my next podcast." He nods and Wesley huffs but doesn't respond. "Go change wherever you want. I'm gay and not going to be looking at…" He swoops his hand around me again, which I take to mean, everything.

"Same," Wesley mutters.

"Thanks," I almost chuckle as I head to the bathroom. Though I'm happy to be on the right course, heading home to save my world, I also feel… I don't know. I search my feelings while tearing the rest of my tunic off me.

Terror. Fear. Those stick closest to the surface of my mind.

What if there was more for me to do? What if I've disappointed my grandmother? What if Wesley Daniels isn't who he's supposed to be?

I haven't known him longer than a few rotations, but he doesn't seem compassionate. He's cold, abrupt, and is hiding something. He doesn't seem interested in Mal Ares or the fate I believe he has.

What if he chooses not to save Mal Ares with me?

My blood runs frigid at the thought. My people need our help and what will I have done for them if Wesley doesn't agree? I can't bear to think of it.

So I tap the bundle that Rubin gave me and it unfurls in my hands into soft, pliable fabric. But it's very small.

"I don't think this'll work, Rubin," I shout through the door. "There's not enough for my body."

Rubin tuts. "Oh, you of little faith, just put it on."

I shake my head. My knowledge of fine clothes is minimal at best, but even I can tell I'm too much for this scrap of fabric. Still, I find the holes for my legs and stuff them inside. The material adjusts, expands, slips up my body like it was made for me. I gasp. The pearls glitter and sparkle. I bring the rest of it up, over my stomach, and then put my arms through. It thickens against my skin, making me feel cocooned and safe.

I stare down at myself in the limited space that now smells like some exotic flower from some exotic world. I'm glamorous. Beautiful.

After a few twirls and discreet giggles, I let a long breath loose. Hope washes over me. I'm going home. I'm going to fix everything and that'll be the end of all of this. We're going to be okay. My grandmother will give me one of her warmest hugs and she'll be proud of me.

I'll unlock the rest of Indigo and we'll reform Mal Ares. We'll make it green again, with glistening rivers and pure atmo. We'll end the reign of the Ilori on our world and we'll be free, finally. I smile. It's all coming together just the way she had hoped.

I hold the universe in my hands and I'm not shaking, I'm not faltering. All of this, everything I am and have done, has been for my people and I'm so close now.

I nearly burst out of the bathroom, full of purpose. Rubin nods in my direction.

"Am I right, or am I right?" He takes my hands in his, twisting me around once. "You look like a holostar. Did you see yourself? Wesley, look."

Wesley tosses me a glance. "Yup."

My eyes narrow on him but I don't say anything about his lack of kindness. The air whiffs of dreams coming true. "When will we be there?"

Wesley sighs. "Actually, right about—"

The ship slows and I prepare myself. I'm going to save the nightweavers and their magic. A smile rushes to my lips. I'm finally going to do something right.

But then the ship stops, and there's a gnawing sense of dread looming in the pit of my stomach. We should be seeing Mal Ares by now. I know this place. I know its location. It's supposed to be here. Though it is small, dark, and almost forgettable on the outside, it is everything within.

Something is very wrong.

It's not here. There's nothing here besides empty space. My home, my life, my people… It's all gone. Only spiraling blackness remains.

How can this be? I don't understand. The Emperor could not have destroyed it that fast. Ciaran said he'd hold it off...

The alarm on the ship begins to squeal.

"Alert. Close proximity."

"What's—" Rubin's eyes widen. "Where's Mal Ares?"

Wesley shakes his head, gripping the thrusters with all his might. He's yanking them back, wresting control from the pull of some entity.

The realization dawns on me. It's a black hole.

My planet has been sucked into a black hole and no one knew. No one saw. No one cared.

I peer closer, ignoring the tug on my heart and the emotions flooding my system. Ozvios was here. He punished my people. He destroyed my world.

They're all gone.

My entire world is gone.

Grandma.

I slump to the floor as chaos erupts around me. Rubin gasps and Wesley groans. The ship shakes and the pressure builds.

"It's too strong. It's too much," he says through gritted teeth. "I don't know—"

"We need an explosion! Zaira, baby, you got an explosion in you?" Rubin bends down, taking my face in his hands. "No pressure but also *huge* pressure cuz we're gonna die if you don't."

I hear the words. They pierce through my roving thoughts, but I can't respond. Everything I am, everything that mattered, is gone. They're all gone. Yes, my people were just spirits lurking in the shadows with nowhere to go... What did they feel in those last few moments? Were they scared?

After the Ilori took everything from them, the nightweavers had dreams of something better. They deserved something better. They deserved something better than me. I couldn't even keep the planet whole long enough to try to sing them back to life. A tear slides down my cheek and my chest feels as if it's going to crack open.

Did my grandmother know this would happen? Had she seen it? Is that why she sent me away on this wild goose chase?

"Zaira, honey. I need you to look at me." Rubin's begging now, pleading. I see him before me. The panic in his eyes. I hear the ship's metal creaking and tearing apart. We're going to die. It's all my fault.

Wesley's hand lands on Rubin's shoulder. "Hold the thrusters, okay? Hold them tight."

Rubin nods, giving me one last glance. "I'm sorry."

The words register but the massive ache in my heart won't let them propel me to action.

Wesley crouches down, putting his hands on my shoulders. "I hate doing this," he says quietly over the siren. "I've never been good with all these emotions, and we don't know each other, but circumstances…" He closes his eyes. "I feel your pain. I feel your sadness. Your anger. I can't see your memories or hear your thoughts, but I feel you, okay? And you need to feel everything. You need that. But right now, *we* need you more."

I stare into his blue eyes. My mouth opens yet nothing comes out.

Wesley continues, trying to reach me. "I'm sorry, Zaira. I'm sorry for everything. But we're not going to survive without you. You can't give up now. Me and Rubin depend on you."

He pulls me up with him and stands me in front of him. His hands once again find my shoulders. He leans into my ear. "You see that black hole. You have to push us away from it. I don't know how your abilities work, but I know you can do all kinds of things. If Indigo is inside of you, can you create an explosion?"

Create? I've never been able to create. The power… All I've done is kill and destroy. That's all I am. I've become my enemy. I've lost sight of Indigo, of who I'm supposed to be, and I've lost my world because of it.

Create. What does that look like?

I dig deep into my thoughts and the fragments of Indigo's memories I've seen, pushing aside the pain that threatens to overcome me. I close my eyes and concentrate hard until I find them. Songs to create worlds that I don't yet know how to sing. Incomplete melodies to create life and flowers and water, things I wish I could have known before on Mal Ares. But there, somewhere, rising to the surface, are a few notes to create something large and powerful. Just what we need.

Though the floor beneath me rattles, the siren blasts through the speakers, and the screen flashes red, I shut it all out. I focus. The notes arrange themselves within me.

My mouth opens and out they flow. Not darkness, not swirls of slithering black like my nightweaver powers. Gold beads of light like stardust. The light whorls and strengthens around us, through us, beyond us. It encircles our ship. Rubin's locs lift off his head as he holds onto the thrusters for dear life. Wesley reaches out and grabs my hand, and that's when I realize we've been lifted off the floor. We're floating. We're creating now.

I am Indigo. Or Indigo is me.

The light outside converges beautifully into a ball, glowing brighter and brighter.

"Hold on," I warn through the song, though we can only hold on to each other. The melody crescendos and blasts out of me stronger than anything I've ever sung before.

The ball outside rips apart and knocks me and Wesley onto the floor. The ship shoots backward. Rubin thuds beside us and laces his fingers through mine.

Wesley tries to get up but can't; the pressure is too intense. He turns his head toward mine. "Who's got the ship?"

"Force, honey," Rubin shouts over the metal twisting and squealing. "Scientists call it force reaction."

My eyes droop as the energy begins to leave my body. I'm crashing hard, and I don't yet know if I saved them, us. All I know is that I failed my people. I failed the nightweavers. I know I don't deserve to be alive while they're gone.

They're lost because of me.

I should be there with them. Maybe I will be soon. Maybe I won't wake up. Maybe—

"No, none of that," Wesley says, grasping my hand tightly. "It's easy to want to give up. I know, I wanted to many times. I still do… I may not have lost everything like you, but I don't have anything either." He takes a deep breath, his hand still holding mine. "I remember playing once in our backyard in Andarra. The water below my feet was lit up with life and the sky was perfect. There was a salty warm breeze, and I was happy. My brother was strumming a funny instrument— I can't remember its name. And my mother's eyes lit up. She told him how beautiful he is, how important he is to her and the universe. So I picked up the instrument, imitating what he did, and when I finally got her attention, she frowned. I'll never forget that. She told me to put it down, step away, go away. No one wants me, she said. Useless, she called me. A mistake. Her words were venom and they poisoned me. I've been flying around galaxies all this time, trying to prove to myself that I'm worthwhile. Sometimes though, I think I could just not exist and no one among the stars would care." He pins me with a deep stare. "But I'm here. You're here. You lost everything, but you're here. You deserve to be here." Slowly, I look at him and grip his hands tighter. "And, I mean, who else is going to help me get Rubin to Earth, huh?"

My smile is bittersweet as my eyes slowly close. I deserve to be here. I'm still needed.

If only I had been there when my people needed me.

CHAPTER ELEVEN

Wesley

Her power did that.

Loathe as I am to care about anyone else in my life, I find myself wanting to care for her. She just lost her world and still she managed to save us from a black hole. If I had anything at all that tugged my heart the way her home tugged hers, would I have been able to do the same?

The pressure in the ship ebbs away and though my body is still held down to the floor, the alerts in the cabin have gone quiet and the screen has calmed down. Though I don't know our coordinates, I imagine we're not about to collide with anything out here. At least not yet.

The cabin's lights brighten. *"Arfabe schti crasata."*

"What's that mean?" Rubin asks, eyes wide.

"Think it means…" I rise slowly, feeling the cabin's gravity and lack of pressure, "that the cabin's pressure has been stabilized."

"Oh, thank the gods." Rubin sits up beside me, scrubbing a hand over his face. "I mean, thank Zaira." He chuckles to himself, then looks at me. "Is she going to be alright?"

"She's devastated, but she's alive." I hold my open palm out to him. He takes it and I pull him to standing, enjoying the warmth of his hand in mine. I drop my arm and move toward the pilot seat.

Rubin's brows furrow as he glances down at his hand. "What do we do now?"

"What we were always supposed to do: deliver you to Earth." I'm surprised to realize my thoughts aren't about the money or the freedom I'll get once I've gotten him on Terra. I can't help but think about Zaira. Why did she believe I would be the salvation of her world? Why did she choose me?

I didn't have time to consider that before, but now her home is gone, and I feel...a little responsible? It doesn't make sense, yet I do. I should have gone to her world sooner, believed her sooner. Instead, I was thinking about melios and my fast ship and being beholden to no one and no thing.

Am I broken inside? Have I spent so much time trying not to care about people, feeling rage, then indifference toward my family, trying to escape from the last of my responsibilities that I forgot how to care about someone other than myself? Have I forgotten what it means to help someone who asks for it?

I inhale sharply and plop down into the pilot seat. A heavy sadness creeps through my heart. I've let Zaira down and I've let myself down. Maybe this is why my mother sent me away. Maybe she saw this cowardly cruelty in me and decided to banish it from her home.

Is it too late for me to change now?

The map pops up on-screen and I sift through the planets until I reach the small green and blue one a solid fifteen rotations away without jumping. Reluctantly, I hit it, and the screen flashes once to tell me the course has been set.

Rubin takes a seat beneath the dash beside my legs and gazes up at me. His perfume smells incredible, and he's right, despite our several encounters with doom, he still looks amazing. "So you're a fan of mine?"

I try not to roll my eyes. Already, he's fishing for compliments? "Was."

"Hmm," he says, suddenly interested in his fingernails. "Why?"

The honest answer comes quickly. "I thought you were one of the only journalists—definitely the only one my age—going out there into the big unknown and asking the tough questions to people who lie for profit." I shrug, gripping the thruster a bit tighter.

"It used to be all I did. I started at twelve." He shifts on the floor and I find myself meeting his gaze. "I didn't have a home, didn't have a family. I had an orbiphone and believed that was all I needed to get the truth out to the people."

Now it's my turn to ask, "Why?"

His lips twitch once, just a tiny bit, as if he's surprised I care. "My parents died on the Ilori colony Balfus. They were helping create the next gen of humanoid labmades for Earth and needed metal at the planet's core. My parents realized that if they took the metal from the core, the entire world would crumble. The Ilori punished them for it."

I straighten, inhaling his sadness and loss. "I'm sorry."

"Me too." He nods at me, his eyes crinkling at the edges. "I was their only kid. They were trying to make enough to buy me a better life. Instead, they died because a true Ilori lost his precious temper and killed them."

Though I desperately want to say something, I'm at a loss for words. What does one say to that without just saying sorry again?

He doesn't care about my lack of response. "It was Emperor 1lv's son, apparently. Did you know he created a humanoid labmade and raised it like family? I still can't believe that."

I huff. "I'd heard, but I figured it was a fluff campaign to make them seem more redeeming."

"I bet he hates the poor thing," Rubin says, looking down at his nails once more. "His wife though, Gl1nd—I think that's her name—she's running the biggest rebellion against her own family. That's why I want to get to Earth. I want to be there on the battlefield when all the Ilori's carefully laid plans fall apart. When they turn on each other, and in one fell swoop, we're all free, baby."

I shake my head, surprised in his confidence. "You don't really believe anyone but the Ilori has a chance...do you?"

"Before I met Zaira, I wasn't sure." Rubin's lips purse as he runs a hand over his tight locs. "My plan was to just get there. Someone's gotta report what's happening, win or lose, right? And the Ilori are coming for me anyway... But with Zaira, our little sleeping god, we could win." He twists his head away. His lip wobbles and I wish, in that moment, that I could hug him. He needs it. Loss swirls around him like blue smoke, touching and transforming everything in its wake. "I'll never get my parents back. I'll never get to tell them all that I've done, all that I've tried to do to make this universe safe. With her—" he nods in Zaira's direction "—we can at least prevent other kids from losing their parents, their friends, their loved ones, their homes, you know? We have a chance to make things better."

I sigh. He's an idealist. He honestly thinks that with a lot of work and good intentions, the universe will be a better place. That the Ilori will lose and just fade away, back to their homeland, and leave us all be. The colonies will gain independence and we'll all live in harmony. Despite my skepticism, I don't mock him. It's nice to have faith in something other than yourself and the ever-present terribleness of civilization.

Instead, I change the subject. "Who was your favorite guest on your show?"

Rubin's cheeks stretch into a smile as he looks beyond me. He's silent a few moments but when he answers, there's a thoughtfulness in his voice. "There was this little brown girl in Major Sidarra who was bossing all these grown adults around, telling them what's what about how to protect the coral reefs. She was so knowledgeable and couldn't have been more than eight years old. Sometimes I remember her when I'm doing interviews, and it gives me a little boost. If she could be that fearless at her age, what's stopping me?"

I nod, remembering that interview. She was a force of nature. No doubt she'll be huge in climate affairs in the future, and Rubin's platform helped get her voice heard.

That's why I always respected Rubin. He knows his reach, how to get people interested in things they might never have thought about before. "Who is one person you always wanted to interview but never had the chance?"

Rubin shakes his head. "There are so many stories out there we don't even know about but need to be told. I could interview you and learn something new. I could interview Zaira and tell the universe that Mal Ares existed, and for some reason, we never thought to save them till it was too late. There are galaxies of tales, Wesley Daniels, and I hope I don't die so I can be there to share them."

Something in my gut plunges and I feel sick at the thought of anything happening to Rubin. Even if he is wearing that ridiculous leotard and keeps calling me baby. I don't want him in my thoughts, and yet here he is, making me want to promise that nothing'll happen to him.

"Wesley Daniels—"

"Just call me Wesley, please," I cut in, my fingers shaking against the thrusters.

"Wesley." He smiles again and his whole face lights up. And suddenly my crush on him is back, just like he knew it would be. "How does an Andarran boy end up in the Outerim, promising to deliver a multitalented space podcaster across the universe? What happened to you that this seemed like the best choice?"

Answers rush to my tongue that I immediately swallow. "Sometimes life is weird."

"Life is always weird," he laughs. "You're a tough one to crack, but I'll succeed. Mark my words. There's never been a person who could resist my charms for long."

"I live to be your first," I manage to say over my pounding heart.

Something wicked flashes in his gaze. "Oh, baby, don't make promises you don't want to keep."

My face feels like a million degrees Celsius and I have to look away from his smolder. Is it hot in here? Am I going to be okay? Bigger question, is Rubin Rima flirting with me? I catch him smirking briefly before he focuses on Zaira.

"You know, when she wakes up, you're going to have to do your Andarran trick of helping her through her emotions again. Empathy really is powerful, huh?"

"It's not a trick." The whiplash of that statement leaves a bitterness in my mouth. "Why do you care so much? Because you want her to fight the Ilori and turn the tides of war?" She lost everything and I don't want to be the one to ask her to give up more. Why should she want to?

"No, Wesley Daniels." There's an edge to his tone now as he pushes himself to standing. "Because I know what it's like to lose everything. I don't know if…if I can help her without ripping open my own wounds. But you…you don't wear your heart on your sleeve. You might be able to give her the best chance at grieving in a healthy way."

With that, he's about to walk off but then the screen lights up again.

His eyes widen. "What now? Every five seconds there's a new threat."

I try to read the Mal Aresian words but I have no clue what they mean. The display shifts, showing the mechanics of the ship and flashes red in the areas where it's…not doing well? Breaking apart? I have no idea but flashing red is never good.

"We're going to need to stop somewhere and figure this out," I say mostly to myself, though Rubin huffs loudly.

"Where's the next safe planet?"

Together we bring up the sky map and we search… There's

only one. Rubin turns to me, lips pinched tight. I feel his terror and his relief. And I know what he's thinking. This should be the easiest decision to make. No doubt the safest too.

My foot stamps on the floor, seemingly on its own accord. "No. There has to be somewhere else."

Rubin nibbles his bottom lip and my gaze flits to it. "Nowhere else that's not a complete straight shot from here if we jump it."

"We aren't supposed to be jumping."

"Well," he says wagging his brows, "we weren't supposed to do a lot of things and I don't think our Zaira is gonna wake up and somehow fix the ship before it conks out."

"Ferk," is all I can say, tapping the screen. Every voice in my head is screaming, telling me to go another way, to go anywhere but there. Those voices are wrong. This is the only way I can guarantee Rubin Rima lives another day to get to Earth where there'll be a big payout waiting for me.

This is the only way.

His fingers brush against my arm. "You really don't want to go there, do you?"

"No," I answer easily. They don't want me there either. They all but forced me out of my home in the middle of the night with a few cases packed with clothes and money. Since then, I haven't seen them. Not once. In almost ten years.

I stare at the big dot on the screen. Andarra. Home of the second oldest civilization in the universe. Where everyone's an empath and eternal. Andarra, home of the Jadu; the sacred creatures that swim on the watery world and nibble the hands of those destined to do great and powerful things. To be bitten by the Jadu means to be given the ability to see the future and past simultaneously. It gives you purpose and responsibility.

On the day I was supposed to put my hand in the water, I ran away. I embarrassed my family. Embarrassed myself. Embarrassed my homeworld. My mother never let me forget how much of a disgrace I am.

So, yeah, it's the absolute last place I want to go, and that's saying something, since my mission is getting Rubin to about-to-be-war-torn Earth.

Rubin watches me closely, unsure of what to say. "Are we going to your family's house to patch up the ship?"

"No," I nearly shout. "There are plenty of places to go where we won't be seen." Rubin nods and stretches out beside Zaira on the floor. He's going to nap, no doubt, because this isn't his problem. Or he doesn't have another solution.

Memories buzz in my mind. Of home, our estate on the hill with the beautiful pond full of Jadu. Of my brother playing an instrument and my mother singing along. Of the bright blue sky, the bubbling brooks and water beneath our feet, and always sparkling stars.

Of my mother saying to seven-year-old me, "Don't come back here, Wesley. *I* don't want you here. You are a disappointment. A failure to the Daniels name."

PART II

WHEN FATE & DESPERATION COLLIDE

HYPERSPACE BRIDGE DISPATCH OUTSIDE OF XIGRA PRIME

Dispatcher: Oxana Raemer (OR)

OR: This is bridge dispatch. Andarran skipper, please identify yourself, your origin, occupants, and final destination within the XiGRa system.

Unknown: (line crackles) This is Morris...uh... Morris of the...uh, this is just Morris. I'm coming from planet Terra also known as Earth. We, um, that is to say, my friend and I—though I believe one might suggest, well I hope, that she is my girlfriend rather than friend which would infer another, although limited capacity, relationship wherein I believe—

OR: Morris, would you please answer the directives without preamble?

Morris: Yes, I do apologize. Origin, planet Earth. Occupants, me and human, Ellie Baker. Final destination, XiGRa prime, as invited by King AnYeck zumBuden to aid in a sound delivery system.

OR: Thank you, Morris. I do have your arrival on my list. One last thing, can I hear from human occupant, Ellie Baker, to establish signs of life?

Audible repetition of human dialect (known as English) numerals.

OR: What is that sound?

Morris: My friend—girlfriend, we haven't really defined our relationship—has anxiety and tends to count when feeling a lack of control. I just gave her a heargo so that she understands other dialects, but I'm beginning to believe that might have been overwhelming for a human. Ellie, do you want to talk to the dispatcher? I promise, you will be safe, and it will be short. It is simply an obligatory assessment.

Ellie Baker: …six, I'm alive. Yes, I'm alive. Bit nervous. But I'm here. In this very shiny and colorful universe. I can't believe I understand alien languages now. Um, super weird.

Ship AI: I am noticing an uptick in overwhelming emotions.

Shall I play The Starry Eyed as previously requested and administer a calming chemicallent?

Morris and Ellie Baker: N—

Ship AI: Administering now. Please enjoy your new calm state.

Background sound of Andarran musical group heard through comms.

OR: (loudly) Thank you both and safe travels. You are now free to use the hyperspace bridge to XiGRa prime.

THE RUBIN RIMA PODCAST

Not broadcasted

RR: Hey, spacers! Been a minute since you heard my beautiful voice on your holos, right? Well, hold tight, this is being prerecorded in a bathroom in the tiniest, oldest hopper I've ever seen, and who knows when I'll get it out?

RR: That said, here's my update. I'm traveling with a reincarnated god, an extremely grumpy although...extremely cute Andarran who is skipping school to get me to Earth, and it has been absolute mayhem.

RR: What kind of mayhem you ask? You heard about that explosion on Outerim 32? I was there. My ship's gone. You heard about the possible legions of unconscious Ilori found in the halls? That was my girl/god, Zaira. Did you hear about a black hole on the edge of space where no one has ventured in centuries and didn't know existed? Probably not, but if you had, we were there. We almost got sucked into the black mass and torn apart. And right now, we're on our way to Andarra because our ship is on its last life. We might not even make it, so if anyone finds this message, please play it on air. I want you all to know I was thinking about you in my final moments and my heart was full of love. It's been one hell of an adventure.

RR: And if I manage to live, I'll be in Andarra soon. Which is apparently the most beautiful planet in the universe, but tell that to my boy Wesley who looks like he's been repeatedly stabbed in the heart. I want to know more about this world. I want to see the Jadu, the crystal clear waters, the hot core that's rumored to be so powerful it could heat entire systems for centuries to come. And I want to see the grime beneath all the shine. This may be my last podcast in a while or for-ever, and I want it to be memorable.

RR: On that note, to my former friends Jacen, Fricara, and Emithe, I hope you all have boring, uneventful lives, you backstabbing social climbers. I knew when you three showed up hanging on my every word that I shouldn't trust you. When my other friends disappeared and stopped calling, I should have figured it was because of you. But joke's on all of you, I've got a god for a bestie and an Andar-ran with the bluest eyes I've ever seen as a potential new love interest if he'll ever open up—which is another story for another time. Anyway, when I die, people will remem-ber me for the truth I told and the risks I took in getting that truth. What will they remember you for, huh? The choice is yours. You're still young, you can turn it all around. But you'll never get me back. Which is a real shame...for you, babes. Because I'm one of the best Zaira-damned things in this universe and you lost out.

RR: Anyway, I'm off to save the universe. Byyyyyyye.

CHAPTER TWELVE

Zaira

"She glowed like the universe lived beneath her skin
Oh, how I wished to see her shine,
Oh, how I wished that she was mine
but it wasn't our time,
no, not yet… But soon."

—Allister Daniels, "untitled"

He takes my hand in his and squeezes tight. Though he opens his mouth, I can't hear the words that come out. His beautiful violet eyes crinkle at the edges. His long blue-black hair hangs down to his shoulders. He's covered in glitter and sparkles and oh, how he shines.

I step toward him, wanting nothing more than to be in his proximity. He and I, we're fate, we're destiny. Somehow I know this, and somehow he does too. His gaze drops to my mouth and he pulls me into him. His lips crash into mine and every part of me feels alive and desired and safe. I let out a gasp, my stomach fluttering.

"Zaira," Ciaran's voice interrupts the sweet dream streaming through my mind. "Where are you, my love? Come to me…"

I bolt awake (again!) with my head on Rubin's lap. He strokes my hair gently, humming an unknown melody. When he sees I'm no longer sleeping, he smiles down at me, and it's a genuine thing that shifts a little of the weight pressing on my heart.

Here I was, dreaming of this mystery boy while my people are gone. My home is gone. It doesn't make sense that I'm alive while they aren't. It's not fair. I should have been with them. I should have saved them… I should have…

"How are you feeling, honey?" Rubin regards me slowly, a slight frown pulling at his lips. He doesn't stop rubbing my head and I don't want him to either. How long has it been since someone touched me in such a caring, loving way?

"They're gone." That's all I can say. Ozvios left nothing behind of my home and people. He destroyed them like the olden times—like when I was Indigo, with a black hole only he can control.

Wait. Ozvios… Something clicks in my head. If Ozvios did this, that means Ozvios exists in an actual form. He's not some powerless bogeyman drifting and devouring through the stars, pulling the Ilori's strings. He's been watching, waiting, all along. A coward, like Halsiba said, but a powerful coward. And that power will call to mine, until one of us is dead. Where is he? And why hasn't he snuffed me out yet?

Before I can answer those questions, Rubin cuts in.

"I was wondering...you used to be able to create life, right?" His hand pauses on my forehead. "Can you do that and bring them all back?"

As Zaira, no. But I'm not *just* Zaira anymore. Indigo lingers in my mind and memories. Some part of them has unlocked, yet it wasn't enough to stop the inevitable. It might not ever be enough.

Long ago, Indigo learned that for every creation, there was a destruction of equal magnitude. That's what caused The First Chaos. It's what created a hole for Ozvios to crawl from and wreak havoc on the universe.

Before the explosion, Indigo hadn't created in this body, with this mind. Things are different now. There's a darkness and anger inside me, threatening to overcome me, yet there's also this new brilliance too. One that requires ancient songs I can't quite remember. They are on the edge of my mind, though I don't think I'm quite ready yet.

If I was able to bring them back, what would I be willing to sacrifice in their stead? Myself? Without question. My new friends and their homes? No. But...what if I can find and sacrifice Ozvios?

If I kill a god, surely I can resurrect a planet. That would be balance. Right?

"Possibly," I say with uncertainty. If I find Ozvios, I can kill him. I can use that power and create—assuming I will know how to by then. Those are a lot of ifs. And since I couldn't save them the first time around, how can I succeed in bringing them back?

Tears fill my eyes and I shut them, feeling the warmth slide down my cheeks. Rubin continues patting my head, a comforting presence without being intrusive.

Wesley inhales sharply from the pilot's seat. "You need to understand, all our lives, we were told Mal Ares was gone. That it was a dead planet and no one lived there. We had no idea."

I shift and distance myself from Rubin. "And no one thought to look? Prove it false?"

Wesley twirls around in the chair, blocking out the flashing screen that must mean something new and terrible is happening. "It was the first Ilori colony. Even if we wanted to go there, the Ilori would never allow it. We know so little about your homeworld, only what the Ilori let us know, which was that it was dead."

Anger thrums in my stomach. "Someone could've tried. My people looked to the stars for aid that never came. The Ilori grounded our ships, cut off communication, isolated us, and my people died alone." My voice cracks. "They lived and died and lingered in the darkness. If anyone would've come, that would have changed our fate. Their fate."

Wesley nods, his eyes piercing mine. "You're right, I'm sorry." We sit in silence for a few beats and my anger begins to ebb out of me, replaced with sorrow once more. At the emotional shift, Wesley exhales slowly. "What was it like? Who taught you about the universe? Who made you feel loved?"

I shake my head, not wanting to go down that path of thought right now. Not ready to be more vulnerable than I already am. "What's wrong with the ship?"

Wesley's gaze doesn't leave mine. "It's breaking down so we're taking a straight shot to Andarra. Nothing we can't handle." At that though, his lip twitches. He's hiding something but I don't press. Not like he presses me. "Please, Zaira. Tell us about Mal Ares. Tell us so we can mourn with you."

"You can't. It means nothing to you—"

"*You* mean something to us," he says quietly. "You saved us over and over when you had no reason to. We care about you. We want to know you. Let us share your grief." And though I don't know what has caused this change in him or if he's telling the truth, I want to believe he is.

"Can I hold you?" Rubin asks behind me. "I'm a hugger and you definitely need one."

"Okay." A lump forms in my throat as he wraps his arms around me and holds me close.

"Mal Ares was a dark planet, right?" Wesley leans forward. "It had no access to a sun? How did it stay warm? How did you, as Indigo, create it?"

I close my eyes for a moment and envision my home before I answer. I remember the crumbled palace on the hill. My grandmother tapping my hands and telling me how powerful I was and am, how she believed in me.

When I open my eyes, I'm ready. "Mal Ares was their first creation… Part of me recalls Indigo making it, but I am *and* I am not Indigo. It's a different life, a different body. But I can still hear fragments of the song. Indigo didn't know you needed a sun at the beginning. They had a lot to learn." I laugh a little at the thought. Back then, Indigo didn't have a body in the way I do now. No, they were a concentration of solid stardust. Their songs weren't sung from a mouth, more like vibrations in a body.

"Indigo created Mal Ares and it was dark and cold and

could have been terrible." The memories sweep through my brain. Mine but not mine. "Just like I did near the black hole, Indigo created an explosion at the center of the world. One that was so powerful it made enough heat for life to prosper. And it did for a time. Grass and trees sprouted from the dirt. Condensation from the heat formed little pools and ponds and a river. It was still too dark, so Indigo lit up the sky with tiny gold stars, which they called twilights. That was what Mal Ares was like. Eternal night with a sky full of golden sparkling lights." I smile, remembering so long ago. I'd forgotten how it used to be, how hard Indigo had worked on making this world. How much they loved it. "But then Ozvios came and they battled across space and time. Indigo won, yet the price was too high. They chose to go back to Mal Ares and fade away, believing the time of gods was over. People had come together to unite and defeat Ozvios. They would do right by each other and didn't need Indigo anymore."

"But they did," Wesley says.

"The universe is a mess, Zaira." Rubin rests his head on my shoulder. "People have forgotten what it means to unite and have compassion. The Ilori stamped down any weakness and took over."

"That's what they did to Mal Ares?" Wesley states it like a question but he already knows the answer.

"Indigo had faded by the time the Ilori arrived. I think…I think they knew Indigo was there and that's why they came." Flashes of my people screaming and running flood my mind. The true Ilori arriving on their ships with their guns raised. "They weeded through the people, searching, killing along the way. The grass died. The trees turned to dust. And then…

my grandmother came to find Indigo. To find me. She had seen the future and knew it was time for Indigo to come back before Mal Ares was completely gone."

"And did she find you or Indigo?" Rubin wonders.

"Indigo had never truly left. But they didn't know how to reform. Their stardust settled in the planet's core, their power keeping the world warm enough for the nightweavers to live. A woman, Halsiba, volunteered to give me life. She never wanted to be a mother… She couldn't bear bringing a child into a dying world. But she would for me. She performed a song that combined Indigo's stardust with hers. Soon after, I was born." I take a deep breath. "The people had thought I would be born with all the knowledge of the universe, capable of changing everything with a snap of my fingers. My skin held a map of the stars after all. Unfortunately, they were wrong."

"You were a new child born from an old god." Wesley stares deeply into my eyes and shifts in his seat. "You had to begin all over again."

I laugh, surprising myself. "I had to learn to walk on legs, see with eyes, and sing with a voice. I had to learn math and geography and all these things Indigo had known before, but I didn't. It was frustrating and I was so angry. My grandmother would…" I see her brown face and vibrant brown eyes. Her curly gray hair and ready smile. "She said we all have to start this way and that I would grow and become wise like all creatures. She named me Zaira because I was bright and beautiful, and Citlali, her last name."

I take the necklace that's been tucked close to my heart since I left. In the center hangs the Citlali star. "She gave this to me, made me feel like I was her family. Like I belonged with her."

"That's beautiful." Rubin gently takes the pendant from my fingers.

"You were loved," Wesley agrees. "But...why did she send you to find me?"

"My grandmother—I never even knew her name—she was Andarran like you. She came to Mal Ares, saying she was bitten by the Jadu and it was her purpose to bring Indigo back. The Ilori had a treaty with Andarrans, so she could live wherever she wanted and they could do nothing about it. Until war was declared. We knew our time was running out." I remember her holding my face in her palms. Telling me that my hands must never shake, never falter. I hold the universe in them. I have a purpose and it's not to die for the Ilori. "In her recent vision of the future, there was a boy with dark brown skin and the bluest eyes she'd ever seen. I would meet him at Outerim 32, and together, we would save the universe. Together, we would defeat the Ilori."

Rubin gasps by my ear. "She wants you to fight the Ilori?"

"Not now," Wesley warns him. "Why me? What do I have to do with any of this? And how did she see me when she's not even here herself? I didn't think visions worked like that."

This time, the truth doesn't hurt. "I don't know. That was the vision she had. I never had the chance to question it. I escaped and came here."

Wesley turns his head, gazing far off. "The Jadu never kissed my fingers. I was afraid of them, too scared to let them thrust a purpose upon me that would dictate the course of my life. So I don't know what the future holds. Weird that someone believed I'd have a purpose beyond piloting a ship throughout the stars…" He trails off and I'm not sure if he'll continue, but he does. "I've never known someone who was gifted a purpose from the Jadu to lie. If she thought the two of us—"

"Three," Rubin interjects with a cocked eyebrow.

Wesley rolls his eyes. "If she believed the *three* of us could defeat the Ilori, then we are exactly where we need to be. Getting you and Rubin to Earth. It's already happening."

"Your purpose is more than that." Rubin sits a bit straighter. "You don't just get to drop us off and leave. We need you too."

"For now, we have to go to Andarra."

"Where you're from," I say quietly, losing myself to a memory. After creating Mal Ares, Indigo made Andarra. Indigo channeled their love for Mal Ares into crafting it, this time fashioning a sun first, which helped life to flourish. Indigo wanted waterfalls and deep lakes. And soon, immortal creatures suddenly appeared in the water—the Jadu. There's more to the story than them suddenly appearing, but I can't remember anything beyond them making the people happy, giving them visions of the future and the past to help the universe prosper. And there was color! Indigo wanted all the colors in existence in one place. Where Mal Ares was dark, Andarra was light. They weren't too far from each other because Indigo saw them like siblings. Opposites, but joined together by joy and wonder.

"Where your grandmother was from," Wesley adds or corrects, I'm not sure. "We won't be there long, but you need to be prepared, Zaira. Andarra might not be as you remember it. While it is beautiful, there's an ugliness underneath.

I have no doubt that when you created it as Indigo, you had fun. You thought you'd make it brilliant and positive. But… when immortals know the future, they manipulate, they lose their compassion. They…hurt each other. My own mother hurt me. That's why I'm here now. It's easy to blame the future for your unbearable present, easy to lie about it to unburden yourself."

"Why would she do that?" Rubin stiffens, his arms loosening around me.

"Because she didn't want me. She already had the perfect son with the perfect purpose. One who didn't run away from responsibility and duty. She sent me away and doesn't want me to come back." His voice falls while his eyes shimmer with tears he won't shed. "This universe is a terrible place with terrible people doing terrible things. The Ilori may be the easiest to point at, but ultimately, we all are villains in some ways. We let the Ilori get as far as they did. No one challenged them because it didn't affect the rest of us. We looked away and focused on ourselves. We allowed all of this to happen because at the center of life itself, there's a desire to let everything die."

"No," Rubin blurts. "You can't believe that, right? You don't have such a gloomy perspective on…on everything, do you?" He turns to me. "Tell him it's not true. Tell him why you created the universe."

I can't though. From what I've seen and experienced in my time on Mal Ares, this is the truth. I may have found love with my grandmother and the dwindling remainder of my people, but beyond that? We were abandoned. Left in the dark to die.

No one cared about us.

The universe Indigo once created has shifted away from unity and compassion to something angry and ugly. Now I'm the last of my kind alive, unsure if I want to save it. Or if I want to destroy the Ilori like they destroyed my people. My fists clench by my sides.

I do. I want to destroy them more than I want to save this universe. I want to hunt Ozvios to the edge of everything and bring my home back. If there is such a way. Though I won't share that ambition with Wesley and Rubin yet. We are just beginning to understand each other and admitting my desire to be terrible and do terrible things—to not only let everything die, but to kill it too—would ruin that.

"The two of you need more sunshine in your life. Thankfully, you got me and I'm going turn those frowns upside down." Rubin interrupts my thoughts. "For real though, I get why you might see things that way, given…everything. But I'm going to show you the beauty of the universe and the stars. Just you wait and see. I've been all kinds of places, met all kinds of people and creatures, and though you aren't the same Indigo that made all this, I'm going to show why you did. You too," he says, looking over at Wesley. "I'm not going to let anything happen to either of you."

"I probably should be the one saying that," I mutter.

"It's implied, really. I don't have powers," he chuckles. "Just a desire for beauty, truth, and love."

Wesley sighs. "Yeah, well, we'll need all three of those if we want to fit in on Andarra and get out unnoticed."

"I got you." Rubin smirks and leans over to grab his little bag. "How tight do you like your pants?"

THE WAR ACROSS THE UNIVERSE

Reported by *Galactic News* correspondents, L'avi Jonu & Nyla Harkibi, recorded and transmitted live from Estrella, Maru Monchuri

L'avi Jonu (LJ): Good morning, allies! Let's get straight to business: today the first transport of the royal Marun army, The Soleil, have reached planet Earth. On the ground, we're told there is a large group of Andarrans and humans forming their defense on the West Coast of a country called United States—

Nyla Harkibi (NH): If it's still called that after Ilori invasion and now colonization, is questionable. The entire world is in disarray; borders and cultures and political turmoil have had to take a backseat now that they have one common enemy. Most humans have been isolated in human housing constructed by the labmade Ilori, and those that are free are on the frontlines, waiting for the war.

LJ: That's right. Though it's only been months for us, it has been over two human years of Ilori control. Swaths of humanity were lost in the invasion, more still lost in the new program established by the Ilori that would make it possible to inhabit a human body while retaining your own consciousness. Truly terrifying.

NH: Yes, but, because of the declaration of war, because of our new Marun royals, the plan to make Earth a vacation destination has been halted. Emperor 1lv is said to be furiously traveling in Mothership IpS1L II between colonies, amassing an army… Things have never been more perilous.

LJ: You're right about that. But there is still hope. Let me say that again for everyone listening: there is hope. More worlds have come out to join the allies, promising armies, supplies, and ships. And there has never been a time in history that so many of us have been united or connected—

NH: Except the battle against Ozvios, if you believe the story of The First Chaos.

LJ: A story we could use as inspiration. Right now, we are sharing knowledge and resources. King Yecki from XiGRa has pledged, along with King Felix and Queen Joy, the First of Their Names, to create the first republic.

NH: Just the thought of everyone banding together like this…
(sniffs). It's truly magical. It makes us feel like not only do we
have a chance, but we have a community outside our system.

LJ: Absolutely. We don't know the future, but we do know,
in times of crisis, who we are determines who we will be. If
we are kinder, braver, stronger together, then there should be
no reason for us to split apart again… That said, a formal in-
quiry has been lodged regarding the explosions on Outerim
32 and the masses of Ilori soldiers taken into custody. None
of our allies are taking responsibility for it, which leads authorities to believe it was a rogue assailant, unaffiliated with
any government.

NH: If you notice outsiders with strange abilities in your
world, The Intergalactic Cooperation would appreciate you
reporting them to your local authorities. There may be a new
enemy in our midst.

CHAPTER THIRTEEN

Wesley

"He was always a good boy, never tough, never mean.
He'd smile big and his laugh was loud.
And he'd look at me and call me brother, and I was proud.
But I knew…it wouldn't last.
Nothing good ever can."

—The Starry Eyed, "Broken Bond"

On the cusp of Andarran airspace, the hopper's siren starts to wail again. After that entirely cheesy heartfelt conversation ended—which, admittedly, may have helped Zaira feel better but made me feel more emotional than I would've liked—things were almost normal in the cabin.

Now this happens. Because we just cannot catch a break.

Zaira's beside me at once, hitting tabs on the screen. "The engine is about to die."

"We can coast on gravity for a little while, right?" Rubin says, leaning in from my other side. "Once we're over Andarra, we should be okay, right?"

"Sure," I lie. If we don't crash into the port, assuming our landing gear still works, or we sink into the water and get lost in the current. Sure.

"I don't feel reassured, Wesley Daniels." Rubin bunches his lips together while he glances down at my vivid red glitter pants he told me I had to wear. They fit nice, but don't leave much to the imagination. "I'm telling you, if we crash, people will want to save you right away in those pants."

"Now *I* don't feel reassured," I mumble just as the comms crackles.

"Where are you coming from, skipper?" The voice is pleasant, the language one I haven't heard in a long while. Maybe too long. Andarran is lyrical and singsongy and far too friendly. "Your ship's shredding metal."

"Yes," I answer quickly. "Had a dust up near XiGRa. Used too much power…"

"Hmm," the voice says. "And how do you feel about that? I sense hesitation and—"

"I'm perfectly fine, thank you." I try not to yell it but annoyance threads my words. Andarra is the one place where they can read your emotions and use them against you. One minute you're flying a plane, the next you're sitting in a therapy session discussing your driving aggression and how it likely has to do with your relationship issues that stem from childhood trauma. No, thanks. I just need to play it safe and keep it short. "Can we dock on the far side of Yumi City?"

There's a pause on the comms as if they're considering.

"You are aware there is an element of minor crime in that area, including but not limited to: pickpocketing, emotional manipulation, street racing, underground fighting rings, up-selling, general lying, and stray animals that will steal your food and/or belongings?"

At that, Rubin's brows rise and his lips curve at the corners. I try to hold in the laugh that's forming in the center of my gut.

"I'm aware, thank you," I say through clenched teeth. "May we dock there?"

Another pause. "You have permission. There are three empty slots on the far left. Happy travels and we here, at Andarra Air Traffic, sincerely hope you do not die." The line goes cold and I shake my head.

They did sincerely mean that, which is honestly worse than if they were being sarcastic. "Ferking Andarra." The curse leaves my mouth quietly, though it's screaming in my head. I don't want to be here. I shouldn't be here.

But this is the only choice. It'll be okay, as long as I don't see my family, my mother. They'll never even know I was here.

I'm immediately racked with guilt. Unlike Zaira, I didn't lose everything. My family is alive, across Yumi City, in their fine home surrounded by their abundant gardens and brooks frequented by the Jadu.

They probably forgot I existed. My mother already had one perfect biological son, and then decided to have one more. Clearly, that was a mistake.

Metal warps and creaks, pulling me from my negative thoughts. As we enter Andarra's atmosphere, the ship lets out a long unhappy groan. We don't have much time till this bird needs to land and get repaired. We might not make it; *that* should be my focus now. Not families and their abandonment. No, Rubin needs to get to Earth. Zaira needs to save the universe from the Ilori. I need to get everyone where they're going and then I can slag off to wherever I want as the world ends.

The blue sky greets us, the sun's rays filtering through the cabin window. The air shifts around us from heavy to light, from sad to hopeful. If only for a moment. Below us, the crystal blue waters sparkle, and beneath their rippling waves, the translucent Jadu swim and make plans for the future. My heart expands—further proof that hearts are nonsensical— relieved to be home. Where I don't stand out and inspire hate.

Here I am. One of them. Another empath bound to live forever...barring sudden death. My eyes don't cause stares, my long body disappears in the crowds of other long bodies. For a moment, I let myself feel welcomed where I could belong.

If they hadn't forced me out.

"It's more beautiful than I imagined," Rubin says beside me. "The colors. Look, Zaira. Look at the sun and the water. You did that."

"Indigo did that," she corrects, though neither of us know why she feels the need to differentiate. She *is* Indigo. "Indigo...loved the two worlds. They had wished... We, I guess, had wished Mal Ares would've looked like this one day, even in the dark." Her voice goes soft and suddenly our cabin fills with sorrow again, a combination of hers and mine.

I need to get out of here, back to the calm nothingness of my life, where my biggest concern was a dead tentacled blob. It's been one disaster after another for the last six rotations, and all I have to show for it is a scary space god and an excitable radio host who wears the flashiest, strangest clothing I've ever seen.

"I've always wanted to come here," Rubin exclaims. I'd ask him why he hasn't before—it's the most visited planet in the universe, without a doubt—but the ship's screens light up again.

"Warning. Close proximity. Warning, engine malfunction. Warning," Zaira translates. "Are we going to make it?"

"Yeah, definitely." I mean, maybe. Possibly. Becoming more unlikely every passing second. "We just need to—"

The engine cuts out and for a moment, there's silence. Everything's so still. Everything's so terrifying. We plummet toward the ground. Rubin screams at a pitch that is entirely too high while Zaira's eyes widen and she tries to grasp what to do. The pressure in the cabin is completely off, but we haven't risen to the roof of the pod—we're just dealing with good ole gravity.

As for me, I keep holding the thrusters like the ship will come back to life and need steering. My body clearly hasn't caught up to what my brain knows. We're going to crash. We're going to die. Unless…

"Zaira," Rubin shouts over the rushing wind. "Baby, now would be the time to do something."

She stares off. "I'm trying… Something shifted inside me the last time. I don't—"

"We have to slow down," my voice finally says, surprising myself. "How do we slow down?" Though I ask it aloud, I'm not expecting either of them to answer.

"Is there a chute? I feel like little hoppers have chutes."

Rubin scrambles over to the dash, searching. "What's *chute* in Mal Aresian?"

"I think… Yes." She bolts over beside him as we freefall over Andarra. "Here."

She pulls a lever and…nothing happens. Just a weird, defeated gasp of an empty chamber releasing stale air.

"Do we think that worked?" Rubin glances around, hands waving. "Wesley, did that work?"

I glare at him. He knows that old thing didn't work. He knows it but he can't accept it. This is why I never travel with idealists. This right here. Always thinking the best is going to happen when there's absolutely no proof it will.

"Zaira, what else you got? Can you do that little singing gold stars thing? I loved that. Are we going to die? Seriously?" Rubin's legs are running in place, while his voice is shrieking, and his arms are thrown across the walls. "I haven't even been knighted yet. I haven't told enough stories. There are places I haven't seen. I only made out a handful of times with like two other podcasters and both times sucked. Christiano Rumeldo hasn't finished that new wardrobe he promised me. I can't die before I wear that!" He stops and stares at the floor like he could see our impending doom. "It's getting closer, isn't it? This is the end?"

"No," Zaira says. "Shh…" She holds her arms out and closes her eyes. She's about to do one of her songs when comms pierces the cabin.

"Skipper, you're coming in hot. Too hot." The same voice as before sounds friendly, almost bubbly, as if they aren't promising our death. "Your metal's all shredded. For the greater good of Andarra, we will need to shoot you down if you cannot slow."

"Um…no, please!" Rubin yells at the dash. "We'll fix it!"

"We've got it covered." My tone sounds confident, though I feel anything but. We're still free-falling.

Zaira emits a slight hum. Her feet lift from the floor. Gold sparks spiral around her and rise to the surface on her cheeks. This is not the same Zaira who fought the Ilori on the Outerim. This isn't the same Zaira that destroyed a missile in the middle of space.

This is the one who saved us from the black hole.

We're both mesmerized by her when the comms crackles again.

"Skipper, you have a three-second warning. Again, we will be forced to shoot if you don't slow. We are sorry for the negativity, you understand."

"No, we don't understand! Don't shoot us!" Rubin's gaze meets mine before he swivels back to Zaira. "Baby, you gotta hurry up."

"Three."

"Zaira, you can do this." I add my voice into the chaotic mix. I don't know if she can do this. She's done a lot of amazing, impossible things, but this could be the one she can't do. Things are different now. She said it herself. She looks different.

"Two."

"Zaira, we believe in you." Rubin's lips tremble as he shuts his eyes and grabs my hand tight.

"One…"

We wait for the shot. We wait for everything to splinter and explode around us. We wait…and nothing happens.

Zaira's eyes are gold and bright. She lifts her arms and the ship stops in midair. Gods only know how close we are to the ground. Well, I guess that god does know. Rubin and I look at each other, afraid to say a word. Afraid that the moment we disrupt the stillness, we'll go back to plummeting to our deaths.

The silence is short-lived. "Skipper, are you there? What happened? Skipper?"

When Zaira speaks, it's in perfect Andarran. "Our ship will fall into the water shortly. Please have a crew nearby to lift us out."

"We can do that," the comms responds quickly, then there's a hesitation. "May I ask who I'm speaking to?"

"Wesley…um…" Seriously? A lie didn't just spring to my lips and save me in my time of need? If I say my full name, my mother will be notified. After all, my brother is an intergalactic superstar doing the gods' work. And my mother…well…

Rubin shakes his head at me, plastering a smile on his beautiful face at the same time. I know what he's going to do—draw attention, smooth things over—but it's not a smart idea. Before I can stop him, he exclaims, "This is Rubin Rima of *The Rubin Rima Podcast*!"

The comms goes blank and I wonder if we've been cut off or if they're already bored with us. Unfortunately, neither of my guesses are correct.

"Oh, my gods! Roooo-bin Reee-ma! I love your podcast. You're so talented! Can I get your autograph ground-side? I'm going to tell everyone—"

"Please don't," I butt in.

Rubin doesn't care though, because he isn't thinking about the fact that the Ilori want him dead. He's thinking about us, about our safety, by glossing over our many issues and any rising questions with his celebrity. "Sure, I can—"

And that's when our ship makes a slower but still plummety descent toward the ocean. One second, we're standing still, held midair by a spooky golden Zaira, the next we're—well, Rubin is screaming again. He's got his entire body wrapped around mine. Zaira, meanwhile, is still holding her arms out as if she's directing our fall.

Maybe she is.

We make a gentle impact in less than a minute, which means we were *so* close to death before. The water bounces around us, and though we're still standing, my legs feel mushy from the panic. Rubin still hasn't let me go. And Zaira... She's back to brown eyes, but the constellations on her skin have shifted from swirly black ink to faint gold. She's more luminous than before, more...alive than before.

She looks like a god. If I hadn't seen the transformation with my own eyes, I wouldn't know she's the same person. She's still tall and perfectly wide, curvy with short kinky hair, but everything else is different. It's like the center of the universe lives beneath her skin.

She is Indigo and Zaira. A god and a girl.

My heart swells looking at her. "This is possibly the fourth time you've saved my life. And each time, I didn't really deserve it and I don't know—"

"You do," she says without elaboration.

I'm not sure it's true. This whole time I've been closed off to her, unkind, and unsure. But I'm going to do better. I'm going to be better, at least a little bit. I have to. Although I may not have lost my world, my family, my everything… not like she did, I did lose my compassion over the last years.

Right here, right now, I vow to get it back. Zaira came to me with a destiny. She believed that, together, we could do huge things. Maybe, just maybe, we can…though I can't imagine how much I could contribute next to an actual god. But I know I can help more. Be kinder.

"Group hug!" Rubin yanks Zaira into us and I let out a yelp as her warm body presses against ours. "You know, I don't have family, but…after near-death experiences with you both, I feel like this might be one? Like, the bonds run deep between us. Me, my god-sister, and my cute pilot—what more could I ask for?"

"Dry land," I say with a smirk, trying not to focus too heavily on the *cute-pilot* bit.

"Food," Zaira admits, meeting my gaze.

A smile reaches my eyes. "Sleep in an actual bed."

"Fewer near-death experiences…"

"Okay, okay." Rubin squeezes us both tighter. "I'm just saying, there's no one else I'd rather be nearly killed several times with." He squeezes one more time and then lets us go. "What adventure will we have next?"

"Figure out how much it'll cost to fix the ship, find somewhere off the beaten path to sleep, fly out tomorrow." All the confidence I wish I felt creeps into my words. I sound like a leader, like someone who knows what they're doing. I'm beginning to think I put on this act for myself more than for them.

Thankfully, my plan should work without hassle. There should be absolutely no reason this doesn't go down how we want it to. We won't need to linger. We'll be smart, make sure no one knows us, and we'll be safer. We'll get in and get out.

We'll travel to Earth and figure out our plans and then I'll leave them when everything's fine. I'll have my life back, but I'll be a better person too.

Easy.

CHAPTER FOURTEEN

Zaira

Indigo is alive inside of me. Memories and power rush through my mind and veins. Their power is unlocking. Slowly. It's as if I was looking through rose-tinted glasses my entire life and now more colors are seeping through as the lenses break. I'm changing. And I don't know what that means, yet. What I can do or who I am. Who I want to be when Indigo is no longer a separate entity, but a part of me.

"The ship's dead. There's nothing that can be fixed." The mechanic looks at Wesley as he says it, his voice snapping me out of the revelation. He ignores me and Rubin, believing that neither one of us knows anything about ships. He's right, but I don't like that he assumes it.

I look outside the open doors. Andarra, even the little bit that I've seen of it by the docks, is beautiful. Crystal blue water sparkles in the distance while multicolored houses and buildings dot the skyline. The warm sun shines down on this world, making everything glimmer and sparkle. When night comes, the water will light up with the bioluminescence of the many harmless sea creatures that flourish in this world. It's all beauty, all the time.

This world was meant to be a celebration of love and life. Of colors and brightness. Of the future and the past. On the surface, it is all of those things…but I wonder what lies beneath like Wesley said.

While Wesley and the mechanic argue, my thoughts turn dark once more. I picture my grandmother in the castle on the hill. I see her standing there, lighting the fires, burning it all down to draw the Ilori away from me. The sacred ceremony—my death—was supposed to happen there.

Did she somehow manage to escape the planet before it was destroyed? Is she still alive? Did the ghosts of my people find peace in their destruction? Is there a way for me to fix them?

I shake my head at the thought, earning a cocked eyebrow from Rubin. I turn away, not wanting the conversation right now.

If it weren't for Wesley and Rubin, I would have never unlocked a sliver of Indigo's memories or abilities—or perhaps it's because of all the near-death experiences. Either way, my mind is changing, my power too. In that respect, my grandmother was right. Wesley Daniels is important. But we didn't save Mal Ares. I unlocked some part of Indigo, yet I still don't know how to bring my people back. I wouldn't have cared what was to be sacrificed for them to live again. They deserved life.

They deserved a better home and a better god than me.

Now they're well and truly lost. And it's my fault. Tears slip down my cheeks and I swipe at them furiously.

Wesley inhales sharply, glancing at me from the corner of his eye. He's reading my emotions right now and he doesn't like it. I'd apologize, but the mechanic is talking and...I'm not sure I am sorry.

"I can give you a used ship, a more modern version of the ship you just crashed, for less money than it is to rebuild one. It's the last one I've got and it'll sell fast." The mechanic sets his hand down hard on the table. He's not an Andarran, whose careers stick to art and expression and the beauty of the world. My guess is that he's an immigrant who realized someone with technical skills could make a lot of money on Andarra. We can use that somehow.

"I don't want to spend my advance on a new ship," Wesley says with a shake of his head. He looks at Rubin. "You're the loaded one. You should buy the new ship,"

Rubin lowers his lips to Wesley's ear, and Wesley stiffens at the contact. "Codrec said not to pay with my own credits. A few people here and there can know who I am, but a money trail would be easier for the Ilori to track..."

"Fine, I'll do it. You better pay me back." Wesley quickly steps away from Rubin.

"What are you all, siblings? Triplets?" The mechanic glances at the three of us with our dark brown skin and garish glittery outfits. It doesn't matter that we are dissimilar in every other way. That Wesley's eyes read Andarran, Rubin's hair is a traditional style from the western colonies, or that my accent is difficult to place and gold shimmers beneath my skin.

"We're family," Rubin answers with a smirk.

Wesley's gaze narrows, avoiding the question completely. "I'll transfer the melios through a cred line—"

The mechanic shakes his head. "No, cash only. Otherwise, you're going to have to go to another shop—"

Wesley turns. "That's fine—"

"Except they're all closed for the Andarran holiday of Nexus," the mechanic cuts in. Though there's a smile on his face, he's not happy about our circumstances. He just wants our money. He knows we're desperate outsiders. Even Wesley.

Wesley grimaces and I step up to the desk, pegging the mechanic with a glare. Something inside me shifts, something new...like recognition. Suddenly, I know he's from Minor Sidarra. A child of two poor mothers. I see flashes of his life. He left home as a teenager, fell into his trade. Brought his mothers here where they became popular seamstresses. I know him as if...as if I created him. And I guess maybe Indigo did, but it's never been like this before. I feel him. I feel the stardust swirling around in his chest. I know his dream—to build ships for royalty—but he never gets close.

I will do this for him. Somehow.

"Midrel," I begin carefully, and his whole body stiffens. "We need that ship. Will you take pity on us and hold it while we find cash?"

Midrel stares at me for a long moment, tapping his fingers on the counter. "Who are you?"

"A stranger in a strange land." I stand tall, keep my voice steady. It's a lie of course; the power thrumming through my veins created this land and most others. It can't be strange to me, only disconnected. Only different than what Indigo intended so long ago in another form, another life.

Rubin slides in beside me, taking my lead. "Haven't you ever felt the same and wished someone would show a bit of kindness to you? We could all use more kindness. Please."

He bows his head to us, and when his eyes meet mine again, there's a warmth in them that wasn't there before. "I can hold the ship, even knock some of the price off if you let me keep the spare parts from your wreck. But I'd need the money tonight."

Rubin nudges me with his shoulder and Wesley's lips twitch.

"We'll do that. We'll be back soon." I thread my arms through Wesley's and Rubin's and lead them out of the shop, into the breezy warm air.

"Where are we going to find enough cash that fast?" Rubin's gaze fixes on the vibrant buildings along the docks where ships, both for water and air, sit idly. Waiting, I'd imagine, for their next adventure.

Wesley's tone is grave when he speaks. "The fighting pits."

Rubin's brows knit together. "You mean, we'll make bets?"

Wesley shakes his head. "No, one of us is going to have to fight." He turns to me, a question in his expression that goes unasked. "And win. A lot."

Rubin throws his hands up. "No. She can't do that. She's a god, Wesley. There must be another—"

Wesley huffs. "If you want to get to Earth, she's our only hope. I know—"

"I'll do it," I interject. "We're family, right?" We have to be because the only other family I have has been devoured by a black hole at the edge of the universe. Their loss lingers so close to my own surface, my pain is so visceral, that I need to hurt something. I need to numb the grief with the senselessness of violence. "Family do what they must for one another to succeed. I can do this for us."

For me.

THE RUBIN RIMA PODCAST

Not broadcasting, in a bathroom in the fighting pits
arena

RR: Hey, spacers! It's Rubin Rima, coming to you *not*
live from Andarra, you know, *the* Andarra; home of the
future-telling color-explosion fashionistas. AKA the
number one destination on my bucket list. It's as beautiful as I imagined, but definitely not as fun. Mostly
because—

WD: Rubin, what are you doing in there? Who are you
talking to?

RR: No one, just talking to myself. You know, like therapy. Self-affirmations and stuff. It's all good.

WD: ... Okay. Whatever. I'm going to help Zaira get ready,
meet me in the arena seating, third seat, second row.

RR: Yep... Anyway, spacers, life's not great. I've been in
nearly three ship crashes, met and befriended a god,
which is also the only good news, and now we're at a
fighting pit. It's super grimy, there's been no mention of
delicious food, the people smell weird—not at all what
you'd expect of one of the universe's oldest civilizations.

RR: Which, on topic but side note, did you know the universe's oldest civilization was Mal Ares? Some of you
have never heard of this world, because up until a few
days ago, it was said to have been dead and gone for a

long time. Well, anyway, the god friend, Zaira, she's from Mal Ares. The one thing I remember reading about Mal Ares is that it used to be home to space witches. They could move objects, do things with their minds through song. Truly scary stuff, or beautiful if you think about it. Anyway, Zaira's one of those space witches with magic... only now she's channeling Indigo's power, which is gold and creates life and stuff. She doesn't really have a handle on it...

RR: Side note aside and back to the business of why I'm hiding in a bathroom. Andarran fighting pits are terrifying. First, they are located beneath the docks of Yumi City. It's dark down here, unclean, and filled with violence. As you all know, I'm a pacifist, so it's not my vibe at all. We've already met a few seedy characters who wanted us to place bets and do other nefarious things. And again, no one has offered us delicious food, which I thought was very much part of the Andarran culture. Like I read in a book that the moment you land, someone will offer you delicious food...

RR: What I'm saying is this is *so* not meeting my expectations. But there's a story here. A story about how Andarra, one of the oldest, most beautiful civilizations, has a dirty little secret below their polished streets and reputation. Maybe knowing the future and the past at the same time has created this sort of...I don't know, disconnect? Like maybe they throw themselves into bad things just to be impulsive, unpredictable...

Unknown: Hey, are you almost done in there? There's a line!

RR: Almost done! Anyway, Zaira has to fight for us to buy a new ship and get Earth-side. Things have never been worse. Like my boo, who has lost her home and family, is going to get fighty on stage just to help me get to Earth. Friends, this is not ideal at all. I feel lost, like a loser who can't make her happy and safe. Who can't even spend my millions of melios to help my friends. You know? So yeah. I guess this is the end of this episode. Hopefully, in a few rotations, I'll be back on the path to Earth and we'll be okay. Hopefully I'll be on my way to report from the front lines of the battle for the universe. Hopefully...my little family is going to stay together somehow. And hopefully someone is going to offer me delicious food. I'm starving.

CHAPTER FIFTEEN

Wesley

Getting Zaira into the fighting pits as a competitor wasn't hard at all. They were desperate for fresh blood, and bonus, with her strong body, she looked like a worthwhile contender. I made her sneer for extra showmanship. From there, they led us down shadowy hallways to the backstage. Torn posters and speckled walls surrounded the cushioned floor and the fighters, most tall and lithe, as they practiced their movements and meditations. We barely had time to glance at the large space when two Dosanis with green tentacles and no-nonsense attitudes thrust a black uniform into Zaira's hands. Then I was politely asked to leave.

After a short nod from Zaira, I left, found Rubin in the bathroom, and sidled into a seat in the arena saved for friends or family.

As I look around, I'm grateful no one catches my eye or

recognizes me here. If they had, my mother would send servants to track me down and bring me home. Or…more likely, to escort me off her planet, as far away from her as possible.

You see, my family has a reputation. Not royal, not even political. Just crucial to the fate of the universe. Because, according to my mother, the Danielses are connected (she says descended but that makes zero sense) to the Jadu, and thus have been trusted to fulfill mightily important destinies. We will be the salvation of the universe. Sounded like rubbish, but people believed it. So did I…until I didn't.

As a child growing up with that mentality thrust upon me, the pressure to be perfect was too much to bear. We had no father; both my brother and I were conceived from donors my mother selected. It was the three of us. My mother, bit by the Jadu when she was a child and given a huge purpose she never shared with us, my brother who would be the catalyst for war on Earth, and me…who was too afraid to be bitten, too afraid to be given a purpose. And therefore was sent away to be forgotten.

Perhaps they have forgotten me. It's been nearly a decade since we were in the same place, so maybe I don't have to worry about being recognized here. I doubt anyone knows my face anymore. They probably don't even remember my name.

The audience cheers and I look up quickly to catch a fighter, a pale-skinned Andarran with white-blond hair, throw a blue-scaled Minor Sidarran into the black cage. Their body zings and pops with electricity. That was a drastic mistake for the Andarran.

The Minor Sidarran ambles to their feet, swaying on its scaly almost-amphibian legs. Their gills, pocking their cheeks, inhale the rank air. If I didn't know what they were, I'd say the Andarran won. The Minor Sidarran, one of the sea creatures from the beach islands, clutches its stomach as if in pain. They aren't though. They're recovering and absorbing. Their home is under the tumultuous middle seas, but they can survive just as fine on land.

And they love electricity. Gobble it up.

The Andarran realizes this as the Minor Sidarran stretches to its full, enormous height. They look stronger than before and their eyes crackle with electrical current. When they open their fists, those too shimmer with electricity. They're maintaining it. Preparing to use it. This is going to be so painful.

The crowd gasps and cheers. The tension and suspense in the arena is palpable. Desire whiffs through the air; desire for harm and action and anything that breaks up the mundane. Andarrans have held the pressure of knowledge on their shoulders too long and they need an output. They need unpredictability. This is it.

The Andarran fighter timidly steps back. If I were them, I would tap out here. Nothing good can come of this. Determination rolls off the Minor Sidarran in waves. The other Andarrans groan around me. If this is their prizefighter, it's about to be over.

The Minor Sidarran stalks forward and I close my eyes. I can't watch this needless violence, even if I just asked Zaira to take part in it so we can get out of here. Some people in the crowd cringe, some moan, some yowl. I try to zone it all out, feeling too many emotions spiral around me, none of them positive.

My shoulders hunch up to my ears, my lips bunched together. A hand wraps around my shoulder and I let out a yelp. Next thing I know, Rubin's voice is in my ear.

"Not into fighting, huh?" There's a smile in his tone. There's probably one on his face too but I haven't opened my eyes. "The Andarran's losing big-time. Minor Sidarrans, baby, they don't lose."

My voice is nearly a strangled whisper. "How can you watch that?"

"These aren't death matches. Also, I pretend every time they get close to each other, instead of punching or hitting or whatever, they'll kiss and love will win." He shrugs, his shoulders hitting mine. "I live in hope. Like, wouldn't that be a huge surprise?"

I shake my head, letting out a giggle I didn't know I had in me given the circumstances. "You're too idealistic. Always believing in the greater good."

He hums beside me. "Better than believing the worst like you."

"I don't believe the worst, I know it. This universe is full of no-good, heartless creatures that have lost sight of what it means to be in all of this together," I grumble. "People need someone like you on their radio waves telling them hope is worthwhile. While people living in the shadows like me prove over and over that it isn't."

"You're too cute to be so pessimistic." Rubin's fingers gently caress the bottom of my chin. My entire body stiffens and I stifle a gasp. "Look at me."

"I don't want to see the stage," I admit reluctantly while also secretly freaking out that Rubin Rima is touching me. He's all sunshine and rainbows—that's why I crushed on him from afar. But up close, that optimism drives me mad.

"Then don't." He gently pulls my head toward him and I inhale sharply. "Look at me, Wesley. I'll shield you from it."

Slowly—on their own volition, it feels like—I open my eyes and stare into his beautiful face. His brown eyes seem to have glitter swirling inside them. His dark brown skin is radiant and his gaze... It's kind. Compassionate. I begin to realize that I unfairly judged Rubin when I finally met him after years of being a fan. He's complex, layered. He's both flawed and perfect. My shoulders unhunch and I exhale.

"See? I got you, babe." He smiles, big and wide, his perfect white teeth gleaming only inches from mine. As the crowd goes wild, all I focus on is Rubin. "Now, I remember you saying you used to be a fan of mine. Am I to take it you still are?"

My lips twitch, unsure if I should scowl or smile. "Don't push it, Rubin."

"I'm a fan of yours," he says softly. "I wish I'd known you existed earlier."

And I don't want to ask, I really don't, but my mouth has other plans. "Why?"

He laughs a little, and if it's possible, he shines a bit brighter. I feel like I'm being held by the sun, and instead of being burned, I'm warmed and cherished and safe. Every bad thought and angry tendency dissipate in his light. "You have the classic protagonist vibe I'm desperate for in my life. Interesting. Gorgeous. The universe has disappointed you and you need someone to stay when everyone else has left. I could be that person for you."

I clear my throat, glad my cheeks aren't capable of blazing red and that Rubin can't hear my heart threatening to pound through my chest. "You probably sweet-talk everyone. I bet you make people feel like...like they've never been seen until you saw them." I tear my eyes from his, staring down at my lap instead. "You just met me a few days ago. You don't know me. Everything's been a mess and you're scared. You're looking for something to make sense."

"You're Andarran, aren't you?" He cocks an eyebrow. "Do you feel anything false in what I've said to you?"

I swallow carefully. I sense fear close to Rubin's surface, but it's unusual. He's... I focus on him and his emotions, trying to forget that he's holding me close and it's making my heart leap in my chest. Right, focus. He's afraid, but beneath that, it's...vulnerability. He's not thinking about our run-ins with death right now; he's afraid that being honest with me means he has opened himself up to my judgment. He's worried that I'll dismiss him. The way he looks at me now, his gaze unbreaking, tells me he knows what I'm feeling from him. When I open my mouth to confirm he's right, the words shrivel on my tongue.

Because if I say what I know to be true...it'd make me vulnerable too.

Thankfully, he doesn't linger on that. "We're alive because of you. And Zaira. Well, mostly Zaira if we're being really real." The crowd boos and something happens on stage. I inadvertently twist in my seat to see, but Rubin holds me firm. "Despite what you think about me, about my fame and sweet-talking, I've never told anyone anything like what I just told you. I can't commit to something or someone when I don't have a bond in place. I'm slow to all of this."

I nod. So am I. I've never felt comfortable enough to share my own emotions with someone else. Never formed strong friendships where I didn't worry about judgment. Never kissed a single soul. Never wanted to either. I'm easily attracted to concepts and ideas of who someone is. Then they talk or do something small that makes me reconsider. Everything has been one-sided in my life. Love. Family. Friends. I wouldn't even know what it would mean if someone stuck with me.

Rubin seems to read my thoughts. "Wesley, you're going to have to ditch this one-man-on-a-mission-against-the-world thing you have going on. You may be able to see the future—"

"I can't," I admit. "Only Andarrans who have been bitten by the Jadu can do that. I never have. Each time I came close, I chickened out. I lost my nerve and eventually my mother told me to stop trying."

His lips lift at the edges as if he's choosing his words carefully. "Maybe that's a good thing. Maybe she had a reason."

"She did." I shake my head. "She knew I can't be trusted to do what's right for the greater good. That I didn't fit here. I don't fit anywhere."

"You fit with me and Zaira. Let us in. She has no one. I have only fakers who want my money and fame. We're outcasts, all of us. But now we have each other and we can change everything. You see that, don't you?" He holds my gaze now, and we're so close his breath skitters across my lips.

"I—"

Someone on stage calls attention to the room and Rubin's face breaks out in a smile.

"See, I told you I could distract you." He says it kindly, letting his hands drop from my chin and neck. "Zaira will be up soon."

I say something inaudible, terrified that everything he said might've been false, just a ruse to make me feel better. Maybe it was. I can't think about that, no matter how much I want to. Instead, I look around. The crowd has changed, now skewing older, more experienced, more dangerous. Bets have been placed. This is the big fight. It'll be Zaira, no doubt, and some popular giant they paired against her.

Everyone but me and Rubin wants Zaira to lose. Things are going to get very, very tense. I feel it in the air. Desperation. Fury. Need. Rubin threads his fingers through mine. And though he can't feel the crowd's emotions like I do, he senses it.

Zaira's in danger. We put her up there for us, and we may end up killing her.

Before I can dart to my feet to find her, tell her there must be another way, the announcer comes onto the stage. They, an Andarran wearing a long oceanic tunic with flared sleeves—despite that being Harcena traditional garb, a group that abhors violence—clap their hands, getting everyone's attention.

Their voice is smooth from years of experience opening fights. "Welcome to the main event of the evening! We have an unknown warrior, Mistress Zaira, of the black planet—that's what she called it, though who knows where that is..." The crowd laughs at what they mistake as Zaira being foolish. "Versus our top contender, Aelib, from planet Faran, known as Indigo's most beloved world. It's been said that Faran is home to the bravest fighters in the universe, and in The Second Chaos, helped defeat the god Ozvios." The crowd shouts their approval and thrums with excitement. "Looking at Aelib, you can almost imagine him there, dealing the lethal strike to Ozvios himself."

If only they knew the truth: that Aelib is going to fight Indigo on stage, the Indigo that made all of this. That Indigo defeated Ozvios with unity, not violence.

But people don't want truth. They want stories that sell well.

"Now this fight is for the big pot. You know the rules: a knockout or tap out in the first five minutes rewards the winner the entire pot. After that, we divide by entertainment value. Got your bets made?" The announcer gives us all a lopsided grin. "And here they are! Mistress Zaira…" Zaira steps onto the stage in a stretchy black cutoff shirt that was probably meant to cover her stomach. As it were, it highlights golden constellations that swirl and spiral across her skin, enthralling anyone who looks at her. Black cargo pants hang loosely around her legs. She takes a deep breath, her hands twitching by her sides. The audience doesn't make a sound. "And our champion, Aelib!" This time the cheers bounce off the walls and people clutch their money and tickets, screaming for victory.

Aelib, the heaving mass of muscle, waves to them all as if he's already guaranteed the win. He's Faran through and through too. I've been there once to make a drop. I was taken in by the rocky landscape, the black waters, the dry air. I'd only docked my ship and walked down the dusty road for a few blocks when I stumbled upon a training center. Farans were outside in courtyards, brandishing wooden staffs, wearing beige flowy garments. Though they were children of all ethnicities, they moved by rote. They were graceful, training together for a war that we all thought would never come.

Now the war's here, and Faran hasn't pledged any of their

warriors. Hasn't gotten involved either way. What was all the training for then? What is the purpose of being prepared to fight if they never do when the time comes?

And I wonder if that's a question I would've asked before I met Zaira or Rubin. Would I care? Would I believe that those who can fight must do so because the universe hangs in the balance?

"Let us begin what will hopefully be a long suspenseful match!" The announcer hops off the stage. And we, all of us, lean forward on bated breath. Zaira stretches before planting her feet solidly on the floor, getting into a fighting stance.

Already, my stomach plummets. What if that Faran hurts her? What if he kills her? What if she loses and we can't get off this rock? What if she loses her power and then can't save us all?

Aelib stalks toward her, slowly, like a massive calef preparing to pounce on the tiny mousare. When he's within striking distance, I want to close my eyes. Shut it out. But instead, I hear Zaira exhale before feinting right. She shouts at him in Faran as he punches air. He grunts back just as she grabs his thick arm, pulling him forward, to step on his knee and wrap her legs around his neck. She swings around just enough to throw herself forward, sending him falling onto her as they hit the hard floor. With her thighs still wrapped around his neck, she presses harder and harder, his face turning a shade of purplish red. He taps his hands, conceding. Her legs loosen and she rolls off him. When she's standing, she extends a hand down to him, offering help. He bats it away.

Momentarily, everyone's stunned. It was fast, concise, unexpected. Even the announcer waits in the wings, unsure what just happened on that stage. Zaira finds my gaze and nods once. She just won. Without even breaking a sweat.

Rubin and I turn to each other. "How much did she just win?" he asks.

"All of it." Air whooshes from my lungs. I push myself to my feet, still clasping Rubin's hand. "Everyone is angry. Really angry. We've got to get her and go before—"

Just then, people in the crowd dash toward the stairs, calling her a cheater. Wanting to enter the ring with her. They thrash at her and she stands there, wide-eyed. Aelib backs away and jumps off the stage, clearly not coming to her aid, though she beat him fair and square.

Some Andarran throws a bottle at her that she narrowly dodges. It's mayhem. I scream her name, trying to get to her, but Rubin and I can't make it through the throng. We're on the outskirts looking down. Hoping she can get off that stage in one piece.

Someone throws a chair. People slam their hands on the edges of the stage. She's standing there alone, surrounded.

"Zaira!" I scream. "Zaira!"

She sees me but already she's changing. The gold beneath her skin fades to black. Back to the way we found her. The nightweaver once more. Darkness wisps from her lips. It smothers the light in the arena. People take note and suddenly back up.

But she's not done yet. Rising above the frantic whispers and shouts is a song. Rubin and I...all we can do is run.

CHAPTER SIXTEEN

Zaira

The song slips from my lips before I even have a chance to consider if this is the right move to make. But I'm too angry, too disappointed to stop. Every time I think I have a grasp on these worlds and their inhabitants, I'm wrong. Anger lights in my chest like a blazing fire.

My grandmother's voice trickles into the back of my head like a whisper. *Zaira, don't.* It's quickly replaced by my pounding heart. I am not Indigo. The rage that's been lingering just beneath the surface is slipping out, and I don't know if I can stop.

Does that feel better? Ciaran asks me somehow in my hallucinatory daze.

Yes, I say. It does.

Andarra was supposed to be the best of them. Like Mal Ares. And look at it. While nightweavers clung to shadowy corners in a crumbling world stolen from them, these people already have everything and still crave more.

Why should I want to save them?

Why should it be up to me to stop the Ilori? Yes, they killed my people. Destroyed my world. But what has Andarra done about this? What has Monchuri done? All of my worlds, even the ones Indigo didn't create, like Earth…they did nothing. They let this happen. They saw the Ilori's horrors and looked away.

Until they were forced to choose a side. Even now, I wonder if they actually believe in what is right and wrong.

I will show them.

The crowd inhales in terror around me as my song pierces the room. Darkness spirals around each and every person who would throw their rocks at me. Everything I felt when I was alone with Rubin and Wesley is gone. The gold is gone. The knowledge. The energy. All that is left are flashes of my home, my people… The only thing that remains is fury.

Fury that demands violence.

The crowd can't see me, can't see anything. They don't know that I am Mal Aresian, using my powers for justice. For defense. For revenge and pain. They can't feel the black smoke as it weaves around us. But I can feel their fear. It makes my blood rise to the surface.

And as the song ends, they—those who would hurt me for melios—fall. They crumble to the floor, clutching their ears. They wonder what's happening to them. They cry, not because I hurt them. I didn't. I just took their senses away from them.

I'll leave them in a darkness as they left Mal Ares. I'll leave them afraid like they left my homeworld.

Even if it's just temporary. Until I believe it is enough, they will learn what it's like to be alone in darkness.

I step toward Wesley and Rubin, the only ones spared. My hands reach toward them, and they both take one, pulling me off the stage onto the floor. Some part of me expects judgment, expects them to abandon me. Surely, now they see me as a monster. They know the anger residing in my heart, ready to strike out at anyone who has made me their enemy. They must fear me. I would fear me.

"How are we not affected?" Rubin tugs me into a hug while Wesley only gives me one of his signature unimpressed looks that means he's thinking about the next steps.

"I felt you…" is all I can say in Rubin's warm, comforting embrace.

"Are they going to be okay?" Wesley glances around at the writhing bodies on the floor. "Not that they didn't deserve that."

"They'll be fine." My head sits on Rubin's shoulder. "We should get our money and go."

"Bit of a problem." Wesley nods his head toward the opposite side of the stage where the fight coordinator is in a ball on the floor beside Aelib. "Think you can let him out of it?"

I step back from Rubin. With a quick nod to Wesley, I stalk closer to the fallen men. The song still clings to all of them. All I have to do… Yes, I know. "Sure, I can—"

There's a sharp pinch in my neck and a hand plops onto my waist. Before I can scream, another hand flattens against my mouth. I twist with all my might to see black-clad figures push Wesley and Rubin down. They scream and struggle to get to me, but already my eyesight gets blurry. My body feels weak. I slump into my assailant's arms.

Just then, there's a whisper in my ear. "I know who you are. Nightweaver. God."

I try to fight, try to break free. I try to sing. I try to reach for my friends, my new family. The only ones that matter now. But there's nothing. My body fails me.

The world goes black.

CHAPTER SEVENTEEN

Wesley

I wake up next to Rubin on the sticky arena floor. The lights flicker overhead and there's a sweaty stench permeating my nostrils. There are several dozens of people passed out around us. Most of them are still under the influence of Zaira's song, but Rubin and I were bashed on the head and left behind.

Zaira.

They took Zaira.

I roll onto my side and my entire body erupts in pain. Rubin's out cold. Mouth open...and snoring. Seriously?

With more strength than I knew I had in me, I shake him. "Rubin. Wake up, come on. Rubin." I put more effort into it until the snoring finally stops. "Hey. Wake up."

When his eyes open, he lets out a blood-curdling scream that makes my entire body curl up into a ball.

"What? Why? Pain. So much pain." He sits up, rubbing the back of his head. "Every five seconds someone's trying to kill us. Why can't this be easier, you know? I'm hungry and tired. And oh…" He twists to touch the side of his very torn outfit. "They broke my outfit." He throws his head back and dry sobs. "This is the most living I've ever done in my life and I don't like it."

I suck in a breath. "They took Zaira."

That stops Rubin cold. "Our girl is gone?"

"Yes." I look down at my feet, deciding what to do next. I brought Zaira here. I'm the reason she's in this mess. Yet, I was paid to bring Rubin to Earth in…just a few days. We aren't even remotely close to our schedule. If I want my money, if I want the life I've always hoped for, I'd have to leave now. This is the moment old Wesley would run. But this new me is different. Better. And as annoying as I once found Rubin.

I glance over at the fight coordinator who is unresponsive on the floor. Ferk.

It could take forever to find Zaira. Neither of us know the terrain, let alone who would take her. Andarra has changed too much for me to keep up. It used to be my world, and now, I don't recognize it at all.

Rubin shakes his head, piercing me with a gaze. "You aren't leaving her behind. You can't. I won't let you."

I bunch up my lips, wiping gunk from my pants. "We aren't leaving her behind. I'm just trying to figure out what we're going to do."

"What are we going to do?" He stares at me and I wish I had a better answer. I wish I could say something brilliant that'd impress him. The truth is I'm going to do the one thing

I never in a million years wanted to do. I'm going to ask for help. I'm going back into the viper's den where I'll be shamed and judged. Where no one wants me, no matter how much I tried to show them I loved them. That I was worthy of them.

"We're going home," I admit quietly. "We're going to see my mother."

There's no way off this planet without Zaira, and there's no getting her back without help. My pride no longer matters. She would never leave me; she never has. And I can't leave her either. I'm going to the family that doesn't want me to save the only family that matters now.

Night begins to slowly fall as we walk up the hill toward the estates of the world's wealthiest and most powerful. We took water tubes—the underwater subways connecting all of Andarra—across town, but the tube doesn't travel here. Lest it disrupt the natural order. Thankfully, walking is nice and I know this place better than the rest of Andarra. Here nothing has changed.

This world is more water than land, but Andarrans found a way to work with nature. Mansions poke through deeply rooted trees that I've been told go as far down as the planet's core. Though the streets are solid, they are translucent, built to hover over the rivers that meander around this area, allowing the Jadu their freedom to explore. The water bubbles and the creatures within awaken. Their bioluminescence isn't dazzling quite yet, but soon, another rotation or so, they'll make this world bright and even more beautiful. And the air, my favorite part—it smells like fresh rain. Even if we only get rain once every month or so.

This area is exactly the same. Unlike me.

I peek over at Rubin, wondering what he thinks of all this. His emotions, like him, are eerily quiet and I'm worried his head was hit too hard. At the same time, he might just be reconsidering this entire endeavor. Wishing Codrec had hired someone who wasn't me. Wishing he were already on Earth, breaking news and finding pockets of compassion in a battlefield. Helping listeners all over the universe understand why there is a war, why it's worth fighting.

Why we need help. Why the Ilori cannot continue this way.

Instead, he's stuck with me on Andarra. Chasing after a god who could be the savior or the doom of us all. He could die in my care because I didn't take him straight to Terra. I wonder if he's beginning to hate me as much as I sometimes hate myself. Emotions certainly swirl around him, but I'm having trouble deciphering them through my own worries. I'm sure the biggest one is disappointment that he's stuck with me.

He turns and tugs my hand into his. "You think our baby's okay?"

I put an air of confidence in my words and let a smile stretch my cheeks, even though I don't feel it. "You've seen her in action. Do you really think she'd go down without a fight? Do you really think anyone can hurt her more than she's already hurt?"

"I have to believe she's okay." Rubin's quiet a few beats, and when he speaks again, his voice cracks. "The three of us, we're carrying around all this loss. Lost homes, lost parents, lost families. Anger. Sadness. We all deal with it in such different ways. I turn to media, trying to uncover the truth because my own is painful. You get into a ship and fly around, building walls around your heart so no one can ever hurt you again... And Zaira, she's... She wants to do great big things, I can see that. She has the power, she has the will. You saw that gold beneath her skin. She was Indigo." He pauses, taking a deep breath before continuing. "But any time—"

"Any time she sees something that reminds her of her home, of how this universe hurt them and left them behind, her anger explodes." I nod my head, thinking. Remembering. I could have told her to stop, I could have told her to try another way... That people can be terrible, yet they can learn to be better too. But I didn't. Because I'm not sure I believe it. I'm not sure I want to put in the work to help make people be better. "Her anger drives her. She's entitled to it, Rubin."

"Of course she is." He shakes his head. "We just have to show her love and hope she gives grace to those who deserve it."

"So few do," I mutter and he tugs my hand, stopping on the sidewalk.

"What did they do to you?" He eyes me closely as the creatures below our feet swim in our shadows. "What are we walking into?"

"My mother... She won't be happy to see me." Breath leaves my lips slowly. "She doesn't want me here. She never did. She made me leave and promise not to come back."

"That can't be true." Rubin shoots me a pitiful look.

"It is." I huff, glancing away from that concern threading his brows. "She made me believe that everything she said or did was important. *The fate of the universe depends on you listening to me. If you don't do as I say, some horrible thing would happen,* or *I've been given the greatest task the Jadu have ever given, you wouldn't understand, Wesley,* or—and this one is my favorite—

love and loyalty, they won't save us. Compassion and sacrifice will. You will never make that sacrifice."

"How do you know she was lying?" Rubin asks gently. "She seems very deep into this whole Jadu thing. Maybe she knows your fate."

I shake my head. "The Jadu only give you glimpses of your future or anything that pertains to your purpose. I never pertained to her purpose, whatever it may be, that has caused her to carry the weight of the universe on her shoulders all her life." Once the words slip from my lips, the anger goes with it. My little rant has no target. If I said any of this to her, she'd scoff and tell me I wouldn't understand. And maybe I don't. But she never helped me try.

Rubin seems to understand and doesn't press. "We're just going to ask for help finding Zaira and getting a new ship, right? That's it?" He steps closer to me, demanding my attention. "Wesley, that's all we're doing, right? It's not going to be that bad."

I nod, staring into his beautiful brown eyes. "That's it."

Sadly though, by the time we meander up the rest of the hill toward my mother's home, we notice a bunch of hover-autos lingering outside. They're lined from the gate all the way up the long drive into the courtyard. All of them fancy. All of them worth more than the ship we were so desperate to buy. Desperate enough to put Zaira in the ring and...

Yeah, I don't need to go over that mistake again.

We linger near the gate. Even the air smells fresher here, more like rain after a warm, hazy day. The sun has set a rotation ago, but still the sky refuses to darken. I look down at our feet, planted on the cushioned translucent ground as little bioluminescent creatures begin to light up. Not gonna lie, I would rather watch them than hit the comms and alert my mother I'm here, waiting outside. I have to pull Rubin back from being in the "see zone," an area around the entire perimeter of the house being watched by several security guards and mini holos that flit about, capturing movement. No one needs to know I'm here just yet. All that talking and we didn't come up with a single plan. Though Rubin only gives me a quick glance before stepping into the see zone and pushing the comms.

My mouth drops open and I stare at him, shocked and terrified.

"Sorry, babe, we don't have time."

I'm about to reply when the comms crackles. An Andarran voice, one I distinctly remember as my mother's assistant, comes through. "Daniels residence, how may I help you?"

"Hi, I'm Rubin Rima of *The Rubin Rima Podcast*. I came to do an interview with…" He looks at me.

"Ka-Alora," I harshly whisper, hoping the comms doesn't pick out my voice.

"Ka-Alora Daniels. I'm sure you have my interview down on your schedule," he says with an air of confidence. I swear, it's so hard to tell when he's being honest or playing. Right now, even I could believe he's on her schedule.

"I'm sorry, please hold—" The line goes dead.

"What's the plan?" Rubin whispers in my direction, teeth gnashed. "Like, do I go in and pretend I'm here on official business or…?"

"Or," I try not to yell, "you could've waited till we had a plan. Or at least figured out what all these people are doing here. You think?"

He furrows his brows. "I'm not going to wait around all day for you to work up your nerve. I'm not even an Andarran and *I* can sense your anxiety. It's not going to get better with time."

"I just needed a moment to—"

The comms cuts back in. "We don't have you on the schedule but Maestra Daniels would be happy to squeeze you in right away. We'd heard you arrived not long ago from Air Traffic, and we're all such huge fans of your show."

There's a smile in the assistant's voice because Rubin Rima inspires that in people. Even in the grumpiest people like me. Though right now, he's really testing my patience.

I glare at him and he holds up a finger. He digs through the clutch strapped to his waist and tosses me a bright yellow hat. Obnoxiously yellow. Could be seen from the Outerim kind of yellow.

"Wear that, no one will recognize you in it."

I try not to shoot daggers from my eyes. "That's because no one will look at my face with this thing on my head." I put it on and I even *feel* yellow wearing it.

"That's exactly right! It's how I never get spotted out and about." The gate swings open soundlessly and Rubin's lip hitches in the corner. "See? Who needs a plan anyway?"

I shake my head and follow him past the holos, up toward the house that is teeming with guests. Not that I'm surprised. My mother always loved to throw parties and have people fawn over her. And with both sons gone, she didn't need to suffer the incessant demands of children getting in her way.

Once we're up to the door, Rubin only knocks once when it's thrown open by some servant. They're in the Daniels home uniform: a traditional wide caftan in a subtle shade of shimmering gold, with two planets—one blue, one black—in a looped orbit over their left chest. I never understood what those planets were meant to be when I was younger but now... knowing Zaira, I realize it is her home, Mal Ares, and Andarra. The twin worlds. One alive and well, the other lost in the darkness forever.

My mother must've have known that Mal Ares existed. But did she care at all about it?

"Please do come in..." The servant whisks us inside, only glancing once at my hat.

Rubin Rima, even dressed in a raggedy, torn sparkly suit has a presence that people automatically respond to. They know he's a someone, whereas my presence is that of a no one. I don't take it personally. The longer I can bask in anonymity, the longer I can plan for how I'm going to approach my mother.

I hesitantly step inside behind Rubin. Even though I can't see them yet, I know from the line of cars outside that there are a lot of people here. But I can't hear them over The Starry Eyed, which of course my mother would be playing during her party.

As I peek around corners, searching for her and her guests, a flash of light from below steals my attention. I gaze down at the translucent floor that hovers carefully over the water world, like everywhere else on this planet. But unlike everywhere else, there are several Jadu swimming lazily in a small school. It's normal to see one or two...never this many. Something is going on.

Rubin points at one. "What are those? Are they the—"

"Jadu," the servant intones with an air of reverence. "They have blessed us with their presence this evening, as you'll soon see."

The Jadu's colors shift and change, but usually they are an amalgam of light. They appear however your eyes can make sense of them. No two people see them the same. To me, they are massive blue creatures with long fins and a mouth full of sharp teeth. My mother once described them to me and my brother as a concentration of colors and magic. Neither solid nor fish. Which honestly, I thought was weird.

Seeing them now though, I begin to wonder why they choose to look like predators to me and hope to my mother. With one glance at Rubin, I wonder what he sees. If he's afraid though, I don't feel it. He's more curious than anything else.

His eyes slide to mine as we're led through the first parlor. The room is all shades of green and everything is gilded in gold. Pictures dot the walls: most of my mother, only a few of my brother, none of me. There's a richness in the home that even melios can't buy. Generations of wealth piled one on top of the other. The Daniels family has done well for themselves. Most are even still alive, choosing to live on beach worlds or serving their purposes elsewhere. However nebulous those may be.

The servant stops outside the second parlor and gifts us both a smile. "You're coming at the most magnificent time." Excitement, wild and fanatical, pours off them and into my nostrils. I step back, something uncomfortable sinking in my gut. But they don't notice my reaction. "We have been given a gift that will change the very fabric of the universe."

Me and Rubin exchange a glance. Before either of us can

ask a question, the servant opens the door. There's at least thirty Andarrans in a circle, standing around…something. Emotions—too many to identify—envelop us, and I feel almost intoxicated immediately. As each head turns our way, I clutch onto Rubin, my legs suddenly unstable.

A path is cleared from us to the center of the room, and through the haze, I can make out two things.

My mother, in a long silver gown, standing over a prone figure dressed all in black. It takes me only a second to realize it's Zaira. She's tied up, her hands close to dipping into an open hole in the floor, where there are more Jadu than I've ever seen in my life. They flip their fins frantically, as if waiting for a treat. As if they know. And they must.

"Mother," I ask, disbelief threading my words. "What have you done?"

"Oh, good, my son is here," my mother's voice drips with disdain and something else… Something I don't quite know. Whatever it is, it's not surprise. She knew I was here. She knew…but how? "The son who has run away from responsibility every moment of his life. Who looked at our Jadu and was too afraid… The son I had left unconscious on the arena floor and didn't take the hint to stay there."

Rubin fiddles with something in his pocket as he stands stiffly, anger blazing in his expression. "What are you doing with my… What are you doing to Zaira?" His voice wobbles, yet he, a pacifist, looks ready to fight.

My mother smiles. Her sycophants turn back, eyes alight with feverish anticipation. "I'm going to save us all."

THE RUBIN RIMA PODCAST

Broadcasting live from an undisclosed location

RR: You better let my baby go. That right there is my sister. I'm not the violent type but I will be if you don't step back.

Ka-Alora Daniels (KD): She is not your sister. She is a reincarnated god who has forgotten her way. We'll show her how best to serve us and the universe again. She will eliminate the Ilori and everything will go back to the way it was. Now if you'll please—

Wesley Daniels (WD): No. No, we won't please let you do anything. She doesn't owe you or anyone else servitude. You knew where she was this whole time, didn't you? You knew about Mal Ares, and you let it die. If she has lost her way, it's because of you. All of you.

KD: My own sister was sent to Mal Ares to fulfill her purpose. She helped bring about the girl, raised her, gave her the tools to become Indigo again and failed, as predicted. She never could separate her heart from her mind. Yet, here Zaira remains, homeless and angry—just as we needed her to be—brought to me by my own son, as foreseen.

RR: Foreseen and done nothing to stop.

KD: We cannot change the tides of fate, child. We embrace them. Zaira will be the doom of the Ilori. But not in this state. She needs to be reminded of who she is. Her power is Indigo's, not the Mal Aresian nightweaving filth she's been using. There's a reason her people were meant to die.

WD: Let her go. I'm begging you.

KD: *(laughs)* You don't get to beg me for anything. You were useless most of your life. A waste of space and time. Your brother, a year older than you and superior in every way, knew what needed to be done and did it without question. But you—

RR: Uh-uh, no, ma'am. Nope. This right here is my boyfriend and you will not talk to him this way. He is one of the most compassionate people I've ever met, and yeah, he's a little rough around the edges because of you, but I'm breaking those walls down, thank you very much. He deserves better than you. He *is* better than you.

KD: He is a product of me. His fear, his lack of responsibility, he is a shame to the Daniels name. We are descended from the Jadu. We—

RR: The only shame I see is a woman in a flawless dress being needlessly cruel to her own child. Because despite you, *he's* the one about to save us all. And, baby, we got this all recorded. People are listening. Everyone's hearing your ugliness. You put yourself in this mansion and said you're special, but I don't see it. Right here, right now, you will be judged.

KD: How dare you! You throw your faith into a boy who chose time and again to turn his back on the Jadu. Who was too afraid. Watch. Watch your boyfriend, watch how he lets his fear rule him. He will disappoint you. *(water splashes)*

RR: Listeners, this lady just pushed Zaira into the water with those big fish. Wesley—

WD: I can't. I can't be near them. They don't want me. I don't want them. Please. I don't... I'm... I can't—

KD: See how he trembles. Weak. Incapable of caring for anyone but himself. A selfish boy who will let you down.

RR: Miss, I'm going to ask you to shut your mouth. Wesley, look at me. Look at me, babe. You can do this. You have to because I can't swim and Zaira needs you. Please, Wesley. Go get our girl.

CHAPTER EIGHTEEN

Zaira

I'm on my knees, chained to the altar. My dress billows in the cool wind. The scents in the air are familiar. Home. Death, darkness, sadness. Loss. The ruins of a once-beautiful world.

Nightweavers circle, whispering though I can't make out their words. Their anger spirals around me. But it's not aimed at me.

No, they don't hate me for letting them down. For losing them.

They hate everyone else.

They hate *him*.

"Zaira… Where is my girl? Where are you, my love?" Something slithers closer. The voice… I'd know it anywhere. My grandmother.

"Grandma?" I ask, my breath stuck in my throat. She doesn't respond. Someone else does.

"Where are you, Zaira?" I don't recognize them and I can't see who they are in the darkness. They hide from me. But there is something…something that registers in the back of my mind.

"I can feel your power growing. The stronger you become, the weaker I feel…" Every part of me stands on alert.

Ozvios.

He's here.

He's close…so close his breath tickles my bare arm. And yet he asks me where I am? "All of the dreadful things that have happened to you have made you better. You clever, clever girl." He exhales slowly. "Indigo found a way back, while I found a way to thrive. You had to learn all over again, but I never forgot. You—"

"You destroyed Mal Ares!"

He laughs, and the sound surrounds me, gnaws on my senses.

"It was such fun. I'd always believed Indigo made that world impossible to kill," his silver tongue intones. "But the nightweavers were weak enough, and their weakness made me strong."

I gasp, wishing I could see his face. Read it. Study it. Find the lies within it. Know my enemy. The altar beneath my knees is cold, unwelcome, and there's only darkness. No sky, no air, nothing but him and me.

"I've come to you with a proposition, Zaira Citlali." His voice circles me and in it…I hear power. I hear screams and chaos. I hear everything terrible in existence, every terror he has wrought upon the stars.

"There's nothing you can offer me. You destroyed my

heart." I try not to whimper like a child. But I am a child and he…he's millennia old. My life is a drop of water compared to the ocean of his.

"Yes, Mal Ares is gone. Unfortunate, yet fitting for a small planet of ghosts. What did you think you could do? Save them?" There's scorn in his voice. "They were lingering spirits. Indigo could only create life, not bring back the dead. And you aren't Indigo."

"I am." The truth of it rings through my ears. "I am Zaira and I am Indigo."

Ozvios takes his time to respond, and when he finally speaks, his tone shifts. "Regardless of who you think you are, stardust once gone from a living host can never return. Life, once lost, is gone forever." He mirthlessly chuckles to himself. "But I digress. I did save one last being on Mal Ares. She calls you granddaughter. A lovely old Andarran, isn't she? Misses you terribly."

My breath catches in my throat and my heart pounds wildly. "She's alive."

There's a smile in his words. "If you want her, come to me. Willingly. Lay down your life and powers, and she'll be free to live out the end of her days in peace." He pauses…testing, waiting, wondering what I'm thinking. "Indigo would never consider trading their life for one person, but again, you are not Indigo. You are Zaira. You are smarter. Better. You see everything as it is, not how you wish it to be. You've seen how far the universe has fallen, and you know it's not worth saving."

"Where is she?" I croak, my mouth betraying me. I know this is wrong. I know, in my head, that there is still hope for the universe. But my heart cannot care. My grandmother is alive. She's alive and held captive because of me. She showed me what love really means.

I can make this sacrifice.

"Since I cannot find you, you must find me… Come to me on the Mothership IpS1L II."

A whoosh of air leaves my lips. "How can I trust you?"

"We are gods." He says it with all the might and wisdom of someone who has lived from the beginning of time. Wisdom I do not possess. "The only two with real power left. You are my only equal in this universe."

I huff. "And you wish to kill me."

"You and I…we are at opposite ends of beliefs. If you give me your power, I can do what is necessary. Bring balance through destruction. It is my time." He stops as if considering his next words carefully. "I'll let some civilizations live. The redeemable parts will remain. Especially the ones that remind me of Mal Ares and its people who were always unfairly treated. For you, I'd let them stay."

And though there is truth in his words, there are lies too. He hesitated. Once I'm gone, he could destroy all of it and I'd be powerless to stop him. I know this but…my grandmother is still alive. She can live out the rest of her days.

"Do you promise me?" There is an edge to my tone, one that will not lie down and die so easily. "Even as you devour everything else, you will let her live? I want a guarantee, Ozvios."

For a moment, there's silence between us. "I will give you one when the time arrives."

"That is—"

"Zaira!" A voice pierces my thoughts, pierces this very real, very vivid dream that must be happening in my head. The altar begins to shake and crumble. The nightweavers slip farther in the shadows.

"IpS1L II," Ozvios whispers. "Feel me. Find me."

I startle awake submerged in crystal blue water. Spheres of light surround me. As my eyes adjust, I realize these aren't spheres of light—they're creatures of magic.

We recognize each other. They know who I am, what I am.

Still they swim closer, nipping at me, and though I kick my legs and wave my arms, one latches on. I make eye contact and it solidifies before me into a vibrant purple fish with golden stripes. It is at once beautiful and terrifying. Its thin whiskers tickle the underside of my arm as its teeth sink into my skin.

My eyes close on instinct as a vision unravels in my mind.

I am me back when I was just Indigo. Sitting on my overworld perch made from stardust and scales, music and magic. I am gold. I am powerful beyond measure. And I am sad. For I have made songs to create worlds, and in my attempt to make the universe vast, I incidentally destroyed some of my older creations. Though I knew my power, I had used too much. A balance had to be struck. Civilizations, stories, creatures were lost. Gone. It was my fault for not knowing my limits.

I refused to sing anymore. Out of fear, out of anger. I forgot my songs. The melodies to create… I pushed them so far down in my mind I could no longer access them. And then Ozvios came. The songs were all too deep to return, but one. One that needed many voices, not just my own. The final song. To defeat Ozvios, we needed unity. I traveled through the stardust, without form, giving the creatures instruments, tools to take care of themselves, knowing my time would be over soon. With their voices, we sang together in harmony. And we defeated the darkness.

A planet may explode into existence; it fades out of existence gradually, quietly. I chose to rest on Mal Ares, my first world, where the core was cooling too fast without a sun. I thought if my power could combine with the dying core… perhaps it could create not just a new planet, but something entirely unique. As I laid myself down, the songs suddenly rushed to the front of my mind. So many songs to create and brighten. To dissipate the black holes, to create events of wonder and power. To save that which has been lost.

And I promised to Mal Ares and myself, "When the time comes—if the time comes—I will make one last creation. I will be born again in a new form. I will give it powers and memories, but it will only remember slowly. One by love. Two by loss. Three by loyalty. It will not make the same mistakes that I did. It will be both joy and anger, creation and destruction. It will learn to balance the two."

Darkness slips from my fingers and the vision changes. I'm Zaira again, my skin lighting up as if the stars live beneath it. There's a boy with me, a boy with long dark blue hair pulled back. His gray eyes stare deeply into my soul and his fingers entwine mine. "I know my future is with you, and I think you know that too, don't you?" He leans close to me, his lips inches from mine. I come alive. My heart threatens to leave my chest. My skin is on fire, a sweet, delicious fire and I want to succumb in this moment.

But arms yank me from the Jadu's teeth and pull me upward. The water swirls around me and…and…

I open my eyes.

Wesley.

He pushes me to the surface as the Jadu scurry toward him. Not one, all of them. They're in a frenzy. I reach out to grab him but he shakes his head at me. The water rushes all around him.

He juts his chin out toward the surface, his eyes locked on mine. *Go*, he says without words.

I don't want to leave him. But this is what he wants. This is what he needs right now. I break through the surface. Rubin's got his hand out for me and I take it, allowing him to pull me onto the floor.

My clothes stick to my body and the air is cold. "Wesley—" I say between gasps. "He's—"

"Finding his purpose." Rubin throws his arms around me. "I'm so glad you're alive. I'm so glad you're here. We missed you, honey. Are you okay? You must be freezing. They aren't going to give us warm clothes and dry bots here. We gotta get out the minute our boy breaks free."

I can only nod while staring down into the water as the Jadu disengage from Wesley. They must have had something important to tell him. Some big purpose to thrust upon him.

Though my heart worries for him, worries for whatever change is coming for him, I have bigger things on my mind. Bigger motivations too…

Like getting to IpS1L II. Everything I've learned doesn't matter. Can't matter. I don't have the time anymore.

My grandmother needs me. She comes first.

CHAPTER NINETEEN

Wesley

When I burst out of the water, the first thing I see is my mother glaring down at me. I barely have time to register anything else when Rubin and Zaira pull me onto the floor. The guests all around us have taken several steps back. Uncertainty coats the surface of the room.

And anger, so much anger.

"You." My mother's mouth hangs open and rage flies out. "You get out of my home and never come back. Never. You hear me?" She turns to Zaira. "You. You serve us. You created this world and you must save it."

From the shadows, security step out from the corners of the room where they lingered. I instantly recognize them as the same security that knocked me and Rubin out and took Zaira. But my gaze swivels to my mother as her lips curl. "Take her."

They slowly approach, my mother's guests moving aside.

I shake my head, staring up at Zaira as she plants her feet on the ground. "Zaira, I think it's time you showed them who you are. Not the person they want you to be, but the person your grandmother raised. Show them."

Rubin smiles. "Look at my family coming together in the face of adversity."

I try not to roll my eyes as I push to my feet.

Zaira takes a deep breath. "Your sister," she says to my mother, "was a good person. She raised me with love and gave me a name. I see now, looking at you, that she was a Daniels, but she called me Zaira Citlali."

"That was our mother's name. The name of the star, the Jadu—" my own mother gasps. "She had no right—"

Zaira's eyes flash and I grab her hand, giving it a squeeze. "She did. Because she raised me like family, she raised me with love. And I wonder now, why you didn't learn from her and treat your own children the same. Why instead you carry this hatred in your heart." Zaira's skin alights with shimmery gold while dark wisps slither from her lips and fingers. Power rolls off her, both god and nightweaver. Briefly, in a flicker before my eyes, she sparkles like translucent stardust. But she's solid again the next moment. "It is not my job to fix you or fix this universe. I'm not the same Indigo that came before. I am Zaira. I am someone new with old powers. I am balance."

The security team stops in their tracks, watching her power unravel and circle the three of us. They can't come any closer; they're afraid of her. As they should be. I would be too, if I was on their side. But I'm on hers.

"And your son—" She shoots me a glance with a smile in her eyes. "He's worth more than a purpose. He's my friend, he's *my* family. He and Rubin—they are what's worth saving. If this universe continues to exist after Ozvios and the Ilori try to destroy everything, it'll be because of people like them."

She reaches out to grasp Rubin with her other hand. We stand united, feeling the power surge from her palms where they touch ours. Power that envelops us, blocks us from the rest of the room. From my mother.

The woman who abandoned me, plagued me my entire life, stamps her foot dramatically. "I was tasked to do this. Tasked to change this war. You can't take my purpose away from me. You can't—" Her voice wobbles and shakes, so unlike the woman who has always believed herself higher and mightier than all.

"Your task," Zaira says, tilting her head over her shoulder, "was to be compassionate to your two children, Ka-Alora Daniels, who would need that compassion to complete their own tasks. One would use it to understand humanity, the other to save it. Despite your failure, your family has succeeded. You are free now. Use your time wisely."

My mother's gaze sweeps across the three of us. "I did everything I could. How could I do more when… I never wanted to be a mother. I didn't fail… Danielses don't fail." Her eyes bore into mine. "You didn't have a purpose… Not until now." She shakes her head, tears sliding down her cheeks. "What did they tell you? What task did they give you? What is your mission?"

"You've done your part, now I'll do mine." I give her a sad smile. "Don't worry, I won't be back, but I'll honor the Daniels name. Not for you—for the aunt I never knew who raised a god, and my brother who, like me, was trying to live up to your impossible expectations. And for my new family, who make me believe this universe could be better."

And with that, we walk away, out of the mansion I once called home. Through the riches and wealth I desperately craved for myself, believing it would give me freedom. Down the same hill I frequently ran crying, trying to escape my mother when she made me wish I had never been born. Into the city I once knew but don't anymore. I'm a different person now. One who chose a new family and found that freedom.

On the underwater tram from the docks, we're quiet. I know what they'll ask, though I'm not sure I fully understand the answer. Still the Jadu's visions float behind my eyes.

"Excuse me." A little child with yellow eyes beams up at me, tapping my leg. Their mother tries to pull them back but to no avail.

"I'm so sorry, they're very stubborn," she says with a shrug, settling back into her seat.

They completely ignore her. "Aren't you the brother of The Starry Eyed guy?"

I smile down at them, even though my heart feels chewed and mangled up. "That's right, I am. Aren't you a bit young to know who they are?"

"I saw them on holonews about the war on Terra. I don't remember his name, but he was very glittery." The child talks very fast with a lot of excitement.

"He does love his glitter," I offer.

"It was *a lot* of glitter," they continue and I have no idea where this is going. "Anyway, I saw him and the band on holovision at the city market, and he said he misses his brother Westen or Wessel. I don't know—"

"Wesley," I add. Rubin knocks against my side, smiling at me. Zaira bunches her lips together, trying not to laugh.

"No, I think he said Westen." The child shakes their head as if that is apparently the right name. "He showed a picture of him with his brother on-screen and said: *I hope he comes to see me soon*. And he told us all that if we see his brother, we should tell you that you need to go to him because he misses you. I'm a very good listener."

"Yes, you are," the mother says with a hint of pride in her voice. My heart breaks a little more. If my mother had treated me that way, who would I be now? Would I be happier?

"Thank you for telling me. I'm on my way to see him." With that, the kid beams a little brighter and scampers back to their mother.

"Is that where we're going next?" Rubin steps a little closer, filling my nostrils with both relief and uncertainty. "What's the plan? What did the Jadu show you?"

I try not to look into his eyes, try not to get trapped in his orbit. The Jadu didn't just show me the future and my purpose; they showed me Rubin. It showed me our connection. It showed me… Part of me heats up at the thought while another part goes cold. I push those thoughts aside and instead focus on the question. What did they show me? Everything. But what do I want to share?

"We have to go to IpS1L II. The Ilori mothership on the cusp of Earth."

"That's exactly where I wanted to go…" Zaira grasps a tram bar, her eyes darting between me and the windows showcasing the vibrant water world passing us by. "Why do you need to go there?"

I take a deep breath. "There's a labmade Ilori named Morris, and a…a human, I think, named Ellie who are about to sneak onto the ship to…do something I don't know. Anyway, they need our help. Specifically, I think they need Rubin's help."

Rubin's mouth drops open. "Are you saying the Jadu have a purpose for me too?"

"You were fated to come into my life and be a part of it. You and me…" The words get stuck in my throat.

"We're destiny," he adds with a big smile. "I don't need anyone, not even some sacred fish, to tell me that."

My cheeks heat and I glance at Zaira, who is standing close but her mind is far off. "The Jadu want us to save the universe. To continue life." The moment the words leave my mouth, I realize the truth in them. "They want us to…just…exist. To keep living, breathing, loving, finding happiness. Do things that make us feel good, useful, valued."

"Because…" Rubin's gaze fills with idealistic hope. "Because existing is our purpose."

I nod. Everything else, every vision the Jadu have given the Andarran people, it's to make us realize how special we already are. I want to laugh, thinking back to the fear that gnawed on me my entire childhood. If I had only been less terrified of the prospect, my life would've been so much easier.

But then…I wouldn't be here today with a boy I like and a girl who's a god. I wouldn't be standing on the underwater tram, traveling at high speed through the water core of my former home, ready to shoot off into space and somewhere new.

It's all worth it—I have to believe that. In the end, I'm in a better place than before. In the end, I'm the Wesley Daniels who has finally gotten closure on what it means to be my mother's son. I can shed this nagging belief that I don't deserve love, happiness, friendship, or family. And although accepting these truths means the end—my end—is nearer, my heart feels lighter.

"So, we have to go to IpS1L II to help some strangers. What else?" Zaira's gaze doesn't reach mine. She's focused on the fish that light up the ground beneath us. A part of her created that, and now, after lifetimes of revolutions and technological advancements, she can see it for herself.

I sigh, not afraid of what the future holds, but that it's not the happy ending we deserve. "We go to Earth, exactly as planned, and we fight for freedom from the Ilori."

"I'll make sure everyone everywhere knows what's happening and how to help." Rubin smiles, not knowing how bittersweet this will be.

"And I'll kill Ozvios," Zaira says, her voice low. "As soon as we get our hands on a new ship."

"Kill Ozvios?" Rubin gasps, startling some of the other passengers. "Babe, last time you tried that, you needed to create universal harmony. No offense, but there's no way you're going to pull that off again. People hate each other. Certain worlds are evil. There's a war!"

"I have a plan," she says, calmly. "Indigo lives within me. Now I know that it's not so I can be just like them, but to be something new. Something new with two forms of magic in my veins, who will do things differently."

"Mm…okay but, like, Ozvios can destroy entire worlds with black holes. You see the difference, right?" He's shaking his head at her, brows nearly reaching his scalp.

"We're going to be alright," I interject, tossing him a glance. "We're in this together."

"When did you become such an optimist?" Rubin asks, genuinely shocked.

Zaira looks up from the creatures below, finally giving us her full attention. "We can do this. Together."

"Okay." Rubin sighs. "But after this, if we survive, you both have to become regulars on my podcast and—" he narrows his eyes on me "—you have to stop wearing so much black. I want color. I want you to show us who you are when you aren't burdened by that woman we left back there."

And I wish then that I would survive this. Because if there was ever a person to wear the most ridiculous outfits for, it'd be Rubin.

STARRY EYED
AND BUSHY-TAILED

I really hope this gets through…

Hey, friends, it's me, Gabby, former blogger, and current occupant in human housing outside of Detroit.

Things are weird.

We're two years into the Ilori occupation… In case you forgot—which I don't know how you could—it all started when the Ilori appeared in our skies one day. We fired at them. They invaded us. Everything basically turned to shit. Those of us outside of cities didn't face too much action. One minute we were watching Allister Daniels strut on stage with The Starry Eyed, shaking his perfect backside (okay, that's what I was doing, everyone else seems to have been paying attention to politics and stuff) and the next, we were forced out of our homes into human housing set up by our new overlords.

Look, I'm going to be honest, the human housing isn't terrible. I know, I know, we aren't supposed to like anything about being colonized (Stockholm syndrome much?) and I don't. None of us do. But…reluctantly, I have to admit there have been some silver linings. Yeah, we didn't pick out this place and yeah, we were forced into little communities as if we're living in a zombie apocalypse. Also the Ilori patrolling those communities are packing electrical charges that can throw us into walls without lifting a finger.

Anyway, if you look past allllll of that, you could almost appreciate our new circumstances. We have homes. *Everyone* has a home. We're talking Ilori-made two-to-four-bedroom houses with backyard gardens, heat, beds, you name it. Capitalism, who is she? We have food. We've gone back to gardening. The Ilori (the labmades as they're called, who have no choice but to follow their true Ilori leadership) have introduced all kinds of new tech to make the most of our land. Nature is flourishing. (Side note: birds are ridiculously louder now). They've even created new bio clothing to keep us comfortable. Weirdly, *huge* human designers have stepped up to add some fashionable flair. Even Beyoncé's involved!

Health care has never been better? Like, make that make sense. It's free. Even therapy! They've shared their medicine with us. Human and Ilori doctors work together. They see people, care about people.

Anyway, a strange kinship has evolved between us and the labmades, which we never thought was possible. We're all trapped in this system together—they by their true Ilori rulers, and us (at first) by them. Knowing that sorta created this… I don't know… We relate to each other.

Which brings me to this blog post after two years of silence. Remember how the Ilori came, destroyed computers and books and music and everything we hold dear? Well, they didn't actually. Yes, they destroyed massive servers and the cloud. But they backed up everything.

They even created a new type of computer called a holo (new to us, old to them). I'm writing on one right now for the first time. Can you believe it? As my labmade friend told me (Her name is Elsira. She's super cool and I think we might be dating? Oh, goodness, I really want to believe we are. She is adorable and funny and...yeah), labmades are handing them out around human housing all over the world. We can communicate again! Heyyyyy!

So, the reason I'm writing—beyond saying hello, how are you, I missed you—is to say, things are weird. *Big* weird. Word on the Ilori street is that a war is coming to Earth. Even weirder, war has been declared *in space*. Civilizations from worlds we never even knew about are coming to defend us. They're coming to save us.

And the weirdest thing yet: you know how my favorite group is The Starry Eyed? Well, they're aliens! I know, right?! When you think about it though, it kinda makes sense? They are all way too beautiful to be human.

Anyway, there's hope. A lot of hope. We aren't in this alone anymore. There are worlds beyond ours with technology and customs and beliefs we don't understand. Soon, maybe we will. Soon...we might even meet. Regardless of who and what they are, *we* have to show up and show out as a united people. We get to choose how we will be perceived.

We've all experienced loss. We lost loved ones, we lost

our homes, we lost control of our world. And, likely, things can never go back to the way they were. I don't think that's a bad thing in some ways. We were divided, angry, suffering before the Ilori came. We now have a chance—assuming we win our independence from the true Ilori—to change Earth for the better.

To start over.

What does that mean for us? What do we want to take from our history and what do we want to leave behind? How do we want to treat people who have suffered alongside us when we're no longer suffering? Not with old hatreds and prejudices, right? Right?!

Here's my homework for you: think about the world before and the world now. How do you want it to change and why? What are you willing to do to make it a better place?

And, if you're like me, how do we get Allister Daniels and his alien pop group to stay on Earth once it's free? *If* it's free, I guess.

For real though, we are in unprecedented times. If we can find a way not to hate the labmade Ilori, can we find a way not to hate each other? Can we stand together on the battlefield for Earth, and choose humanity?

I hope so.

CHAPTER TWENTY

Zaira

By the time we arrive back at the mechanic's office after finally collecting my money from the fight, *The Rubin Rima Podcast* from the Danielses' house has gone viral.

My grandmother whispers in the back of my mind. *Zaira... save me.* My knees shake where we're standing by the docks and I grab onto Rubin a little tighter. My mind is playing tricks on me, that's all. I want to save her so bad. But no. I need to focus.

Wesley fumes. "The Ilori will know where we are from that livestream. What were you thinking?"

Rubin taps his toe, impatient as the mechanic prepares the ship. "My entire job has always been exposing the truth. Your mom was very clearly in need of having her truth exposed. I did this so you know that you aren't—"

"Oh, my G00287! Are you Rubin Rima?" A passerby

stops in front of the three of us, head tilted. Though they are dressed in Andarran garb—a long caftan painted like the sea and dotted with creatures—they are very noticeably not Andarran. They are not any creature that Indigo created. They are tall, pleasantly plump, with a painted face and translucent panel along their left jaw. "I just heard your latest episode and I... I'm sorry, why are you staring at me?" They stand straighter, putting a hand on their hip and glaring at me. "Can I help you?"

"Sorry," Rubin cuts in with a smile. "Please don't take offense. I don't think she's ever seen a labmade Ilori up close before."

"You've been created in labs? By the Ilori?" I try to ask politely, but how did they do this? Why? How did they channel Indigo's power in this way? "Who is G00287?"

"It's the Ilori word for god, specifically Ozvios," Wesley answers by my ear. "That is who they worship."

My brows furrow. When I was Indigo, I created Ilor, giving them a beautiful home and incredible power. Power to be eternal and channel electricity—not just channel it, but they could use it to connect to each other, to collectively charge each other. And the Ilor system was diverse, with caves and volcanoes, wide trees that could reach the edge of atmo, creatures called calef that would supply nutrient-rich juice, fields of grass, small oceans full of vibrant life. They should have been happy there. Satisfied.

What changed? What made them into the monsters they are today?

"Labmades have been created for the last few hundred years." The labmade's expression loses its sharp angles. They assess me for a moment, taking in my damp clothes and the exposed constellations swirling on my skin. If they recognize me, they don't say. "The Ilori said they extracted power from some dying world... Mal Ares maybe? And they channeled it into creating new life forms to serve them. But they haven't been able to make more after the last batch of humanoid labmades seventeen years ago. The final generation."

Wesley turns to me. "They used Indigo's power?"

"No," I say, shaking my head as tears prickle at the corners of my eyes. "They extracted it from my people." I run a hand over my kinky fro that hasn't been maintained in days. I remember my people, how they, like me, were forced to wear Ilori-made bracelets to dampen their powers. Not just to dampen...but to collect. "They stole the nightweavers' power and then killed them all..."

Flashes of home flicker through my mind. The bodies of the elders I stumbled upon days ago, buried and left to rot. They looked drained—but I couldn't make sense of it at the time. Just like I couldn't figure out why the Ilori would colonize Mal Ares in the first place. Why would they be interested in a dark planet with no resources the Ilori needed? But there was a resource—within its people. Nightweaving. Magic.

But seventeen years ago, not long after I was born, the Ilori killed all the remaining nightweavers. My people died and the Ilori had no power left to fuel their experiments.

I am the last living nightweaver. This is why Ozvios wants me to die. Because I, with the power of Indigo and of Mal Ares running in my veins, no longer need Ozvios for balance. If I don't need him, he will not exist. He was created in reaction to me. I just might be the most powerful being in the universe.

I swipe at the sudden tears sliding down my cheeks. All this pain, destruction, death… For what?

Rubin wraps his arm around my shoulders and smiles at the labmade, asking, "How did you break free?" His voice carries a hint of wonder. "How did the true Ilori let you go?"

"It wasn't easy." The labmade shakes their head. "I broke my panel and escaped before they sent me to Earth. Took a job aboard a Dosani planet hopper. Been hiding out here ever since. Can't use the power or charge, but at least I'm free."

"Wait a minute," Wesley interjects. "Dosanis have tentacles. They can't planet hop…"

The labmade throws their head back and laughs. "That's what they want you to think. Tentacled creatures planet hop all the time… It's just that when they do, they shift forms. They emit a gas that stabilizes their matter, but in the process makes them and anyone aboard their ship untraceable. Illegal."

"Untraceable…" Wesley repeats. "Well."

"Oh, no, you've got a strange look in your eyes." Rubin grimaces. "Zaira, you see this?"

"Uh-huh." I nod. Wesley's got a plan. And from the looks of it, it won't be a fun one.

After Rubin signs the labmade's holo and thanks them, we stand at the edge of the dock as the mechanic sets our new ship down. It's bigger than our last and far more advanced. The metallic panels flicker and rotate as the ship touches down.

"Dang, that's nice." Rubin clasps both mine and Wesley's hands. "Let's try not to crash this one or get sucked into a black hole. Agreed?"

"Agreed," Wesley and I say at the same time.

Finally, I ask the one question that's been on my mind for a few moments. "What are you thinking, Wesley?"

"I'm thinking we have a way to use bridges and flyways now. I'm thinking I know how to get on the mothership without detection." Wesley smirks. "It just involves a quick pit stop to my academy."

"Please tell me it doesn't involve taking on a Dosani crew," Rubin winces as the mechanic flounces down the ramp and throws the keys into Wesley's outstretched hand. I break Rubin's embrace and walk over to the mechanic, handing him more melios than we agreed. We have more than enough.

"Thank you," he stutters. "Thank you. I—"

"You should tell your mothers they raised a good son." I shake his hand warmly. "You are very lucky to have love like that in your life."

"I am," he agrees and pins me with a smile. "Next time you're back here, I'll get you a better ship, promise."

I laugh and stalk back to Wesley and Rubin, who is still complaining.

He puts a hand on his hip. "I don't know if I have room in my heart for another found family member just yet, Wesley. You two have taken up a lot of space, as is."

"We aren't adding another crew member." Wesley shoots him a glance. "We're going to pick up my good buddy called Blobby." He points a finger at Rubin. "And you're going to make sure he doesn't hit me in the stomach again. That little blob has a temper."

PART III

IT ALL ENDS HERE

THE RUBIN RIMA PODCAST

Not broadcasting, but will be released in a podcast series
when we're not trying to sneak by the Ilori

RR: Hey, spacers, it's Rubin Rima, coming to you from a
new ship with my new fam. First there's Zaira and she's
a god! Can you believe? Say hello, Zaira.

Zaira Citlali (ZC): Um...hello?

RR: Love her. She's terrifying but in the best way. And
sitting beside her is my new boyfriend—

WD: We are not boyfriends.

RR: I told your mom we are.

WD: You were defending me. And—

RR: But I meant it.

WD: ... You never asked me. Shouldn't that be something
we mutually agree on?

RR: Wesley, wanna be my boyfriend? I'll admit, I'm not
very experienced at it but—

WD: Okay.

RR: I like you and you like me so we should do it. The

universe could end, and we could all die. Wouldn't you rather live and be with me than die alone in space?

WD: ... *(inaudible)*

RR: Speak up, babe, the orbiphone didn't catch that.

WD: I said yes.

RR: Yay! I have my first boyfriend, and, spacers, if you could see him. Wow. He's so handsome. Bright blue eyes, gorgeous dark brown skin, and he's tall! Wait till we go on a universal tour. You'll see him and you'll believe in love and magic and—

WD: Universal tour?

RR: Yeah, after we save everyone. And you know how exactly we're going to save everything? Because we have a new family pet!

ZC: He's not a pet.

WD: He's a weapon.

RR: He's our family pet and his name is—

ZC: *(inaudible)*

RR: Zaira, I didn't know you spoke that language.

ZC: I speak all languages. Part of me once created the entire universe, didn't I *(inaudible)*?

WD: Stop calling him that, his name is Blobby.

RR: We are not calling him Blobby. We're going to call him...Sir Bonesby.

ZC: That's disrespectful.

WD: He is a blob who sometimes sheds his bones. We are not calling him Sir anything.

ZC: *(inaudible)* He doesn't like it.

RR: I'm sorry, did you just communicate with him?

ZC: We are all creations of the universe.

RR: He doesn't like Sir Bonesby?

ZC: *(inaudible)* He does not.

RR: Well, then, what's his name? Does he have a name?

ZC: *(inaudible)* Yes, he prefers Blobby.

WD: See? Even the creature agrees that name should represent him.

ZC: *(inaudible)* He likes Wesley very much and hopes they go on many adventures together.

WD: That's weird.

RR: Yeah, tell him we're a package deal. That's my boy-friend, if anyone's going to cuddle him, it'll be me.

ZC: I'm not saying that.

WD: ... Are we going to cuddle?

CHAPTER TWENTY-ONE

Wesley

I hope when he finds himself surrounded by love
He doesn't let it pass him by, never tries to say goodbye,
He can keep it close till the end of time,
And I'll be there, I'll watch him shine.

—The Starry Eyed, "Find Yourself"

Zaira's taking care of Blobby in the back of the cabin while Rubin nods off against my shoulder. And I'm wondering... how did this happen? How did I, the loner whose own family loathes him, find two people who needed someone in their lives as much as him?

One of whom is an actual reborn god, and the other a space radio host...who is now my boyfriend? What are the odds on this? Why is the universe so mysterious? And why... *Oh, no.*

A vision flashes in my mind. I close my eyes and let the details sink in. I'm in the ship... The screen is lit up in red.

"Missile impact in twenty-seven seconds," the AI says solemnly. "Would you like me to take away your fear and pain?"

"No!" I yank the thrusters hard and veer right. "I need help. AI, ask...ask...ask the—is there anyone...anyone left to help?"

The vision fades and I'm left gasping for air. That's what it means to be bit by the Jadu. To see slices of the future and not know what to make of them or how to change them. All I know is the current path we're on leads to me closer to death.

The AI, the same one from the vision, the same one in this very Andarran ship, dings on the console. "Prepare to take the planet jump or would you prefer another method of travel?"

"Prepare to planet jump," I say, already dreading the stench that'll fill the cabin. "To the edge of Planet Terra, Earth."

Zaira coughs. "When we arrive, we will have to move fast. Ozvios is there. He—"

I take a deep breath, worried we might be going for two very different reasons. "And so is this labmade Ilori and human girl. I know you don't believe it, but they are more important than anyone else right now, even Ozvios."

Her voice climbs. "If I kill Ozvios, the war is over."

"You could kill Emperor 1lv and the war wouldn't be over." I shake my head, swiveling carefully in my seat so as to not disturb a dreaming Rubin. "The Ilori have hundreds—maybe even thousands—of colonies spread across the unknown universe. They connect them with their internal communication system Il-0CoM, controlling them using their minds, and taking their life energy. And this labmade, he has a plan to neutralize them all by breaking Il-0CoM. He could free them, Zaira."

Zaira turns her face away from me. Frustration rolls off her in waves and settles on my skin. Frustration and something else... Something I can't quite read. She's keeping a secret. Possibly a mission the Jadu gave her.

Possibly worse.

My mother's voice flits into my mind as I clench the thrusters tight. *He will disappoint you.*

Does Zaira believe that to be true? I wouldn't blame her if she did. Perhaps I haven't proven myself yet. In our short history, I've oscillated between wanting to be a lone skipper on missions around the universe to collect enough money to have a ship to call home, and being a decent person, willing to do the right thing even when it doesn't benefit me.

If I were her, I wouldn't trust me either.

I am telling the truth though. I close my eyes once more, letting the image of Morris—an Ilori labmade with light brown skin, long brown almost-black hair, sparkling brown eyes, and a blue-lit panel along the left of his jaw—flit through my mind. Morris is standing in a hallway with Ellie, a short girl with brown skin, a purple hat, black-rimmed glasses, and a slight frown on her face as she regards him.

"Morris, are you sure about this? We've just snuck onto the most dangerous ship in the universe, and you think it would be a good idea to rest in a cupboard?"

Morris shakes his head. "Not rest—charge. Sneaking onto this ship took seventy-eight percent of my power. And you haven't slept since we left XiGRa. We can't do what we need to do if we are exhausted, Ellie."

"I don't think this is a good idea," she whispers harshly near his ear. "The longer we stay, the likelier they are to catch us."

"Without power, if we get caught, I cannot defend us. And although you saved me once, humans are easier to threaten than a ship full of true Ilori." He smiles down at her like she's the only important thing in his life. Though I'm watching this in a vision, I feel like I'm interrupting a private moment. I shouldn't be here, but still I can't look away. I've never seen a love like this, never seen people look at each other the way they do. "I won't let anything happen to you."

"Yeah, well..." She looks up at him, eyes misty. "I would prefer if you said you won't let anything happen to *us*."

"I won't lie to you. I can't. Not again." He rests his head against hers. "But I can say, I want nothing more than to live with you for the rest of time. Know that I am motivated to save us both."

She sniffs. "Hopeless romantic."

"Not hopeless, remember? You've given me hope." He pulls away and smiles, leaning closer. They kiss, and although it's a really lovely moment, I don't know why the Jadu are sharing all of this with me. I thought they only showed patches of my own future and past.

A pounding of footsteps sound nearby and they pull apart. Morris glances up at the comms flickering in the corner.

"They don't know we're here. I've been interrupting their comms since before we boarded the ship." He drags her into the dark cupboard quickly and pulls the door closed. "They aren't here for us... They—"

Ellie flicks a light switch and the small cupboard reveals

itself to be a comms room. "This is just what we need, isn't it? This is where you can do the broadcast..."

Morris steps up to the console and lets a long breath loose. "They've reconfigured the system... I can upload but it has to come from... There's a key. I don't—"

The vision cuts off and I know what I have to do.

The Jadu showed me this because they want me to fix it. And the solution is asleep beside me. If anyone knows how to broadcast something important, if anyone can get the Ilori's attention, it's Rubin Rima. Public Ilori Enemy #1. I just know it, in my heart and mind, that he and I were fated to meet, fated to do this together. That's why the Jadu are leading me to Morris and Ellie. Everything we've done has put me on this path.

As we take the hyperspace bridge to the mothership, Blobby releases his extremely potent gas. Even Rubin shifts awake, eyes wide.

"That? That's the smell that's going to make our body signatures untraceable?"

I nod.

He tightens two fingers around his nose. "Oh, no. Is it going to seep into my clothes? This had better be worth it."

"Now you see why he's named Blobby?"

"More like Stenchy," Rubin adds.

"He's very sensitive about his odor, be kind," Zaira says, putting his bones in a neat line around the cage. She sounds positive, as if she's not fuming angry with me about our plan... but I know the truth. When the time comes, I will disappoint her like I've done everyone else.

And she will abandon me, like everyone else.

★ ★ ★

When we leave the hyperspace bridge, we're on the far side of Earth's moon. It's so small and gray and white, and pocked with craters. Beyond it, there's a small blue and green planet spinning lazily on its axis. It's new and pretty. I wonder if or when we would've discovered Earth if the Ilori hadn't first.

The Ilori.

Their ships—cruisers and some small pods—sit stationary in the space between worlds. As if waiting for something. The Ilori have always traveled predictably too. Fleets for acquisitions. Cruisers for their scientists and ecologists who make the world suitable for the true Ilori to come next. And then the cleanup crews start to leave from the pods. It's all very rote. Except…there. A massive shadow darkens an ocean below. IpS1L II.

"Oh, my…Zaira," Rubin mutters, staring at the front window in awe.

"Ferk," is all I can say. It's the largest ship I've ever seen. All smooth metal carved and sleek for an emperor.

We're supposed to sneak on there? There must be thousands of Ilori, labmade and true, onboard. What was I expecting? This was always going to be near impossible, dangerous, terrifying. But seeing it up close in person… I'm not prepared. I'm not as brave as I want to be.

"Stealth mode still activated?" I ask the AI, even though if it wasn't, we'd already be blown to smithereens.

"Stealth mode still activated," it confirms. There's a twinge in my chest and my breath feels short. I rub a hand through my short nappy hair.

Rubin threads his fingers through mine. "You don't look good."

"We can't do this—the Ilori—Rubin, they—we have to wait, we have to plan. We can't rush this. It's too—"

"Let me do this," Zaira says, pushing to her feet. "I don't need either of you. I don't want to risk either of you." She hits the ventilator switch, opening the atmo converter and refreshing the air inside.

"Zaira." Rubin twists around. "We need each other. We just gotta readjust our plan…"

"Don't," I warn both him and her. "Don't do this."

"I have to," she says, her gaze resting on the massive ship in the distance. Memorizing every line and angle and hatch. "And now I know how." Her skin lights up, gold and swirling. Her eyes widen, and slowly she becomes less and less solid. She looks like…like…stardust. Her garbled, mighty voice fills the cabin. "Go to Earth. I will fix everything. There will be no war. You'll see."

Before I can even get out of my seat, tell her to stop, tell her we need her more than she needs to kill Ozvios, she begins to dissipate. As I rush to say that there is no easy solution, no easy fix to this—she explodes in a storm of gold. *Poof.* She's just…gone. Through the vents, into space.

There's a moment of silence between us until Rubin breaks it. "Did she just…?"

"I don't… I don't think she needs a body." The truth leaves my lips breathlessly. "She chose to have one. That's what those old stories say, right? Indigo chose not to have one… They could change forms. Indigo could appear as a creature, a constellation, stardust. Zaira is more than just Indigo, but they have the same power." I sound so smart and knowledge-able, but the truth is, I'm neither. "She needs to see where to go, like with the missile. Remember? She has to map it in her mind, that way she can pinpoint exactly where it is. She needed us to get her here so she could—"

"Go after Ozvios." Rubin shakes his head. "Zaira is going after Ozvios, who never faded, never lost his powers. She's... She was desperate to get to that ship. She knows something we don't."

"You're right." I take a deep breath. "What if it's a trap? She may be powerful, and whatever happened in Andarra might've changed her perspective, but she's like us. She's not experienced. Not against the Ilori."

Rubin trembles beside me, connecting the pieces like a terrible puzzle where the complete picture will devastate us. "She's going to die, Wesley."

"No." I take the thrusters in my hands and shoot forward, across space and around the moon. "We aren't going to let her."

His eyes meet mine. "Are you sure about this?"

"Absolutely," I lie. Because truthfully, I know I'm going to die in this skipper. I've seen it in the vision. So, at this point, going to the Ilori, going on the mothership where there's a thousand enemies around every corner can't be my death. That makes perfect logical sense, right? "She needs us."

CHAPTER TWENTY-TWO

Zaira

The stars freckled and swirled like constellations on her skin
She was powerful, determined, undeniably fierce
And though she believed herself invulnerable
She was trapped in a shell, no one else could pierce
—Allister Daniels, "She Who Breaks The Stars"

This ends here. Nothing and no one will stop me now.

Come find me.

Ozvios is on that ship and he will give me my grandmother. And he will pay for everything he has done. The Ilori will fall and I... I can leave this universe once and for all. Fade away again where there's peace and quiet, where no one expects me to save them.

I dash through space in a cloud of stardust, traveling over the moon and Earth. It wasn't until I was bit by the Jadu that

I knew I could do this. That I knew I was strong enough to use Indigo's power.

The hatch is right there. I saw it in my solid state. All I have to do is reform within. All I have to do…is move with the flow. Feel for an opening, find the heat and warmth and life. And there it is, on the edge of the mothership, in a little slice between the sleek metal. Just a crack. But that's all I need.

I sweep inside it, dust by dust, and I land on my knees, reformed and gasping for air. Air that's a trickle of atmo. Once my lungs fill and expand, I look around my surroundings. I'm in a compartment of… The breath leaves my lips now. On both sides of the room, lined along the walls, labmade Ilori rest in individual pods. The panels across their jaws flicker blue and white. Consuming energy.

Though I'm prepared for a fight, I think it's best to keep my arrival quiet while I can. My energy belongs elsewhere. Gingerly, I creep toward the sliding doors, scanning the panel. There are too many Ilori numbers, too many variables, and I'd imagine one mistake would be one too many.

My fingers hover above the keypad. Getting onto the ship was supposed to be the hardest part and yet I don't even know how to open the door.

I nibble my bottom lip. Maybe if I could find another opening between the rooms again—

A voice pierces the silence and sets my heart pounding. "Who are you?"

I turn slowly, hands ready for violence. There's an Ilori, a labmade, I think. I glance down at the number on their chest; the true Ilori on Mal Ares wore them too, and I should be able to translate it. They use she/her pronouns and is considered upper-level command. The rest of the numbers mean nothing to me. She adjusts the panel on her jaw, and instead of glowing blue like the others, it settles into place like skin. She has long black hair, bright watery blue eyes, and a pale white complexion.

She limps toward me but stops. I take a breath, sniffing for any sense of familiarity on her. These creatures were built using Mal Aresian magic—surely, they must sense me as I do them?

Her eyes flash as she takes in my constellations. "You are nothing I've seen before."

"And you," I say carefully, "are using magic stolen from my people."

She smirks. "We do not get to choose how we're created, god."

"You know who I am." Now it's my turn to smile as wisps of black seep from my fingers. "Are you telling the others I'm here—with your…?" I wave my hand around, referring to her panel. That's how they communicate, right? That's how they stay connected and serve the true Ilori.

"No." She limps closer. "It is a pleasure to be in your presence. I am 0rsa, first generation humanoid. Your power sings to me, makes me feel at home."

I let that last sentence slide by, unsure how to respond. "What do you want, 0rsa? You could communicate, alert them of my presence—but you know I could end your life with a melody, yes?"

"Why would I do this?" Her lips quirk. "Who would benefit? I am quite interested in my own preservation."

"And yet," I say, stepping closer until we're inches apart, "you still have not told me what you want."

If she finds my nearness intimidating, she doesn't show it. "I know why you're here. And I know you cannot open that door. It's true Ilori tech made to keep us labmades locked inside, unable to get out. We're being punished, you see, for not succeeding at our directives. I've been stripped of my command and left here to rot."

"That sounds sad." I watch as her lips wobble.

She shakes her head quickly. "There is no emotion."

"The power you've stolen from my people reacts *only* through emotion. Didn't you know that?" I laugh mirthlessly, feeling anger rise up my throat. This is what the Ilori killed my people for? A labmade who has no idea of the power they wield? "I'd imagine that little panel is made from the bracelets the nightweavers were forced to wear to dampen their abilities. It connects you to the true Ilori, lets them control you and siphon your energy. They conditioned you not to feel so you would never break it and find your own power within. True Ilori—"

"I am true Ilori," she whispers harshly. "I deserve to be. I should have been."

"If that's what you want, I can kill you now." I let power stream from my mouth along with the words. "I have a thing against true Ilori. Not a fan."

She tilts her head to the side. "Is that what you're going to do? Kill all of them?"

Funny how she doesn't say all of *us*. Suddenly, she's not so certain she wants to be clumped together with murderers worshipping a god bent on destroying the universe. "I don't believe in genocide. I believe in justice."

She considers me for a few moments in silence. "That door is impenetrable. If any of us try to break through, enter the wrong combination only once, they will open the hatch and let us die in atmo."

Hmm. I chose the wrong place to enter the ship. I stalk back to the panel, staring down at the numbers sparkling up at me, waiting for me to make a mistake.

Her voice is soft as she limps up beside me. A silver dagger glimmers by her hip but she makes no move to use it. "I can open it for you—"

"If you could open it, why are you here?" I cock an assessing eyebrow her way.

"Where else would I go?" The same expression meets my own. "I'll require payment."

I glare at her openly. "And what would that be?"

"Since I was created, all I ever wanted was to be true Ilori. I wanted it…" Her voice cracks. "I wanted it so much, I believed it. I was prepared to sacrifice my own race to succeed. But after Earth, after Morris chose not to leave me for dead, had his brother bring me back here—I've realized I want to be more than them." She stares at me now, tears filling the corners of her eyes. "They told me not to feel, that it is a weakness. They told me I can never be one of them. They told me I deserve to be eliminated for what I did, letting Morris go."

I watch her carefully, unsure of where she is going with this. What does she want from me? What is it this broken, confused Ilori girl thinks I can do for her?

"I've… I was not always a good person. I imprisoned humans on Earth, hurt them. If I am to feel, then I must feel everything, even the emotions that make me…" She trails off, her eyes darting away from mine. "I want to choose my own fate."

And there it is. Finally. I let air sail between my teeth. "You want me to sever Il-0CoM." If that's the case, isn't that what Rubin and Wesley plan to do anyway? Help this labmade Morris and human Ellie destroy their mind-connection system? Before I can tell her as such, she shakes her head again.

"I can break my panel and go off the proverbial grid on my own. But doing so would mean I don't have power. It would mean losing everything I've built and sacrificed for my entire life." She glares at me as if I understand. "I cannot lose my power. I *will* not. I don't want to be free of the Ilori—I want to rule them. I can take us into a newer, less cruel age after the 1lvs die."

I stand there mystified for a moment. "And again, I ask—"

"When all of this is over, don't oppose me in my bid for leadership. Endorse me if asked." When she notices my expression, she juts out her jaw. "I will break up the empire, I will free the colonies, I will do my part to pay for what my people have done… But I need the position and power to do so."

"So you're asking me to spare your life and let you lead the Ilori."

She smiles, and in it, I see ambition and desire. "You were always going to spare me. You don't have the look of a killer. And if you want out of this room, the solution is easy. When this empire crashes and falls apart, let me put it back together as something new and better."

Every time I think I understand creatures in this universe they surprise me. They've strayed so far away from love and compassion and wonder. Now they're all trying to get power. With another quick glance at 0rsa, I nod. Sure, she can lead whatever she wants.

If this all goes according to plan, I won't be here to see it. I'll free my grandmother, kill Ozvios, and let these worlds decide their own future free from gods. Perhaps they'll find unity or perhaps they'll destroy each other. That's not my problem.

I'm not meant to serve this universe. The only reason I left Mal Ares was to save my people and I failed. Killing Ozvios won't bring my people back, he's right. What is lost is lost forever. But I can save my grandmother. I can do one right thing and not care about all the wrong things.

0rsa hits a series of numbers into the door. "This will be a fruitful alliance," she says, mostly to herself.

I don't respond, having already regretted coming to this one room on this ship and meeting someone who has the potential to do great good or great evil. I can't tell. Once the door slides open, revealing a gray metal deserted hallway, I nearly bolt outside.

0rsa watches me from the doorway, and as it slides shut, she smirks. "I really hope you don't die."

Out of sight, I exhale. Wow. She's intense.

But I don't have time to think about her or the future she wants. I look down both sides of the hall and decide that anywhere is better than here. I take a left, treading quietly on the soundless floor. There are doors embedded along the walls, but no knobs, only keypads. This must be a prison. This must be where they send anyone who dissents.

At the end of the long hallway, there's a pull in my body to the right. As if something within me wants me to move in that direction.

Ozvios. He's here. Our power is reacting to each other.

I pick up the pace, moving at a slight jog now. Doors remain closed, not another Ilori in sight. There must not be any comms watching me, recording me, alerting my arrival to lackeys on board.

And I know, I know, something's wrong here… These halls should be flooded with Ilori. They should have been alerted when a new sign of life just suddenly appeared on board, but my mind is going a meter a minute. Over and over, I see glimpses of my grandmother.

Her wailing in pain. Her begging me for help. Her telling me to save her.

I need to find Ozvios. I need to set things right. This universe doesn't belong to me—it never did. Indigo created it, and part of me is Indigo, yes, but I've lived through experiences that have shaped me, that have made me Zaira. Experiences of cruelty, hatred, anger, living in darkness. But my grandmother, she was the light guiding me in the dark. She loved me when I thought love didn't exist.

I cannot leave her here to die. She can be the light again, for someone new, someone better. Someone who deserves her.

"Zaira, come find me. Zaira…" my grandmother says, maybe in my mind, maybe outside of it. I can't tell anymore.

My feet pick up their pace and my heart gallops. A door slides open and I bolt inside of it, sure this is a sign. Sure this is where I'm meant to be. She's here. She's waiting for me. She's...

The room is black. The walls are dark metal and the door shuts behind me. There's no one here. It's empty. Not a bench to sit on, not a screen to watch.

"Zaira, are you here?" The garbled voice comes from the corner...where there's no one and nothing. Not even a speaker to broadcast the sound. "I thought I'd better keep my distance since the last time we met, you threw me into a wall."

"Ciaran?" I speak into the void. The confusion must be seen on my face somehow because he laughs, loud and riotous, making my skin prickle. "Wh—are you being punished for helping me? I'm sorry, Ciaran. I can get you out."

"Oh, Zaira, how could you?" Before I can ask what he means, why I'm here, he slinks from the dark corner. I don't understand how he could've appeared where there was nothing moments ago. How he... "I watched you form and reform. Tricky magic, that. But you did it. Means you're progressing."

His blond hair's slicked back against his scalp. He's wearing traditional Ilori garb: a black tunic and silver threaded pants. His orange eyes meet mine and I'm reminded of how not long ago, I considered him a friend. How he saved me. How he's always been there for me, and that has landed him in a prison. I open my mouth to apologize again, but the words freeze in my throat.

The violet aura vibrates around him like all true Ilori. Power and experience. Only this time, in a darkness far different than my home, I really see it.

Before, on Mal Ares, his power read young. My age. The older Ilori become, the thicker the aura. He was new.

Now, the power hovering over his skin is almost solid. He's old. Terribly old. Older than he should be.

As he watches my brows knit together, he smiles. "I needed to stay close to you. I needed you to trust me and care for me. I was your best friend, your only friend, and still..." His voice trails off with an edge of anger. Still, he doesn't say, I never let him in. Never let him be more than a friend. Never let him into my heart. He sighs and stands straighter. "I've had a long time to perfect this. I can change forms just like you. Though I do admit, this one's my favorite. Young and easy to fit in. I've found people respond well to it."

"Ozvios." The name tumbles from my lips like poison.

"Indigo. No, not Indigo—Zaira. Two forms meshed together in one body. One with emotional magic, the other with power that can create the universe. *Could.*" He smiles wider, stepping closer to me. "I want to kill Indigo, you see. Indigo is my greatest enemy. Indigo's stardust would be delicious. But I want to save Zaira."

I stumble back, feeling his power wash down my bare arms and around my back. Holding me in thrall. "Why?"

"Zaira is the last nightweaver. Zaira is the only one of her kind left in this universe. That makes her special. Our powers together, we'd be..." His eyes roam over my body lasciviously. "I've wanted this for so long."

My body stands rigidly in place. "My...my grandmother?"

"Gone." He smirks. "Just like Mal Ares."

Melodies rise in my throat but my lips won't move. Can't move.

"Oh, you can't do that here. I've had a long time to learn about nightweaving and how to control it. I can't recreate it, and I don't know how powerful it can truly be. But these walls are made from the same materials as the bracelets we clasped around your wrists. I had to drain every nightweaver I could to study your weaknesses. Once I understood the power Indigo created in their first world, I found a way to use it. Channel it to power my armies." He gloats, smug. "I bet you thought 1lv did that, right? No, he's far too ignorant. A very annoying supremacist. I just went where the resources were. Creating Il-0CoM was my greatest tool of destruction; it provides me with a steady diet of life force. The labmades were a stroke of genius.

"After Indigo faded away, I had nothing but time. It was boring without them to challenge me, I'll admit. So I had to do something." He huffs, shaking his head. "And then Indigo was reborn on Mal Ares, their first world. They became you. I thanked the universe and gave you a lifetime of suffering. You don't see it now, but Indigo had it too good. It made them foolish. Suffering, though…it made *you* smart. It made you worthy and my equal. It made you see how terrible this universe is without someone guiding it in the right direction."

I want to ask a million questions. To hurt him and punish him and make him pay for everything he has done to me, my world, my universe. My grandmother.

"I can feel the anger rising within you," he says, now only a few inches away from my face. His breath, sweet and hot, brushes against my skin. "Zaira is beautiful. Zaira's anger is seductive. When she uses it, she does bad things, doesn't she? She hurts people and causes chaos. She's like me—destruction runs through her veins." He laughs, the sound grating my ears. "You like it, you crave it. Soon you won't aim that fury at me anymore. And I'll never hold you back."

He runs a cool hand across my cheek. "Oh, so soft and pretty. You will love me. You will. Maybe if I do this?" He snaps his other finger and his Ilori appearance changes—he's now an Andarran with crisp blue eyes like Wesley's. "You like Andarrans right? That's why you travel with one? Or maybe this?" He snaps his fingers again and this time he's something else. Something I've never seen before. His body slumps a little, his eyes a light green. "Human," he says, as if reading my mind. "Very fragile things. Easy to kill. You didn't create them. They were a happy accident after you faded away. They're very cute, aren't they?"

I can't speak. I can't move. I can't scream and shout and throw my fists at him. And though I feel his power around me, I'm beginning to feel the cracks. He has found a way to control the nightweaver within me, but not Indigo. I just need to… I close my eyes. Digging through memories and melodies.

His hand wraps around my neck, yanking my head toward his. "I don't want Indigo's magic here. I want Zaira. Be Zaira for me." When power flares alive in my blood and rises to the skin, gold and shiny, Ozvios sighs. "Just when we were having fun."

His hand, still holding my neck, thrums with strength. His eyes meet mine. I'm about to open my lips and break through his hold on me… And he throws me hard into the metal wall.

My body bounces off it, my limbs crying out in agony. My vision blurs, but I see him bring two fingers to his lips, kiss them, and blow it toward me. A haze falls around me, this one impenetrable. My body flattens against the floor. My eyes slowly close. I can't… I can't do anything.

"I'm going to Earth to watch everyone kill each other. It's going to be a spectacular feast of stardust. Then I'll be back and we can decide how to rule this universe together. Sleep tight, my love."

CHAPTER TWENTY-THREE

Wesley

As we're stealthily slipping by the Earth's moon toward IpS1L, the sky fills with Ilori ships. Hundreds of Ilori ships. I pause with the thrusters in my hands as they rush by us toward Earth.

"What are they doing?" Rubin's body is pasted against mine, his eyes wide.

"They're going to war," I say. "The battle must be beginning." And just as the words leave my lips, more ships appear out of hyperspace. Huge ones bearing the crests of Andarra, XiGRa, Major and Minor Sidarra, even Faran. I can't believe my eyes. And... I gasp. Even the sigil of three mighty warriors, their swords clashed together.

"Is that—is that the Juxto warlords?"

I smile. They decided to come. I think about Dax. I wonder if he's aboard one of these fleets, ready to fight and die for freedom from the Ilori. I hope not. Before I can respond to Rubin, even more fleets arrive. The space around us is packed tight and I grip the thrusters, weaving through all of them.

The largest fleet I've ever seen nearly lands on top of us and I swerve out of the way just in time. I look up, my eyes catching on the label. Three gold suns layered in purple.

"The Soleil," I mutter to myself.

Monchuri. The solitary Qadin crest is gone, replaced by a new symbol; one featuring all twelve worlds belonging in the Monchuri system. The Hamdi Abara governance. The new republic. The end of a monarchy and beginning of a democracy.

"They did say they would show up with a might of their own," Rubin laughs beside me. "They're so ferking cool. You think they're on there?"

"Queen Joy and King Felix?" My mouth flops open in wonder. "No doubt." My stomach flips. There are more armies here than we could have imagined. More people who have decided to fight than we could've believed. United to save this one little planet on the edge of space. United to kill an empire. As the ships rush past us into Earth's atmo, landing and setting down, the sky half empties.

This is our chance.

"IpS1L will be too busy to see us coming. They have a war to fight, one they thought they'd win easily. We have to get to Zaira and find that labmade. We might have a chance…" I can't even finish the sentence because if I did, it would be real. And I don't want to have hope just yet. I'm already surprised how wrong I was, thinking that people have lost compassion. That they could never unite.

Right now, our girl needs us.

I gingerly zoom past motherships holding royals from across the galaxy toward IpS1L. Soon, these ships will be on the defense as the fight moves to the air. But I'm getting ahead of myself.

The landing port is still open on IpS1L from the fly-fighters deployment, so we rush toward it, full speed ahead. The hangar's empty, no one there to shoot at us. No one there to even notice us just yet. Blobby's stealth mode is legit saving our lives.

I land us quickly and carefully. With a few flicks on the console, the ramp hits the Ilori ground and I toss a glance at Rubin. "We might need some stunners. Do you have one?"

"Baby, I always have something in my pack here." He opens the pouch clinched on his waist. "We got stunners, we got these little pods that explode into a fruity haze—" He notices my expression. "I like to either make an entrance or a disappearance. Very important."

He shifts some things around and waves me over, then shoves two little silver tabs into my hand once I'm close enough.

I look down at them and then back into his perfectly brown eyes. "What are these?"

"They're called Painless. If something happens—if you— we are…" His voice cracks and trails off. And I… I do something I've never done before. I take his head in my hands and try to stare at his eyes instead of his perfectly plump lips.

"Nothing is going to happen to you, Rubin. Hear me?" I exude all the confidence I can and I hope it's enough to give him comfort. "You're going to make it through this."

Me, on the other hand? My fate will lead me back to this ship and that'll be it.

He nods, his skin soft and warm in my hands. I almost pull away when the AI's voice crackles through the comms.

"Ilori have been alerted to your presence. Do you need a calming chemicallent?"

"No!" we both shout at the same time and then smile at each other.

He leans into me. Our noses touch and my heart is racing. I know what he wants; I want the same. I'm just… I'm not sure I can give him what he deserves. I'm too new at this, so uncertain. My time left is too short. But when our lips meet—and the suspense doesn't manage to kill me—this kiss is everything I could've imagined. He's so soft and careful. There are mini explosions in the pit of my stomach with every brush of contact. It's warm and hot and I think my legs are shaking.

Desire rolls off him. I'm sure it's rolling off me too. Maybe even more so. There are millions of things we could be worrying about, doing, running from—but in this moment, we're two boys from two worlds kissing for the first time. My first kiss. The best kiss.

He opens his mouth enough to let me in. Suddenly, there's fear coursing through my veins; I have no idea what I'm doing, if this is right, even though it feels absolutely right. We stay there like this until the panic gets the better of us. Until we know we have to move, we have to be responsible and determined. We have to find Zaira, save Zaira. Remind her that she's never alone, that she has family.

"Damn, you are good at that," Rubin mutters breathlessly as our fingers entwine and clutch tight. We run down the ramp together, stunners in our free hands. Prepared for violence even when neither of us believe in it.

But no one stops us. No one comes for us.

It's not until we bash the panel against the hangar wall and slide through into a hallway that we slow down. I glance up at the corners of the ceiling where tiny comms perch, watching us. Who knows how many Ilori there are on the other side of them. I give it a wave and shoot at it with a stunner. Missing wildly. Not even close.

Rubin aims and catches it in one go. Then hits the other three in quick succession. "I'm a celebrity. I need to be good at aiming."

We don't have the time for me to question how exactly those two things go together. Instead, I cock an eyebrow his way and then pause in the middle of the hall.

We've reached a fork. Right or left? We have to start somewhere. Zaira's on this ship. My purpose is on this ship.

Shouts sound to the left, followed by heavy footsteps. Right it is.

Rubin and I bolt. He's breathing heavy beside me as our bodies sync in quick motion.

"I really should exercise more," he says between breaths.

I give him a smirk as we pass by cool black metal walls dotted with seamless doors and tiny panels. "You are perfect. Everything about you."

His lips twitch. "Don't say stuff like that to me. It'll make me like you even more."

"Even more?" I laugh despite our worsening circumstances. "We wouldn't want that."

The corner of his lip hitches as he inhales air greedily. We make it down another hallway until…

"You! Stop there!" An Ilori holds a stunner level at me. "Drop your weapons!"

The Ilori is true; a faint violet haze clings to their skin. Their pale orange hair is held tightly back in a bun, and their eyes are a shade of vibrant red. Terrifying. Rubin drops his stunner right away and I begin to lower mine when more shouts sound from down the hall.

The Ilori turns away from us, though their stunner remains aimed right at me. We look past them down the empty hall as screams echo. The true Ilori's hand begins to shake. Deciding that between us, the unknown assailants are more threatening.

Rubin steps back and grabs his stunner while I prepare my own.

With a quick nod, I try to nonverbally tell Rubin that we should run. He makes a face that clearly says, *What?* I jut my chin in the direction of the other hallway. His brows furrow. I swear to the gods, namely Zaira, that we are on two very different wavelengths but damn if I don't get flutters when he looks at me.

I point at me, I point at him, I point at the hallway. Understanding dawns in his expression. We slip back carefully without alerting the Ilori and nearly make it to the metal sliding doors when shots ring out on either side of us.

We both fall to the floor seconds before the Ilori thuds unconsciously between us. I look up as another Ilori, this one covered in a black mask, stalks forward, holding their stunner. They bend down, taking the pulse of the fallen guard, and then meet my gaze.

Behind them, another person with a long black hood covering their face walks up to them. "Who are they?"

The masked Ilori tilts their head back and forth. "More like *what* are they?" Their voice sounds stiff and their language, though translated by my heargo, is unlike any I've ever heard before. "Andarran and...Balfian?"

"Wait a minute..." Rubin squeaks from the floor. "How did you know I'm from Balfus?"

The Ilori pulls their mask off and long brown-black hair falls beside their deeply tan skin, stark against their bright blue panel. "I've read many books about Ilori colonies and the people who lived in subjugation. I feel it's always a good idea to know different cultural and physical differences between—"

"You're...Morris?" I stare up at him. "You're the labmade who's going to break the true Ilori's hold on labmades?"

"Shhh," the person says behind Morris. "I can't believe these little bug things even work. Like this is wild that I can understand aliens."

"We're all aliens here, Ellie, even you." Morris glances over his shoulder, his stunner suddenly trained on me. "How do you know my name and mission, Andarran?"

I raise my hands in the air, putting all the weight on my chest. "I mean no harm. I was bit by the Jadu and saw that we're supposed to help you."

Morris holds my gaze for a long moment and then lowers his stunner. "I'm not convinced I can break the labmades free of Il-0CoM. The system is different now, and I'm unsure if I have the compatible programming."

"That's why we're here," I say, reaching a hand out to Morris. He takes it and pulls me up to standing. "Me and Rubin are going to help you."

Ellie, the human I've seen from the visions, stalks closer.

She pulls her hood back, revealing brown skin, curly hair spilling from a purple hat, and a pair of unusual dark-rimmed frames around her eyes.

"How are *you* going to help us?" She puts a hand on her hip, eyeing us both intensely. "Morris, this is a trap. That King dude said people aren't always what they seem. And we both know not to trust anyone. We are the only ones we can count on. Nobody helps for free."

Anger circles her aura. Anger and hurt. I feel flashes of regret, betrayal, and more emotions that I can't isolate and understand. Humans, it would seem, feel too much. With a peek at Morris though, this labmade feels his emotions just as intensely. His gaze slides to hers. Where she's anger and distrust, he's adoration. He is deeply, completely in love with her. Her lips twitch and she looks away, warmth spreading up her cheeks. She's in love with him too. Though quietly, carefully.

I take this moment to appreciate that. It helps knowing that neither of them are blasting violence into the air. Neither of them, despite taking this guard down, seem to be violent by nature. I help Rubin up and clasp his hand tight, saying, "My brother lived on Earth for a few human years and is probably down there now, fighting for your world."

Ellie's gaze narrows on me. "Who is your brother?"

"Allister Daniels… He's in a pop band called—"

"The Starry Eyed," Ellie and Morris say at the same time. They both exchange a wide almost-giddy smile and Morris laughs.

"Well, brother of Allister, I think it's time you told us how you can help."

THE RUBIN RIMA PODCAST

Broadcasting from an undisclosed location

RR: Hey, spacers, it's Rubin, coming to you live from a very dangerous ship outside of Earth. And, spacers, listening near and far, here's the update you've been waiting for: the war against the Ilori is bigger than we ever thought it would be. Everyone is here—are you? Are you going to hop in your ship and see the biggest battle in our starry history? Now is the time! I don't want to predict too quickly, but the Ilori aren't prepared for a united front. And that's exactly what we'll need to defeat them.

Unknown: Who are you talking to?

RR: This is my new friend, Morris. He's a labmade Ilori who is extremely adorable and very taken. Morris, say hi to everyone.

Morris: Uh…hello?

RR: Morris is traveling with love interest, Ellie. Do you want to say hello, Ellie? She's a slightly short human with a head full of curls, and dark brown skin. You'd be the first human ever on my program.

Ellie: No.

RR: She's a bit prickly but I have a feeling we're going to be best friends after all of this. Anyway, I'm here teaching them about how to broadcast across different platforms simultaneously using updated systems that are finicky about letting you upload onto them. Now most of you are wondering why this is a topic, and I can't say! You're just going to have to take my word for it that it's super important and necessary at the moment.

WD: Rubin, you stay here and help them. I think this room is secure. I'm going to go find Zaira.

RR: Wait! You shouldn't go alone. You don't even know where to look, where she'll—

Morris: If you are missing a friend aboard this ship, they will most likely keep them in a cargo compartment with impenetrable walls, that doesn't allow Il-0CoM, panel charging, or transmission. It would be toward the left quadrant, end of the second sector. That's where prisoners stay under security. Especially labmade ones.

WD: Security?

Morris: Yes, there will be a few true Ilori guards and comms. You will need to bypass them in the first sector.

RR: You need me. I should—

WD: No, you stay. You help them. How long will this take?

RR: Looking at this system, half a rotation at least—

Ellie: How much is a rotation again?

Morris: About three human hours.

RR: Aren't these two cute, everyone? She's wearing the most precious purple hat. Inquiring minds want to know, where did you get it?

Ellie: ... My dad bought it for me under the Brooklyn Bridge. My dad who is down there, messed up because of the Ilori. So while you're making cutesy conversation, try to remember that there is an entire planet fighting for its freedom and autonomy.

RR: Oh, baby, we've all been fighting the Ilori—wait, Morris, don't put that there, use the other port, the one marked insculpulator—for as long as we could. Our homeworlds are massively older than yours. But here's something I never told my own listeners. When I was seven years old, my own parents were executed by the Ilori when they couldn't fix the unfixable problem of making more labmades without destroying a world. Now, you're probably all thinking that I alluded to this many times over podcast history. But I never told you that I was there when they died. My mother screamed my name when the Ilori scrambled her mind. My father told me to never stop looking for the truth. He was a broken man beside my mother's corpse, ready to die alongside her. So when you say that we don't know what it's like to see the very real devastation of the Ilori, we do. Many of us do. The only difference is that Earth was unprepared for it.

Ellie: I'm sorry. I shouldn't have assumed.

RR: You're allowed to be angry and ready to unleash all the hurt you've endured. You deserve that... So do we. We've been hurt too. Most of the known worlds in this universe are here right now, fighting for your world and theirs. So let's keep that anger for when the Ilori fall and we get to decide how we want to experience the future. Channel it into making the universe a better, more united place.

Ellie: Do you really think that? Do you really think we can win against them? I've seen the Ilori roll over my world in days. You can't—

RR: I have to believe we're going to win. What's the alternative, Ellie?

WD: Besides, we have a secret weapon—I just have to find her.

Morris: Weapon?

RR: Yeah, we just gotta find her and get her down to the battlefield. One more kiss before you go?

WD: *(inaudible)* ...definitely.

CHAPTER TWENTY-FOUR

Zaira

Time is running out, I remember my grandmother saying. Time is running out and yet, I'm here, weak, trapped in a black room with no doors. Trapped by my enemy who destroyed my home, killed my people, killed my grandmother, and won't stop until the universe is a fragment of what it once was. Ciaran, my friend, is now and has always been Ozvios. The guilt I felt for never loving him the way he seemed to love me… The time I spent letting him share my life… It wasn't real. He toyed with me from the beginning. He lied, he manipulated. And now there's nothing I can do to stop him.

I try to lift my arm but it sits still on the floor, lifeless. There's no energy. No hope.

I failed my grandmother. Failed Mal Ares. Failed at being Indigo. Failed Rubin and Wesley by running off, proclaiming that I knew what I was doing and that I would fix everything. I was overconfident, so sure of myself. With a small laugh that stays inside my throat, I think about how I believed I could kill Ozvios.

He has spent centuries creating and devouring. Growing wiser and stronger. What chance did I have? I may have all this power within me, but I'm still too new. Too inexperienced.

My eyes drift to the far side of the room that is enveloped in shadows. I think of home.

Let myself sink into my memories. Of hobbling on short legs to reach my grandmother. The vivid image of it that washes over me would make me gasp if I could open my lips. I close my eyes, hoping the memory will thicken and fill with color. But there weren't a lot of colors on Mal Ares. Not in the end. The nightweavers darkened the corners in death because they couldn't let go, couldn't move on. They whispered their anger into the cold air. And I was a baby. A child. Maybe I still am.

My grandmother's voice had bubbled with positivity and faith as I struggled to find my footing in my young body. *Come to me, Zaira. That's right, you can do it.* She'd smile, piercing through the whispers. *Such a big girl.* I'd opened my mouth but words were hard. I couldn't form them yet. And they didn't make much sense anyway. She kissed me on my forehead. *You don't need to be more than you are. You simply need to be. That is enough.*

On this cold desolate floor, I wish I could sniff, cry. I wish I could see her now. Instead, I think of another memory. This one not as old.

I was wearing the Citlali star, working it back and forth across the silver chain. Books, outdated and damaged, were strewn all over the gray stone floor. A cool draft wafted in from the window. The nightweavers' whispers were there, always there, but not as clear. I walked to the window and stared out at the landscape. It was cracked and broken. Like my people. Indigo's first creation—my first creation—was collapsing around me, although I didn't consider it mine at the time.

Ciaran didn't knock, simply opened the door and strutted inside. He was a child, like me. Maybe a year older. He stared at me until I turned around, giving him all my attention.

"It's your birthday," he stated with a smile. There was joy in the pronouncement, like he really cared. "Do you feel any different?"

I shook my head. Words weren't necessary for the lie. Truthfully, I'd begun hearing new melodies in my head when I turned nine. Flashes of memories appeared then too, not necessarily mine, but belonging to the nightweavers. They could change my reality, let me live within theirs. They stayed with me, connected with me. They told me about Indigo, explaining as if I was *them*, but I knew I wasn't. Still, I wondered at Indigo's abilities; how they could take stardust and shape worlds in their hands. How they had so much and poured it all into Mal Ares. Yes, they'd made mistakes, but it was perfect just as it was. Indigo's heart—my heart—was here in this world.

"Zaira," Ciaran had said, watching my face on my birthday. His hands fidgeted by his sides. He looked younger then, less powerful too. I wish I had seen through his illusion. I wish I had made different choices in this memory. "Are you remembering?"

I shook my head again, looking down at my sack of a dress. The material itched my skin and didn't keep me warm in Mal Ares's cold endless night.

Ciaran stepped closer, beaming at me until I met his gaze. "You do, don't you. What do you remember? You can't fool me, Zaira. I can read your face like a book. You and I, we are too similar. We are made from the same stardust. That is why we must always be close."

"Sometimes," I said carefully. "I see glimpses of the universe as nothing but darkness."

Ciaran smiled. "Those times are gone now. The universe is full. Perhaps, too full. Worlds you didn't craft have sprung to existence. They hate each other. They fight. Only Ozvios can save the universe. By culling those that would end it all."

I knew that wasn't true—Ozvios couldn't save the universe because he thrived on destruction—but I nodded again. That was what the Ilori wanted from me. They needed me to accept my fate. My death. They didn't want me to fight it… They knew that if I did, I would break free. I would change everything. I would…

My eyes burst open.

I've been in this position before, back on Andarra. I came out of that water renewed, confident, believing that *I* was balance. Both Indigo and Zaira. Both god and nightweaver, creation and destruction. I thought I was meant to be the most powerful being in the universe. I was sure of it—as sure as I was that walking onto this ship would solve everything.

I was wrong.

Indigo didn't want to be reborn the same god so they could get their second chance. No. Indigo gave me their power, gave me their memories, because they wanted me to do something new with it.

They wanted me to *be* something new. Because Indigo had shaped worlds into existence but could never live among their creatures. They wanted me to feel connected, a part of a community. And I did on Mal Ares. They wanted me to love that world and see something beautiful and precious through that darkness.

There was a lesson in that: not all things are what they seem. Look beyond the surface. Yes, there are terrible things in this universe, but there's magic too, in between these stars. In between me and everyone else.

Indigo didn't want me to unlock their power to create new worlds. They wanted me to care. To find love. To see the good. And help make the universe better—not from up high on a godly perch, but within it.

Seventeen years I've lived in this body, with this mind, with memories my own and theirs, and finally...*finally*, I think I understand.

I'm not the god of creation. I am the creation of a god. No, not a god. A higher being. *Higher beings?* I want to unravel that thought, but I don't have time.

Right now, I have to go down there to Earth and save them—the humans, the creatures, *the good*—from the Ilori. Unite them. Be with them.

As I try to lift my arm again...nothing happens. I scrunch up my nose and then realize I can scrunch up my nose. If I can do that, I can do more.

Using all my effort, I push my fingertips into the floor. They're cold, they're sluggish, but I push and push and push until the momentum gives me the strength to sit up slowly, painfully. With my head hanging toward my chest, I take as deep of a breath as I can. No one's coming here to save me; I've got to save myself.

It takes long moments and a few tears until I can fight through the fog Ozvios left to keep me weak. It's like being underwater in Andarra again, the fish fluttering around me, blocking out the light and enclosing on my body. But this isn't water, it's power, and I have it too. I am strong too. Otherwise, he wouldn't have hunted me across the galaxies and locked me here. He wouldn't have spent all those years pretending to be a friend when he was my enemy. He let me leave so I could learn to harness my power, but not be so confident that I could beat him.

My feet plant on the floor and I slowly elongate my spine, panting as I draw closer to the ceiling. When I'm standing—not tall, not strong, just standing—I let out a little scream of victory.

The door whooshes open on my left and I let out another scream, this time afraid of who will join me in the shadows. Afraid in this weakened state, I can lose.

A voice calls from the doorway. It's too bright for me to focus, but I'd recognize the voice anywhere. "Zaira? Are you here? I swear to all the gods, including you if you're here, that I hate the dark."

He stands there in the light of the hall, his gaze sliding from me in the dark to the panel just inside.

"I'm here," I croak. "Please, I'm here."

"Wait there, there's something wrong." Wesley's words catch. "The air feels thick, the pressure is too much. Let me see." He slowly crosses over to the panel and fiddles with the buttons.

"Careful, the Ilori are—"

"I know," he says with an edge of calm. "I got this." He hits a few more buttons and the room brightens at once. I throw my hands over my face at the harsh light, only realizing under their cover that it was easy to do. That the haze is clearing. That I'm free.

Wesley pulls me into a hug. "I found you."

Warmth trickles down my cheeks. He holds me tightly and a sob escapes my lips. And then another. And another. They burst free as if there's been a wall there, holding them in this entire time. I'd always felt that allowing myself to be afraid, to embrace my sorrow, meant I was weak. I see now that I was wrong; letting myself feel means that I'm letting myself be free.

Wesley doesn't say anything. He rubs my back and holds me there. He's a rock on which I can lean and doesn't require anything in return. I don't know how long I cry on his shoulder, but when I eventually pull away, there are tears glistening in his eyes too.

I clear my throat, my fingers swiping at the tears on his cheeks. "Are you okay?"

"I feel what you feel…"

I nod. That's right, Indigo thought it would be special for an entire civilization to be in tune with their feelings and those of others. They thought compassion and empathy could only be good for the universe. I understand now that it can be a burden too. "Because you're Andarran."

"Because…" he says with a sigh, "because none of this has been easy or okay. We—all of us—told ourselves that loss and abandonment and pain are acceptable and bearable, but they aren't. We deserve more. We deserve better."

"I'm glad I have you," I say, looking into those impossibly blue eyes that light up his face.

"I'm glad I have you too."

"Rubin!" I blurt, looking beyond him to the doorway.

"He's okay. We're going to be okay." His lips twitch when he says it though. As if he's holding in something terrible, something he doesn't want to share. "We have to go."

He tugs my arm but I hold my feet firm. "Ozvios. My grandmother—"

"I searched every single one of these prison cells, Zaira." He holds my gaze. "You were the only one here."

"No." I shake my head. "She's…she's dead. Ozvios killed her. He lured me here… I believed him. That I could save her. I have no one."

"Zaira," Wesley breathes softly. "You have us, and we have to go. *You* have to go. There's a war below and they could use your help down there. They need you more than I need you. Don't let Ozvios win by focusing on death instead of life."

I lick my lips, salty and tear-stained. They need me. He's right. Ozvios is down there, soaking in their destruction, getting stronger. And the stronger he becomes, the likelihood grows that there won't be a universe left to save.

Mourning my grandmother can wait. Earth needs me now. I cannot shake. I cannot falter.

THE STARRY EYED:

"A SONG OF SALVATION"

Written and Performed by Allister Daniels,
Whisper Landsome, Rupert and Cecil Montague

Fish that bite, skies that bleed
Girls who battle, boys who believe
The cosmos is changing, the colonies fight free
Honey, who will we be?

Gather the universe, take to the stars
Zoom past Andarra, dash past Mars
Over the moon, and beyond the sea
Darling, it's waiting for you and me

If we lose, my dear, we lose it all
If they win, my dear, they'll make us small

We sing it now, we sing it for our lives
A song about destruction
A song about creation

Brought together by fate and flames
We never knew each other, only the names
They crafted the universe from dust to star
He was a singer from verse to guitar

She came to him then, with a song in her mind
He saw her there, his heart entwined
She said this is it, boy, we've got to unite
He gave her his voice, he added his might

If we lose, my love, we lose it all
We'll lose each other, our worlds will fall
We sing it now, we sing it for our lives
A song that begs for love
A song that begs for peace
A song about destruction
A song about creation
A song of salvation

CHAPTER TWENTY-FIVE

Wesley

Back at the control room on IpS1L, I kiss Rubin one more time. "I'll be back," I lie easily, even if a sob threatens to break free. "We will see each other again." He clasps his arms around my neck, his forehead resting against mine. "Besides, I don't get paid unless I bring you to Earth, remember? Codrec would be pissed." I try for a bit of levity, but Rubin ignores it. His heart is hammering, lips wobbling. Sorrow circles around us and some part of me wants to pull away from it as I always have. A larger part of me wants to remain, feeling and embracing.

"Please, Wesley," he says quietly, his breath skimming against my lips. "Please don't go. Wait for me."

Ellie and Morris sit across the room, their heads huddled together as they arrange items on the floor. They whisper, their gazes locked. I want what they have, and I want that with Rubin. Even though we haven't known each other for very long, I can already tell it was going to happen for us. It already was happening. He's one of the greatest, kindest people I've ever met and he has let me into his heart. He has changed me. He has given me something I've been searching for my entire life.

I'll always remember this. We'll always have this one moment.

He'll have more. Replace me. Forget me. As he should. But for me, this is everything.

"I'll be back," I repeat again. "You have to help them, and the moment you're done, get off this ship. Get out of orbit. Go anywhere else."

His brown eyes pierce me. "What about you?"

"I'm going to bring Zaira down, and I'll do whatever else is needed of me. We will meet when it's all over and done, and we're free." My voice nearly cracks, his fear seeping into my skin through his shiny, glittery suit.

Zaira throws her arms around us both, inhaling slowly. Rubin disengages slightly from me and kisses her cheek.

"Be careful down there, both of you. Don't let anything happen to him." Another tear slips down his chin before he turns back to me. "Don't let anything happen to her."

Another few minutes pass until we can actually part ways. I don't mind it; I know the future. I've seen it. I can enjoy this sweet goodbye because I won't get another. This is it.

Zaira and I run down hallways in silence, no stunners needed. I'm with one of the mightiest beings in the universe. What can anyone do to me with her by my side? We reach the ship after only one quick interruption from some poor Ilori, who Zaira easily dispatched by putting them to sleep.

"I'm tired of hurting people," she said as they slumped against the floor. "There's enough pain already. I was created to do more than this. Be more than this, just like you." Her voice trailed off and we found our way to the ship.

Now she's sitting in the back with Blobby and I'm holding the thrusters and we're lifting off. My hands shake on the grips. I'm going to Earth. Somewhere I've never been. This is getting close to the end of my journey. My brother is down there. My family. He probably doesn't want me either, not the way I wanted him. He probably never did. The only two who have ever cared about me are Rubin and Zaira, and I'm going to lose them both.

"You know, Indigo created Andarra because they thought it would make the universe better to have a civilization that was programmed to care…" Zaira's voice is soft as she strokes Blobby through the bars of his cage. "Indigo had such grand designs for everyone and everything. It wasn't until they almost lost to Ozvios that they realized having big beautiful ideas doesn't mean big beautiful things will happen. Indigo didn't want to believe in negativity and…and suffering and rage and hatred, or that their creations were capable of hurting one another."

I twist in my seat, unsure what prompted her to tell me this. "What happened when Indigo realized that balance will always find a way?"

She glances up at me, a sad smile tugging on her lips. "They faded away. They chose to. Everyone—even me— always thought Indigo faded away after the battle with Ozvios because they were too weak to carry on. But no. Indigo had an epiphany after the defeat: their idealism, their rosy disposition, their privilege—it didn't benefit the universe anymore. They didn't understand their own creations anymore. They were disconnected. And so they decided to create me. Someone born in that darkness, who had the light inside of them all along."

I exhale slowly. "They created you to see the world as it is. The beauty and the pain. All of it."

She nods, shoving one of Blobby's bones with the heel of her foot. "That's why I was meant to find you."

My brows knit together as we begin the descent into Earth's atmo. "What do you mean?"

"Warning, incoming communications" the AI's voice calmly notes, "from IpS1L…"

"IpS1L?" Zaira and I both say at the same time. Rubin, he must be hurt. I shouldn't have left him. Oh, no. Oh, no, no, no…

"Brother." One word. One voice. My stomach sinks and I gasp. "Follow these coordinates to me. I need you here."

Zaira's gaze meets mine. "Your brother?"

I huff. "The one and only."

The coordinates pop up on our screen as if Allister has commandeered our skipper. I know that he put that call out into the galaxies to get me closer not long ago—how could I forget that child reminding me on the underwater tram. I think back to all the letters and songs he sent to me on Fer Asta over the years, all of which I left unopened on my bedroom floor. I couldn't risk finding out if he sent them out of pity or obligation, not because he actually cared.

But maybe if I had taken the chance, everything would be different.

I hit the dash, agreeing to the new location, and we shoot through stars and into clouds.

Zaira comes to sit beside me, eyes wide. "Look how beautiful it is."

Our little ship fills with the sound of a million things happening around us. Ocean waves crashing against each other. Sea creatures emerging from within, hitting the water hard. There are schools of others, hopping in and out of their watery paradise. They look nothing like the ones back home. We see trees, not oversized ones typical of other worlds; no, these are rather small, with simple roots. Rain pings against the window, tiny droplets of water that Zaira watches closely in wonderment. Has she ever seen rain? The clouds darken and there's a boom that echoes across the sky.

"What's that?" she cries out, smashing against me. And I laugh despite the sorrow of her loss, and the tension in our circumstances, because she's so powerful and yet she's still afraid.

"I don't know," I answer. "It sounds like nature."

There's a flash of light, of electricity, in the sky as we begin to set down on a sandy knoll. All we can do is look and watch as the blue line sizzles through the clouds, and a few seconds later, that booming sound happens again. Zaira yelps and I... I sit there, stunned.

We watch the sky light up for another few moments until we realize we're beside another ship. A mothership almost identical to the one we just left.

IpS1L the first. But unlike its successor, this one is black and rumpled. The metal is shredded. Debris is scattered all along the edge of the ocean and the sand. And there…just there…I see him.

I punch the tab to open the hatch, and without saying a word, I bolt outside, leaving Zaira behind to collect herself. My legs take me a meter a minute down the ramp, through the warm almost-humid air. Toward him. He looks at me. Tears glistening in his eyes. His hair is longer than I remember. And bluer too. He left Andarra as a child, but now he's older. His skin looks just a little too pale. His body just a little too skinny. And his clothes… He's wearing blue pants and a white shirt. So very subdued and unlike the Allister I remember.

Though I feel a million things about seeing him here, seeing him now, remembering our past and the way he left… I run into his arms. Like I used to.

He's my brother. He knew me before I knew myself.

We hold each other, him tighter than me. He's stronger than I remember too. And taller, maybe. How did he get to be so tall?

"Wesley," he murmurs near my ear. "I've missed you."

"I…missed you too," I admit, not letting him go, not even a little.

But he pulls back, his lips lifting into a smirk. "You did, didn't you?"

"You were always better at reading emotions than me," I laugh a little.

"She was wrong, you know, to do what she did. I wrote you so many times to tell you that you're worth more than a purpose from the Jadu. You're worth more than the Daniels name. But you didn't read them, did you?" He smiles down at me. "No, I didn't think you would. I'm just happy you're here now."

I swallow down the emotions threatening to overwhelm me. "There's a war," I say, changing the subject as I hear Zaira slowly coming down the ramp. "Where is it?"

"All over." He points beyond the sand and trees. "The Ilori don't come this way. They think this ship is cursed. Very superstitious for a people that don't believe in feelings. Need me to have someone collect anything from your ship?"

"Yeah, a little tentacled blob is caged in the cabin." I sweep a look over my shoulder at the skipper and catch Zaira staring down at the sand in wonder. I wish I could enjoy this with her, but there's too much happening. "Tell your folks to be careful, the little thing has a backswing when it gets rid of its bones."

"You have a…" He repeats the creature's species name and still I have no idea what he says. "That's very lucky. They don't tend to bond easily."

"Yeah." I laugh, though it's more from nerves than anything else. "Everyone's here, Allister."

Allister shakes his head, nibbling his lower lip. "I can't believe it."

"Neither can I," Zaira says, coming up to us slowly, still looking down at her feet in the sand. She jumps when the sky lights up again and booms. "What is that?"

"Weather," Allister says, his whole body freezing up against mine. "Lightning, thunder. Earth is wild, and there's beauty in that." He says that last bit while staring hard at her face. "You're…Indigo… Zaira?"

"Zaira," she affirms, finally lifting her head to meet his

attention. When she does, she steps back, her mouth falling open. "You're real?"

He takes a big breath, though his words still come out breathlessly. "I am."

"I've seen you before." Her eyebrows furrow, her hands planted against her thighs. "In my dreams. The Jadu... I think..." She doesn't finish the thought and she doesn't need to. Seeing someone in a vision from the Jadu means something. And the way he's looking at her means he saw her too.

She clears her throat. "I'm here for Ozvios."

He nods, swallowing the very strong feelings he has about her presence that I politely try not to read. "If he's here, he's on the battlefield inland. The air assault is about to begin. I'm happy to see you, brother, but I need your help too. And we don't have time." He loops his arm through mine. "I knew you'd come today. I'd seen it. It feels like I've been waiting forever down here on Earth."

I can't keep the incredulity from my voice. "You were waiting for me?"

"You are my brother. I wanted to spend my life growing up beside you, not here on Earth with Cecil-ferking-Wright— now Montague... Though I'll admit, I'm a superstar here. Being rich on Earth is like... You can't have it better. The privilege. I could buy several homes bigger than ours on Andarra and do whatever the hell I wanted. No one would stop me. They still don't even know I'm an alien." He chuckles. "It's been fun, but it's not what I really wanted."

I stop, my feet sinking into the sand. "You wanted me... in your life?"

Allister huffs, shaking his head once more. "Of course I

did. I knew who our mother was before you did, and I didn't do enough to make you feel loved. And I'm sorry for that, Wesley." He sniffs. "You were always the best part of my life on Andarra. I want to spend the rest of my time in this universe getting to know you again."

The old me would scoff at that, would never believe he or anyone else would want to spend even a fraction of their lives in my company. The new me, the one who confronted my mother, got bit by the Jadu, kissed my dream boy, boarded the Ilori mothership and escaped without a scratch, can't help smiling. Zaira shifts beside me.

I want to be a part of his life too…but fate already has other plans. And I can't tell him that. I can't tell anyone that. It's for the best. Everything I do from this moment on will be for the best.

"I would like that," I admit, trying to shake off the sadness. "So where are we going?" Thunder cracks overhead again and Zaira jumps, breathing heavy.

Allister throws a glance at her, nibbling his bottom lip as we continue walking. Desire, probably the easiest, strongest emotion to read on anyone, trickles off his skin and swirls around us. He sees me watching him and he cocks an eyebrow. "I find you very annoying right now, Wesley."

I stifle a laugh. "I thought you wanted to spend the rest of your life getting to know me again."

"Stop reading my private emotions. It's very rude and frankly unfashionable," he says, rolling his eyes.

"Stop making your private emotions so easy to read." I chuckle, peeking back at Zaira, who has fallen behind out of hearing. "How do you know her?"

He looks at her quickly and sidles up closer to me, his voice a whisper. "I've dreamt of her for most of my life. I've seen her in my visions of the future. I've loved her before I knew what love was. I've been waiting, wondering if I'd ever..." His voice trails off. He takes a deep breath and nods at a building just beyond a sandy dune. "Come on. There's a war, lest you forgot."

Back at Allister's house—no, I'm sorry, this simply isn't a house, it's a compound—everyone is congregated in the kitchen. Which is the size of my academy on Fer Asta. It's got a big table jutting from the center, and people sit on stools, heads down, looking over documents. There's food everywhere, and others graze, talking quietly to one another. Zaira meanders slowly behind me, taking in every single detail.

I'm barely in the room when Cecil locks me in an embrace, mumbling my name. As per usual, he's not wearing a top, preferring to show off his rose tattoos. His pants are tight and black. Same old Cecil. Even back when we were kids, he had a flair for all things pretty. "There he is! Oh, my little cutie. Rupert, look, it's Wesley. He's gotten so big. And those eyes, wow, what eyes! You could break hearts with those eyes."

"Oh, do shut up, Cecil," Allister says over the din. "He's already uncertain about being here, I don't want him running away from me...again."

The *again* makes my gaze snap to his. It's been nearly ten years and still he remembers when I ran away from him as he prepared to go to Earth. He stood there beside Cecil, Rupert, and Whisper, begging me to tell him goodbye. Begging for a hug. He was just a child—so was I—and I acted like it more than he did.

"Ah, yes, he is very tall now," Rupert says, sizing me up. "Eyes are the same. Good proportions on him. Could use more muscles. People like muscles. I'm assuming you've met your love interest, yes?"

I try not to gag. Rupert has always been odd. Even by Andarran standards. "Yes. He's up on IpS1L II. You'd like him."

"Of course, we'd like him. He likes you, which means we have to like him." Cecil narrows his eyes at Allister but gifts me a smile.

Looking at them now, the same back and forth, reminds me of happier times back home. When the four of them were running around the house, and I would watch them pretend to be rock stars.

"Finally," Whisper declares, yanking me into a hug. "I've missed you. These three are the worst. Terrible, honestly. You may have been younger, but you were always a voice of reason."

I smile at her. Whisper is in what I can only call a full ball gown that takes up ample space in the kitchen and knocks people into the table. Not that she cares. She never did. She's a free spirit. Of all Allister's friends, Whisper has always been my favorite.

A white girl with dirty blond hair, pink-glossed lips and a black-and-white striped jumpsuit pushes past Whisper's dress. "This is the brother you were telling us about, Allister? Oh, he's...um... He doesn't really look much like you except maybe the..." She points to my nose.

She's not wrong. Allister has tan skin, long straight hair

and very Daniels features like my mother. While my dark brown skin, blue eyes, and build must've been gifted from my donor father.

"He looks exactly like my brother, Alice," Allister says, popping some weird orange thing into his mouth. "Are you hungry?" Though he asks me, his eyes scan beyond to Zaira as she makes her way into the room. The others turn to look at her too.

Her brows quirk and she steps beside me. "I haven't eaten in a very long time. What are these things?"

Whisper and Rupert exchange a glance.

"Finally," Whisper says again near my ear as Allister leads Zaira over to the counters spread with food. "He's had several brief relationships with humans—Rupert, remember that Sidra girl, the supermodel? We had to keep reminding him that Zaira was coming, but he was losing hope. Thank goodness she's here."

"This is seriously the most I've ever seen you talk to one person." Alice, the human who's got her hands linked with Whisper, gives me a once-over.

"He's my favorite Daniels. Don't tell Allister." Whisper gives me a conspiratorial wink and then saunters off, hitting people with her dress where they sit. "I'm going to check the comms, get the news."

"You're Allister's brother?" An Ilori, ferk, a true Ilori turns from their seat. The haze surrounding them isn't so thick; they must be a few decades old at most. Nothing for a true Ilori. Still considered a child. They have brown skin and piercing gray eyes. "My name is Brixton. I'm here to lead the rebellion against my father, heir to the Emperor." He notices me cringe and throws up his hands. "I will not hurt you. They'll vouch for me."

Cecil and Rupert nod. "He's okay. I mean, still Ilori but any brother of Morris is a friend of ours."

I look at him a little closer. "Morris? The labmade?"

His eyes light up. "You've met him?"

I take a seat beside him and tell him everything I know about Morris and Ellie. About Rubin and the song they'll broadcast, which should break Il-0CoM. It's not until I'm done talking that I realize I have everyone's attention. Humans, Andarrans, Ilori alike.

"Morris and Ellie. They're heroes," Brixton says, lips twitching. "My brother has always been the best of us."

"I'm sure he'd say the same about you." Because if there's one thing I know about people like Morris, it's that they genuinely see the good in the world, even when everything's terrible.

"Yes, well, that's enough of that," Allister cuts in, taking a seat next to Zaira who has a formidable plate of food in front of her. "Ozvios is working with Emperor 1lv. They have leveled the state of Texas and are battling there for the rule of Earth. Soon the fight will take to the skies. The Ilori fly-fighters haven't arrived yet."

"Allister says you're the best pilot he knows." Brixton shoves a map toward me. "I know you're not a soldier, but we could use your help creating an offensive strategy here. I can't plug in to Il-0CoM, but I know this is where they'll go."

I stare down at the map of Earth at some weird little patch of land called Texas. Thunder claps overhead and every eye is on me but Zaira's.

"You know how the Ilori will run this," I say to Brixton. "I've seen them on my travels. They're ruthless but always sensible. They'll shoot down any armies the moment they arrive. You need a blockade up there." I point at the ceiling, hoping he grasps my meaning. "Good news is that The Soleil is ready, as is all of Monchuri. The Ilori's hangars are empty—"

Whisper dashes into the room. "Ilori fly-fighters are engaged with the Juxto warlords already. That's who they're fighting in the sky. That's why they haven't arrived yet."

"The Juxto?" Brixton's brows reach his scalp.

"The Juxto are good warriors. And Minor Sidarra is up there too. If you want to win, you go to them. Split them up among allies. Don't give them a chance to even reach Earth." I tap the map. "I'll go to the Monchuri leadership. I'll help them form a strategy. I can help coordinate, get everyone on the same page."

"No," Allister gulps. "I won't allow that. Someone else can go."

"It's my purpose, Allister. I've seen it." I give him a sad smile. "We will win if we do this right."

What I don't say is that we will win, but I'll lose.

CHAPTER TWENTY-SIX

Zaira

"Wesley, I don't think you should—"

"I must," he interjects. He pulls away toward the skipper and I grab his arm, stilling him.

I take the chain off my neck with the star suspended inside and shove it into his hand. "The Daniels name doesn't define you. It wasn't something you had to deserve or earn. You are a Citlali too. Okay? Take this—it's good luck and it'll bring you, the rightful wearer, the best of luck."

A tear slides down his cheek. He yanks me into a hug and then quickly climbs into the skipper before I can try to talk him out of it again. He leaves me standing there on the sandy field as thunder crackles and makes my muscles bounce.

He leaves me.

Allister stands close but not too close. We watch Wesley's ship take off together.

"He's going to be okay," Allister says quietly. "Wesley always wanted to be in a ship exploring the stars, probably because a ship was more hospitable than our home and the universe more welcoming. I don't know this older version of him, but I do know from rumors that he's…an incredible pilot."

"He is." I turn to him. "But when this all began, it was the three of us, together. Me, Wesley, and Rubin. And now we're in different places… I feel like… I feel like I can't control the outcome without them with me."

His lips quirk. "I don't think anyone can control the outcome, Zaira."

"I can. I *will*." I nod to myself. If anything happens to the two of them, I don't know what I'll do or who I'll be. Rage stirs in the pit of my stomach just at the thought. "I have to find Ozvios. I have to stop him from getting stronger."

"That'd mean taking a pod over to Texas, and those things only hold two people at most. If you wait, we can—"

"No waiting. If we stop him, we can stop total destruction." I can defeat him. Ozvios, Ciaran, he deserves punishment and justice. Only I can give that to him…

Allister watches me closely. "I'll get the pod ready."

I reach out, staying his arm. "You shouldn't come. Your people back at the house, they need you. I can fly a ship alone." Poorly, but he doesn't need to know that.

He leans into my touch. "You are my people." He laughs. "I'm aware how presumptuous that sounds, I really am. It's just, I know my future is with you, and I think you know that too, don't you?"

My cheeks heat and I drop my arm from his. This scene has

played out in my dreams so many times and now that it's here, I don't know how to feel. "The thought of that scares me."

"Which thought?" His eyes bore into mine. "I'm not going to chase you, Zaira. I do want to know you though. If you'll let me…when the time is right."

I swallow and nod. "When the time is right."

"Great," he says with a beaming smile. "Because you're going to love me. I mean, not in that way, though kind of in that way, one day…" he rambles on, and laughs. "I'm normally better at this. People constantly turn to me for advice, and I always have the right words. I'm very zen, you know? Wise beyond my years. The moment it's my turn and no, nothing. It's embarrassing, that's what it is. Complete failure. Me, Allister Daniels, of The Starry Eyed. We've gone platinum with every record. People quote my love songs. And I'm standing in front of the girl I've dreamed about my entire life, and…"

I touch his arm again, shyly. "I… I've dreamed about you too."

That seems to calm him for a moment and then he cracks an even bigger smile. "I'm not going to screw this up."

"Then let's try not to die," I admit, changing the subject. I'm not ready for whatever he will be to me. There are too many responsibilities at the moment and none of them involve love. Besides, I don't even know if someone like me—a half god and nightweaver, a person who has never known a life of joy and ease—can fall in love, can kiss or be kissed. Can do anything but exist and try my best.

Allister leads me along the beach—he calls it—through the hulking piles of charred metal that was once IpS1L.

"This used to be Santa Monica." He dodges something

sharp and steers me around it. "It had a pier and boardwalk, Ferris wheel and corn dogs. I loved it."

"I have no idea what any of those things are," I admit as the thunder continues to crack above us. I cringe but try to keep up, try to act unafraid. "Was it pretty?"

He turns, his gaze meeting mine. "Very."

Again, my cheeks heat and I want to lose my form, become stardust and shoot off into the sky aimlessly. But I don't know how long I can keep that form, and I'm not sure I don't enjoy Allister's attention either. Which is extremely useless right now. The universe is ending and some silly part of me wants to get to know a boy?

My home has been destroyed. My people are gone. My grandmother is gone, and now Wesley and Rubin are too. Both to do their part in defeating the Ilori, and I'm standing here enjoying little compliments and smiles? I don't deserve this happiness. And I have to stay on task.

Even if I had dreams of him. Even if the Jadu showed me his beautiful face and how he'll adore me. Love me. But nothing is guaranteed. Fate can still change. The universe can give and take. Indigo could too and look what happened to them. Nothing, even the future, is set in stone. Before this, I had a grandmother on a planet full of ghosts. Now I have a little found family; Rubin and Wesley mean the world to me. I don't know if I can let myself lose focus for Allister. I can't.

"You seem like you just figured something out." He tilts his head to the side.

"I'm just preparing for battle," I lie. Because what am I supposed to say? *I figured out the future can change so there's no point allowing myself to be interested in you and the feelings you evoke?* No.

"Good, because here it is." He throws his arms out. "Ta-da!"

It's a small pod with scorch marks up the sides. It has a tiny window and half of the Ilori 1lv crest remains as if someone tried to tear it off. I grimace.

He notices my face and shrugs. "Okay, so it's not much, but it'll get us there relatively quickly." He punches a few numbers into the panel, opening the hatch. The ramp creaks and lowers midway but stops before it reaches the sand. "Well, it isn't in great condition since the fire, but it'll work. I think. Maybe."

I cock an eyebrow and stifle a chuckle. "Let's go."

We hop up the ramp and into the tiny pod. There's only one seat and no room for me to sit elsewhere, so we stuff into the chair, my entire body mashed against his. There's no embarrassment about how much space my thick body takes up—my body is mine, and it is strong. I'm happy with how present it is in this universe. Still, there is something else about being this close to him. I've shared small quarters with people—namely Rubin and Wesley—yet this...this feels different. My skin prickles and warmth spreads through the pit of my stomach.

Allister hits a few buttons and...nothing happens. "Just a sec." He hits the same buttons a few more times. And then a few more. I'm close to getting out of this thing when the engine rattles alive. "Ah, there we are. See? Working condition." The dash barks out a command in Ilori and Allister rolls his shoulders. "Manual."

It refuses to acknowledge he spoke.

"You're saying it with too much of an accent." I sit up

straight and let out a breath. "Manual," I say in near-perfect Ilori, which sounds like a numerical code.

"Manual accepted," the dash responds.

"Show-off." Allister grabs the thrusters and gently eases them back. "Okay, I haven't flown in a really long time. Don't judge me."

I laugh a little…the sound unexpected. When was the last time I laughed? Truly laughed? Rubin. Rubin makes me laugh. Nightweavers on Mal Ares, who would hide in the shadows as I tried to find them.

"Are you ready?" He lifts the pod off the ground. "We're going into battle, you know that? And I don't want to downplay my own significance but I'm not a soldier or a fighter or even someone good at self-preservation. I almost died a few weeks ago trying to harvest tomatoes around a wasp nest. So…"

I laugh again. "I won't let anything happen to you, Allister Daniels. Stick with me, okay?"

He smiles, bouncing his leg against mine. "Okay, Zaira."

The ship shoots lowly across the sky, and though it creaks and groans, I can hardly care. My adrenaline is pumping. My brain is preparing for this. My body is warming up. Songs push to the front of my mind as I look out below at the land.

It's brown and tan. There's nothing, only nature. A world Indigo didn't create but it was created just the same. It's different yet beautiful. A reflection, I think, of the humans who inhabit this land.

I'm enjoying the quiet when the ship takes a sharp flip to the side. I flatten against Allister and let out a gasp. He holds the thrusters tight as the view in front of us changes from tranquil landscape to…war. Ships of all sizes, from smooth slate metal to black, carrying crests from different worlds and kingdoms, litter the sky above. A chorus of shooting and blasts make me nearly jump out of my seat. The sky is gray as if it too is engaged in a battle for sovereignty. My eyes can't follow the ships rushing after each other, shooting down below… where soldiers dressed in all kinds of colors, of all different kinds of species, are locked in battle. Blasters ring out, explosions boom. Shields form and reform.

There have to be hundreds of thousands, millions of them. And it's not even equal. The Ilori vastly outnumber everyone. They're dressed in their somber black gear with black masks. Using their electrical power, they bat humans aside like they are flies. Meanwhile, on another side of this massive field, there are Monchurans, The Soleil, Farans decimating swaths of Ilori. Their movements are graceful, coordinated, but they can't outlast the sheer number of them forever.

I don't see Ozvios. Yet, I know he's here. He's watching up high, eating up all this destruction. Letting it fill him with energy. If I don't find him…

"We have to set this down outside the fighting. Any closer and they'll hit us." Allister begins the descent and I'm realizing now, as a beam of sunlight beats down on everyone, that to get to Ozvios, I will have to cut through this battle. As we land onto the dry dirt, Allister turns to me, his expression grave. "Welcome to the battle for freedom."

THE RUBIN RIMA PODCAST

Broadcasting from an undisclosed location

RR: Hello, spacers! It's Rubin Rima, coming to you live from IpS1L II, the Ilori mothership currently over planet Earth. I bet you weren't expecting that, right? Well, me and my friends, Morris and Ellie, are here. And we're about to do huge great things. Just you wait and see. Morris, do you want to explain what you're doing?

Morris: In order for you to fully grasp what we are doing, you must know what we have done. First, I am Morris 1lv, grandson of Emperor 1lv. Second, I am a labmade, created from the genetic material of my mother, Gl1nd, and my brother, Brixton. Third, I was created to lead the revolution against the true Ilori. Fourth, that meant playing a role within the Ilori acquisition of Earth, a role which I deeply regret. I went to Earth with the purpose of obtaining high command, gaining their trust, and sowing the seeds of their defeat. I failed, however. In that time, I made life difficult for humanity. And though now I am close to seeing my plans come to fruition, it was not without challenges.

Ellie: Morris is good at feeling guilty about everything he's done. And I get that, I do, but at the same time, we wouldn't be in the position we are in now if it wasn't for him. Yes, he has done things he will spend a lifetime trying to rectify. But he also gave us, humans, a better chance at taking our freedom back. We are only having this war now because of him.

Morris: You don't need to defend me, Ellie.

Ellie: Uh, yeah I do. I'm not letting you take all the blame for this. If you didn't do all of that, another Ilori would have and they would not have made anything easy for humans. And it's worth noting that humanity was in a bad place before the Ilori even arrived. If they didn't try to destroy us, we would have destroyed ourselves. I'm fairly certain about that.

RR: Are you listening, folks? These two are the leaders of the revolt. And they're also deeply in love and it's adorable. Enemies to lovers! We love a trope! Anyway, let's get back on topic. What are we doing, Morris?

Morris: As a means of destroying the empire, I created a vaccine that would allow true Ilori to use human bodies as an interactive vacation experience. Which would involve combining humans with Il-0CoM, the communication system that connects all Ilori. I had planned to have my grandfather, the Emperor, shift his consciousness into a human and then I would broadcast a song I created that would destroy Il-0CoM. However, after failing the first time on IpS1L, grounded on Earth, I realized my plan needed, as Ellie says, tweaking.

Ellie: We met with King AnYeck zumBuden on planet XiGRa. He had been told of our plans from The Starry Eyed—doesn't this all sound weird? It is weird, but follow us. He said 1lv would never expose himself to a human body or allow himself to be weakened. King AnYeck and his girlfriend—maybe wife, Queen LaTanya, helped us reformat Morris's song.

Morris: Now it would not rely on the humans being vaccinated and the Ilori entering their subconscious. It would attack anything and everything connected to Il-0CoM.

Ellie: Also, really funny here, but it wasn't just King AnYeck who helped us. There were two humans, Rashid and Sarah from Florida, who had been stranded in Monchuri somehow? Rashid is a genius with computers and stuff, and Sarah...she's incredibly kind.

Morris: And Yecki has a lot of money and resources.

RR: Collaboration!

Morris: Yes, exactly. So now, me and Ellie and Rubin have broken into IpS1L II and found a patch around their new operating system. To broadcast our song that would dissect Il-0CoM, we would need—

Unknown: You three! What are you doing? Put your weapons down. *(unknown sounds)* Get down. All of you.

RR: *(whispering)* And now for the final act. *(disconnects)*

CHAPTER TWENTY-SEVEN

Wesley

The sky outside of Earth is filled with ships bearing all sorts of crests. Monchuri, Juxto, Sidarra, XiGRa, Andarra, and so many more. More than I even know about. Maybe I should've gone to class after all...

Nah.

The comms crackles, a transmission incoming from one of the big cruisers lined up along the far side of the moon. "Andarran skipper, state your name and position."

The vision from the Jadu sparks in my mind. I'm in this ship. The sirens are wailing and I'm twisting to the side, squeezing off a few more shots at the Ilori fly-fighters. They're surrounding me. And I know my time is coming now. I know this is the end. I think about Rubin. I think about his kisses and what kind of future we could have had together. I think about his smile and his desire for truth and beauty always. Then I think about Zaira. The hardships she's faced. The power that lingers beneath her skin. I consider finding her, asking her for help. But I don't. Some part of me clings to my mother's words.

He will disappoint you.

Coward.

Foolish child.

My screen lights up, flashing red and there's a boom. That's it. That's my end. Remembering the love I craved and didn't receive and wishing for the love I could've had but will lose.

"Andarran skipper. Come in. Name and position." The comms crackles again. The language is Monchuran, I'd know that anywhere.

I shake the vision away. "Wesley Daniels. Position, wherever you need me."

There's a pause on the other end that extends a little too long for comfort. I'm imagining them shooting me down for some reason, even though I know that's not the end. "Come aboard the Hamdi and Abara skyport, please. Your presence is requested."

The coordinates pop up on my screen and I hit the tab, allowing the ship to redirect there. Moments pass in an anxious haze. In all my life, I've never done anything like this. Never consulted on war with generals and people who matter.

I glance back at the compartment where Zaira and Rubin would be sitting. Where Blobby was throwing out his bones and the three of us were navigating this strange universe together. I'll never see them, any of them, again. My heart cracks a little but I refuse to cry now. Not yet.

The skipper autopilots onto the Monchuran hangar and I'm greeted by Soleil the moment my hatch opens.

"Come with us," they say in accented Andarran and I smile at the attempt. Nice of them to try.

I don't have time to feel anything as I'm led through a pile of ships into vibrant multicolored lit hallways with plush carpeting and sparkly chandeliers. The doors have knobs here. Not a prison, like the Ilori mothership. The vibes are definitely different.

I'm led to a large room where two empty thrones sit perched on marbled stone. It's lavish in tones of white and silver, purples and blues. The air smells floral, clean, lovely. And weirdly, calmness washes over me. As if there's a chemicallent coming in through vents.

"You are Allister's brother?" A girl in a long mint dress comes in through a side door. She's gorgeous, with dark brown skin, a head full of bouncy curls strewn with pearls, and there's a genuine smile on her face. "He said to expect you. Felix—"

"Yes, Joy, my dearest?" A tall lighter brown-skinned boy comes in behind the girl, wearing an outfit similar to what I'd seen Allister wear—dark slacks, white shirt, sleeves rolled up to the elbows. Maybe it's Earth fashion. He winks at me when he catches me gawking at the two of them. "There's a resemblance in the eyes, I see."

I try not to gasp. That's Felix Hamdi. Failed singer, failed playboy, sorta king of the biggest system in the universe. I can't believe I'm meeting him. And holy ferk, he's as hot as they all say. Wow. The gods really blessed him and I want to laugh because Zaira would never have made someone this attractive.

Joy smacks him in the arm. "Will you stop joking all the time? We are actually in a war right now."

"And that's my fault? You were the one who said we had to do what was right, remember? *The humans can't defend themselves…*" He stops, looking around quickly. "None of them are still here, right?"

"No, Sarah and Rashid said, and I quote, *if we can lead a cheer team at Florida State Nationals, we can lead an army.*" Joy shrugs and Felix's lips quirk.

"Thank the gods for that. Humans…wow." He shakes his head and instead of taking a seat on a throne, he pulls up a chair from the dining table and gestures for me to sit in it. He and Joy lean against each other as I do. "So Wesley Daniels, brother of Allister, pilot extraordinaire. You've come to help us?"

"I'll do my part, your majesties," I say, planting my butt into the cushions. I try not to sigh at the luxurious softness. My muscles need to relax for a moment.

"Good. We have a fleet of ships ready to take your orders."

"If you want to," Joy cuts in. "There's no pressure here. You have a choice, always."

It's nice to be told I have a choice, but I don't. Not really. So I smile up at them. "It is my destiny; no one gets to choose differently."

Joy crouches down, putting a hand on my arm and looking into my eyes. "We all get to choose our own destiny, Wesley. Remember that. No one gets to define our lives but us."

There's determination in her words and true, genuine belief. When I look up at Felix, there's only love. Nothing else. No anger or worry or concern about war and death. Just love for the girl crouching down on the floor, talking to a commoner as if she isn't a queen. Rubin would love her. I hope they meet one day. I hope he gets to interview her and tell her story.

She threads her fingers through mine. "You don't have to do anything."

I stare into her beautiful gray eyes. "I want to. I need to feel like I'm doing something good for once. I need to do something right for this universe. Maybe if everyone does the right thing instead of what's easy, it'll be a better place."

"I don't want to see you harmed," she says, squeezing my fingers.

"Joy, we can't actually keep everyone from harm during a war." Felix caresses her shoulder. "Wesley, it's your decision. We'll do our best to keep you safe but there are no guarantees."

I nod. "I want to do this. Let me do this."

"Okay." Felix signals to a guard in the corner. "Bring them all in. The new commander and DiOla." He turns to me. "Let's mobilize the ships."

Joy stands and steps back into Felix's waiting arms. "We will be with you, on your comms, the entire time. You're never alone out there."

Seconds later, the hall fills with nearly a hundred pilots and commanders and people looking to me for answers.

Answers I can give. "The first thing we need to do is keep the mothership safe while Morris and Ellie broadcast a message that'll disable Il-0CoM. We do that by getting the attention of every single one of their ships, pods, and their army down below. We do that by—" I point at the projected space around Earth "—bringing the fights here, and here."

"We'll have to coordinate with all of our allies. They have their own command—but it's worth saying, none of us have seen a proper war in centuries. Only the Ilori have been invading, colonizing, and battling. We're disadvantaged." A woman's voice echoes across the hall. She marches up to us, her eyes narrowed on the map.

"DiOla, this is Wesley Daniels," Joy says with a nod. "Wesley, this is the head of The Soleil."

DiOla glances back at me in acknowledgment and turns her attention back to the royals. She doesn't bow. And I don't think they're the type that want people to bow either.

"It's an advantage," I say loudly, getting back on topic. "Because the Ilori follow predictability. If we're erratic, defying their expectations and good sense, their empire will crumble."

People nod and the morale changes instantly. They believe me. They're relieved. They want to win. And I want them to.

CHAPTER TWENTY-EIGHT

Zaira

Allister's nearly thrown to the muddy ground by a stray stunner, and I reach for him, pulling him back into the bubble of safety I've created with song and power. There's a gash on his forehead and I want to pause, take him back to the ship and find a medikit there, but the only way now is forward.

We step over bodies of Ilori and Andarran and Monchuran and Sidarran and more and more and more. Terror boils in my blood and I want this all to cease but the field is too big. Too vast. A stunner zings past and I push Allister out of the way on impulse, even if our little bubble protects us. In the process, I see a small group of labmade Ilori looking toward us. They raise their weapons and I stand in front of Allister.

I don't want to do this.

I don't want to cause more pain.

But I'm good at it. And some part of me...some part of me enjoys this. Whatever part that is, I'll have to deal with it later.

The song leaves my lips in a wave of black. It streams forth and I raise my shaking hands, letting my power find its targets. It seeps into the heads of twelve, fifteen, twenty soldiers. My song grows louder, angrier. Whispers plague my thoughts, and I hear them. The Ilori. We're connected now. I'm inside their heads. Tasting their thoughts.

Momentarily, I'm confused because their thoughts aren't theirs. It's something bigger. A hive. Those who are controlling these labmades believe in their supremacy. They are the murderers. Colonizers. They take from these labmades just like they take from everyone else.

They are villains and perhaps I am too, because I want violence. I want their pain.

They are so powerfully attached to the labmades their energy is thick and difficult to pierce. I bypass the labmades in front of me to the true Ilori somewhere waiting in the distance. They stand in a group, eyes closed, power pulsing, controlling. I enter their minds through the labmades, through Il-0CoM. I get them to swivel their bodies and aim at one another. They scream out, their voices echoing across the field. They're afraid now. Allister's hand touches my shoulders. He feels what I feel and I feel all of them in their minds.

They shoot each other and tumble to the ground. Dead. My legs wobble and my stomach flips and flutters. I just murdered a group of true Ilori, creatures I created in a different form, a long time ago. I'm going to be sick. All that delicious food at Allister's house has turned in my stomach.

The labmades once under the true Ilori control halt, unsure of what to do with their freedom. They slowly lower their weapons, but I know that their minds will soon be controlled again. I can't hesitate. We're still connected. I'm still inside their minds. I put them to sleep, shutting their brains down like I'm flipping a switch. They'll wake up later; maybe they'll be completely free then.

I may be a murderer, but I won't take any life I don't have to. These labmades don't have a choice. I do.

There's no time to consider my deeds. I swallow my disgust and pull Allister along with me. We make our way through fights, with bullets from the humans' weapons disintegrating before they even reach their marks since the Ilori can easily destroy metal. We dodge batons and blades. Andarrans and Farans engage with Ilori in elegant, dangerous dances of brutality. Sidarrans bang the ground, throwing Ilori off balance. Dosanis wrap Ilori in tentacles, smothering them.

So much pain. So much violence. The air smells of blood. The ground is speckled with it too. Red, blue, green, yellow mixing together in the dirt like a rainbow.

We break through to the middle of the battle—the space between us and them. The Ilori stand firm in lines, waiting. There are too many of them. More than the armies from all the allies combined.

They wait patiently, knowing victory is theirs despite the carnage.

I turn to Allister. "Stay behind me, okay?"

He nods, swiping at the green blood dripping down his forehead.

Indigo's power lives within me, but it's not necessary for me to create worlds and people anymore—no, it's necessary for me to save them. Save those that already exist. And right now, I have to fix this.

A melody pushes from the back of my mind to the tip of my tongue. I let it take over, let it lift me off the ground. The sun beats down on me and sweat drips down my back. My arms rise. All the while, I know Allister is here. He's safe for the moment, below me. That's important.

A song, soft at first, begins in the back of my throat. Out of the corner of my eye, gold prickles along my constellations, bright and shiny. This is power. Not to hurt. To save. I glance down at the Ilori staring at me. Mouths moving. Stunners trained on me.

The song grows and grows and it branches out from me, encircling the others—the Sidarrans, Andarrans, XiGRans, Monchurans, Dosanis, humans, all of Indigo's children. They stop, opening their mouths, and we begin to sing the song together. Not everyone is perfect, but that's why it's perfect.

A memory flashes in my mind of Indigo on the battle-field of stars during The First Chaos. This was the song. The song of salvation. A song to save us all. Ozvios, like the Ilori, formed and reformed but couldn't escape it. It made him weak. Our unity made destruction too difficult.

The Ilori cry out below us, throwing their hands over their ears as if the music is a knife to their minds. They beg for relief. They drop their stunners. The fights halt. Thousands, millions sing with me.

We harmonize. And the power of that unlocks something inside me. Indigo created. Ozvios destroyed. But all of us can create and destroy, even the humans. All of us can choose to do great or terrible things.

I still don't know what I am, or why I am, yet I know that I carry the memories of my people, of the nightweavers, inside me. I carry their anger, their hurt, their love within my heart. I also carry Indigo's memories of the universe within my mind. I open my eyes and see beyond this Earth into... everything. I see worlds spinning, worlds not yet discovered. Worlds that, like Earth, sprung up by chance. The universe is vast and unending. It is a miracle. It is potential and opportunity.

Ozvios and I—I know now that we were simply chosen by chance. We aren't meant to be worshipped, to destroy, or create. We were meant to spread the stardust. Help the universe grow.

To exist. And help others exist too.

I am not a god. Ozvios isn't either. We never were.

Yes, I think. Yes, I'm so close to understanding. I'm so close to doing what I was meant to do. The song grows powerful, twisting and beautiful.

Arms wrap around me and the air whooshes from my chest. My sight narrows from the universe to Ciaran—to Ozvios. He grabs me hard and flies with me away from the battle. Away from Allister.

I scream out, but Ozvios whispers his power into my ear. "Go to sleep, the worlds will die when you wake."

"Allister," is all I can manage to say as his darkness spreads through my mind.

CHAPTER TWENTY-NINE

Wesley

The battle in the skies began only moments ago, and yet, it's already precarious. The Ilori outnumber us at least two to one. Their fly-fighters arrived from the hyperspace bridge shortly after they decimated the Juxto fleet. They're fresh from victory and swooping down over Earth, prepared to destroy that army too.

All that stands between them and humanity is me and a bunch of Monchuran pilots who don't know what we're doing. No one has ever seen war. We're scared, and this fear could lose us this battle. We circle the planet, blocking them from getting past us. Shields up and connected, all we have to do is take all their heat until Morris breaks Il-0CoM, giving us a fighting chance.

"Hold the line," I shout into the interconnected comms of

a hundred ships. "No matter what they do, no matter how they come at you, hold that line. We're stronger together than apart, and the moment one of you leaves, the more vulnerable we all become."

Nerves rattle in the pit of my stomach. How did I, Wesley, the fastest runner this side of Outerim, somehow end up commanding an armada of a ragtag group of pilots from around the universe? Sure, I have experience dodging authorities and I know how ships work better than anything, and yeah, I understand strategy…but too many people are putting their faith in me. How do they know I'll do what's right when the time comes? Why should they trust me?

No idea. But here we are. This is where I'm meant to be. This is where I prove that I'm not a coward. That I'm worthy of love and attention.

One of our ships takes a hit and swerves right, nearly crashing into a smaller one. Shouts come through the comms.

"Keep those shields up. Hold that line." I hit a few tabs on my console, the dash refitted quickly to handle long-range blasters. Honestly, the idea of hitting a ship—even an enemy—with one of those missiles makes acid climb my throat.

My screen lights up. "Warning, we're being targeted by two Ilori vessels."

"Yup." I send a flare out to collide with both bombs in midair, exploding before they can hit me. But I can't keep doing this forever before I'll run out of ammo.

"We should go on offense now," another pilot screams into the comms. "We can't just wait around for them to break us."

"Not yet," I respond. "Wait. It's almost time."

"For what?" another screams. "You're going to get us all killed."

"We are all that sits between our soldiers below and the Ilori who want to annihilate them and win this war. Wait. Just wait. You'll see." I pray I'm right. I pray Rubin was right when he said it would take half a rotation to broadcast that signal because time is up and if Morris doesn't do whatever he needs to do to break down Il-0CoM, we're all going to die up here.

The Ilori ships fire on us, over and over. The shields hold when we're joined together but the moment we break apart—

"We have to go on the offense!" a pilot screams back at me and breaks the line, throwing the shields off. More follow after him and I curse. Time seems to slow down as we all realize we're sitting ducks now. Either shoot or be shot.

"Ferk," I mutter aloud to myself. "Well, here we go." I pull the thrusters hard, and follow a ship that breaks through, speeding to Earth.

Will this chase be how I die?

THE RUBIN RIMA PODCAST

Broadcasting from IpS1L II

Commander 1lv: I should've known you would fail our family, Morris. You are a waste of Ilori genes. You, your brother, and your mother. She's locked away for her crimes and your brother will die among the peasants and inferior creatures below. But you... I will murder you in front of Gl1nd's eyes just to show her that she never had a chance against me. To break her spirit once and for all.

Morris: Please, Father. Please don't.

Commander 1lv: Do not call me father, labmade! You are no 1lv. Father, I must apologize—

Emperor 1lv: Do not call me father in front of others, Commander. And there is no need for apologies. His mind has been turned by the human... An ugly thing. Chain them both. I want to focus on this one.

RR: Oh, finally. I remember you taking great personal offense at my podcasts and I think it's time we cleared this all up.

Emperor: I did not take personal offense. I am the Emperor of Ilor, and I do not feel such unnecessary emotions. Your little podcast created dissent among my subjects. You must pay for your crimes if I am to succeed in keeping control of our assets.

RR: So...what you're saying is that you didn't care about the whole "bathing in blood" picture I drew and had plastered on billboards everywhere I could?

Emperor: Take this...Balfan away. Prepare a chamber for his death.

RR: Actually, I thought I might make a podcast. I can apologize, tell everyone how great you are. I can even have you share your side of the story if you want.

Emperor: I do not need to share my side of any story. Such insolence—

RR: You're right, but people are going to hate your lot after the war. Wouldn't it be best to preemptively strike, get a little more public sentiment on your side? After all, many Ilori will be lost after this, and loss makes people not as...evolved as you, angry.

Commander 1lv: Perhaps he is right, Father. Public perception still matters. We may rule with an iron fist, but we must also take good publicity wherever we can. Our empire has never been more divided.

Emperor: ... Fine. But take the labmade and his human away. And clear the room.

RR: Actually, we're already live. Say hi to everyone!

Emperor 1lv: How did you... Did anyone search them?

Take his recording devices! Call in the guards. If I speak publicly, it will be on my own terms. Seize him!

RR: *(muffled sounds)* I keep my orphiphone in my teeth, helps when I'm in sticky situations. But those little smoke bombs you just took and activated, they're going to go off in three...two...one. *(commotion)* Morris, now?

(commotion intensifies)

RR: Thanks for letting us into the command room. We rigged your entire system but couldn't broadcast without your key first. Which we now have. Are you all ready?

Morris: Here it is.

Ellie: Morris! The guards!

(further commotion, a strange melody plays)

RR: Morris, you made this yourself? It's gorgeous. Who was your inspiration?

Morris: *(muffled)* Queen, for sure, The Starry Eyed, and David Bowie.

RR: Friends everywhere, if you're hearing this, blast this song as loud as you can. Put it out windows, in the streets, in your bathrooms. Everywhere. Let's give the Ilori our best.

Morris: It's working. It's—the labmades are disconnecting everywhere. They're—

Ellie: Morris! Your father is... Wait. Is that—no.

CHAPTER THIRTY

Zaira

Ozvios's power filters in my ear and for a moment, it pulls me under again in a haze. But it's only for a moment. His grip loosens around me, and I push away from his arms and plummet over the field of soldiers.

After a few seconds of free falling toward the battle below, I reform into stardust and fly back to Allister. He's in the middle of the milieu, hands over his eyes, and I scream down to him.

"Allister, I'm—"

Ozvios shoves me. I zoom through the air too fast to catch myself, crashing into the ground outside the field. I form back into my body, one knee in the dirt, the other perpendicular. My fists clench by my sides.

Ozvios reforms in front of me, his teeth gnashed and feet planted. He's prepared for a fight as if we are recreating the great First Chaos. Yet…as I look closer at him, at his body and his eyes, he seems weak. He seems less than he was on the ship.

"I know what you are, what *we* are," I say, my voice thick with anger. The realization slams through me. I almost connected it before, but now I understand. "The Jadu, they were never fish, were they?"

Ozvios snorts, his movements slow. "They are supreme beings. *We* are supreme beings. You don't remember, do you? Indigo's holding some memories back from you. Indigo must not trust you."

I shake my head, taking a step back. He's wrong. As Indigo, I created Mal Ares first as a test. But not one that was judged by me—it was the Jadu who determined it a success. The Jadu were the ones who then let me create Andarra. The water there… It wasn't just water. It was the new stardust from a new world in a growing universe. The Jadu needed it—the stardust—to survive. And that's why they still call Andarra home.

"We were chosen to help."

"Serve them?" Ozvios smiles, his face twisting into an ugly sneer. "We've been worshipped like gods since the beginning of time, so why shouldn't we rule? Why should we take orders from the Jadu?"

"We weren't made to rule the universe, we were made to serve." I slowly pull myself up, watching him for any sudden moves. "That was our purpose."

He steps forward and I step back, saying, "Before us, there was a vast nothingness. And then, by a miracle, there was a flicker of stardust and life. The first Jadu. They could see everything, could do anything with stardust, but they needed more of it. Instead of watching the universe slowly expand into life, they created Indigo. Indigo was something new, young, ambitious, wondrous." I take a deep breath, remembering Indigo's stardust. It was blue. That is why they took the name Indigo. "The Jadu tasked Indigo to create new stars. New creatures. As long as Indigo kept them safe."

Ozvios huffs. "Indigo was a fool. They were meant to shape stardust into new planets and then step away, so that there could be a constant cycle of life and death. Balance. But then Indigo went too far in their desire to create a beautiful, full universe. They couldn't bear the thought of their worlds dying." Ozvios swallows. "When Indigo did too much too fast, there wasn't enough stardust left. The Jadu panicked because they couldn't survive without stardust. The Jadu made me to clean up Indigo's mess. Destroy worlds, to bring back the balance. To free up the stardust. And when my job was done, I was supposed to retire on Andarra like all of our kin. A purpose complete."

My shoes dip into the dirt as the story finally unfolds in my mind. Visions of Indigo creating worlds, never stopping, never allowing old worlds to die. The cycle of life and death disturbed. Ozvios coming into being to get the universe back on track. I see it in my mind, the memories Indigo held close until now, afraid I'd judge them as callous. Afraid I'd be disappointed too.

I could never be disappointed. Their actions, though flawed, showed an abundance of compassion.

"Your purpose was to bring balance. But after you completed it, you came for Indigo, believing you should be the ruler of all. You didn't stop destroying once you achieved balance." I inhale sharply. Hearing the thousands of screams of worlds being swallowed whole by Ozvios. Ripped apart by his black holes. Torn into pieces. "You defied the Jadu."

"They aren't like us. They created *us* because they didn't want to get involved. They wanted to just exist and let the universe take its natural path. They were lazy." His hand fists by his side. "And they created me to just clean up your mess and fade away. I deserved more than that. Much more. I deserved the honor Indigo received." He stares daggers at me now. "After The First Chaos, I was weak but still alive. I went to Indigo's many worlds, devouring their stardust. If that was how the Jadu lived eternal, it would have to work for me. The more death and destruction, the more stardust was free. But it wasn't enough. Still, I began to fade. So I infiltrated Ilor. I created Il-0CoM to feed me. The Ilori love death, love killing and colonizing. When I was finally strong enough, I went looking for Indigo on Mal Ares, but their dust was gone. I tried to devour the power of the nightweavers, but Indigo was too clever for that. Their power was like poison to me."

I exhale slowly, looking down at my feet coated in dirt. "I bet you wanted to devour Andarra too, but the Jadu would kill you long before you even made it there. They made you and could just as easily unmake you."

He grits his teeth. "As I pushed the Ilori to decimate everything in their path, I still couldn't touch Andarra. Even had to make a treaty with them just to keep the Jadu from coming after me."

"Destruction is the only way you can survive." My hands fidget by my sides.

"Destruction tastes delicious, you should try it." He takes another step toward me. This time I don't flinch. Don't give him the satisfaction of showing fear. Ozvios scoffs. "Indigo chose to fade and become something new for the sake of the universe. I chose to keep existing. I did everything I could to stay alive… I had to destroy over and over again just to keep existing. It's never enough."

He crumbles to the ground, landing on his knees. I didn't realize how weak he had become after my song.

"You can't kill me, can you?" I ask, gingerly moving closer. "Indigo saw the future. They knew that if a creature was formed with Jadu stardust and nightweaver magic, it couldn't die. It didn't need stardust to live."

He shakes his head. "Indigo found a way to defeat me in the end."

"Unless I chose to share my stardust with you. Because you and I are the only two beings like each other in the universe. You need my stardust combined with my Mal Aresian magic." I stand in front of him. "That's why you inserted yourself into my life. Why you tried to be my friend. Why you helped me escape. You wanted me to give you life. Give you part of myself. Because you realized it can't be taken from me, only given."

He looks up at me, hope sparkling in his gaze. "Are you going to let me die? You and I are the last of our kind left. We're the only ones who have ever been able to change the universe. We're alike in more ways than how we were made. You have that anger inside of you, the very anger firing in my veins. Together, we would never die. Together, we would rule them all."

I let a long breath loose that swirls around in the dirt at our feet. "I don't want to do anything with you."

His eyes flash. "Without me—"

"Without you, I'll continue on." I smile down at his fake Ilori face. "You cannot deny nature. Stars explode into life, and they fade from it too. People are born, and people die," I say carefully. "You're dying, and when Il-0CoM is finally broken, that's the end for you. But you have a chance to do one right thing before you go. Stop the fighting below. Stop the Ilori. Stop the destruction and disharmony in the universe."

He pushes to his feet and his eyes flash. "Look at them." He points to the battlefield. "Look at them dying. I may not have long left—" his skin begins to sallow, becoming lackluster as if the stardust is separating, prepared to redistribute itself and become something new. He's fading "—but this war should sustain me long enough to kill your friends."

He rushes at me and I block him, spinning around on my heels. He recovers fast, lashing out with a strike into my stomach. I double over, the air knocked from my body. His fingers clasp around my neck and he lifts me up like I weigh no more than a feather.

"You should've saved me. You should've loved me as much as I loved you."

I shut my eyes and let the power out. Let it mark my skin in gold and black, let the darkness leave the tips of my fingers and seep into his skin. He drops me, scrambling back.

But I don't stop, I can't. I let my power reach out at him, encircling him. He fights me off, forming and reforming from dust to solid, yet it's not enough. He's weak.

I lift him up with the darkness and hold him above me.

I'm deciding how to destroy him when the battlefield erupts in cheers. I suspend Ozvios there and watch as the Ilori—no, the labmades—turn on the true Ilori in the beating sun.

Suddenly, the true Ilori are outnumbered. Overpowered by their own creations. Ozvios crumbles above me. Weakness spreads through him. He's so close now.

I glance up at him. "Your war is nearly over."

Ozvios smiles down at me, gloating as if his body isn't beginning to disintegrate. "Not yet." The sky fills with ships shooting and blasting each other. An Andarran ship zooms past. Our ship, followed by three Ilori pods firing at it.

"Wesley!"

CHAPTER THIRTY-ONE

Wesley

I've got three Ilori on my rear, and though I've shot down a fair share, they won't quit. As ships peel off in the distance, turning around and attacking their own, momentary relief washes over me. Rubin, Morris, and Ellie must have been successful.

Unfortunately, there are still too many true Ilori here. Down below they may lose, but up here... They command the skies. And it seems, as I stare out the window, that I'm alone. Every squeeze of the trigger sets my heart pounding and my stomach churning. All my life, I never contributed to the violence that plagues our universe, and here I am, dog-fighting against true Ilori, preventing them from shooting down on the armies below.

After firing two shots, I grip the thrusters hard and swoop

to the side, flying through the explosions around me. Briefly, I'm surrounded by fire. On the other side of it, more ships drop down into view.

I let out a groan. Where's everyone else? "Comms, I'm getting heavy fire. Is anyone there?"

"We're a bit preoccupied! IpS1L II has launched their attacks—"

My brain short-circuits at the thought. Rubin. I flip the thrusters and turn around fast, putting my back to the Ilori fly-fighters. I have to get back up there. How are they going to get off the mothership? What if they got caught? What if...

I'm shooting faster than my ship can handle for very long, and metal starts to shred around me. I don't care. I'm on the cusp of atmo when my ship rocks from the back.

The dash lights up. "Missile incoming."

I swerve, hitting my tab for a flare, but I'm too late. There's no ejection button, and if there were, I'd die out in atmo anyway. The missile hits, tearing off the end of my skipper. This is it. Fire erupts around me. The sirens go from squealing to eerily silent. The bottom falls out beneath me and the dash sparks and crackles.

I scream as smoke trails up my nose. Hacking coughs seize me as I try to disengage the safety belt holding me in. But I'm trapped. Everything's breaking and broken. If I don't explode in this inferno, I'll crash into Earth in a blaze of glory.

The smoke burns my eyes and my chest hurts. This is it now. My fate plays out just like the vision.

I close my eyes and try to preserve the last few moments I can.

A flash of Rubin lights up my mind. Our kiss. His laughter. Our strange, dangerous adventure together. I wish I could have known him better. I wish I could have gone on that terrible tour around the universe and been introduced as his boyfriend.

I think of Zaira. I think of her small smiles and big losses and the secret longing that rolled off her in waves. I think of her hugs and power. How she called us family with her entire heart. I wish I had more time to help her, to be the friend she needs.

And then I remember racing after Allister as we followed the Jadu upstream in our backyard. He tells me I'm the best little brother he could've asked for. He tells me he loves me. I tell him I love him too. Because he's my best friend. Because he's kind and tucks me in at night.

How did I forget all of this until now? Why did I forget?

Maybe it is easier to forget love that is lost when you're hurting.

I wish I had spent more time with him. I wish I had gotten to know him.

My wishes mean nothing as sparks grow and fire licks my skin. I scream, the pain white-hot. My fingers latch onto the necklace around my neck, the Citlali star. It wasn't so lucky after all. I hold it firmly as the fire dances around me.

Any moment now. Please, any moment now.

CHAPTER THIRTY-TWO

Zaira

I bolt upward and onward after Wesley's ship. And I know I should not have let Ozvios go. That I should have found Allister. But I have to be here now. I can't let anything happen to my friend, my family. Everything he has done... He can't die. He can't.

I can't lose him.

Despite how hard I try, how fast I fly, it's not enough. The ship's hit and the back sweeps out, nearly striking me. I bolt past the debris, reaching for him as the skipper plummets.

I can't feel him, don't feel any life at all. He's...gone.

There's a sudden burst of light but no sound or explosion, and for a moment, it's all shredded metal and fire and something else...something strange. I try to dart inside what remains of the ship to somehow bring him back...but fire and sparks and noise pierce the air all around me. I open my throat to sing a song of movement, to help me, to save him, to find him. Only the smoke crawls up my throat.

"Wesley," is all I can croak. "Where…are you?" I finally push my way inside through all the pressure and find him… different.

He's surrounded in…in…stardust. In a cocoon of nothing and everything.

He's alive. He's okay. I feel like I can finally breathe again when my eye catches on the shining star in the center of his palm. Citlali. It saved him—is saving him. He looks at me and I smile even as the fire singes my flesh. Wesley's going to be okay. He's—

There's a series of sparks and the fire grows hotter, climbing up the walls. There's a cacophony of noise as the metal creaks and groans. The ship begins to burst apart, and I barely register the floor dropping out beneath me when Wesley rushes forward.

With Citlali in his grasp, he yanks me into his arms before pushing us off the ship into the sky.

THE RUBIN RIMA PODCAST

Broadcasting from a stolen Ilori pod

RR: We're on our way to Earth after some real drama, which I'll tell you later! Codrec, if you're listening, my boyfriend, Wesley, got me here on time. And helped us win the war. Already, the forces on the ground are saying the fighting has stopped. The true Ilori have surrendered. In the sky, the true Ilori fly-fighters have gone back into the mothership...where we're being told—hold on, we're being hailed. I'm recording this.

Unknown: Emperor 1lv and his son were found dead in their throne room, their throats slit. Believed to have been murdered by...M0Rr1S 1lv and human Ellie Baker. We would like to broadcast that the Ilori will surrender completely, will go home to Ilor and await their trial for colonization and egregious crimes against species. You will not have any more fight with us.

RR: Cool, cool, cool. Who am I speaking to?

Unknown: This is Orsa, we met on the ship. I'm the newly appointed Commander and Leader of the Ilori people.

RR: Okay, Orsa. But I have to say, Morris and Ellie are sitting next to me right now. And as you know, when we left the throne room, the Emperor and son were alive. We have recordings to prove—

Orsa: What matters is that the Emperor is dead and our people are free. To the colonies listening, to the people who have lost loved ones for a war they were forced to fight—I am here. I and my new government will help you transition to your own autonomy. Your ties will be severed from us, but we owe you a great deal to establish your independence. A debt we are willing and are desiring to pay. With Il-0CoM broken, true Ilori have become weak, their life energy depleted. Their immortality is no longer secure. It is up to us—labmades—to help ensure a new world of unity and peace.

RR: I mean, you promise, babe? Because no doubt, there are a lot of people listening who won't believe you.

Orsa: I cannot change the past. I do believe we will be able to change the present and future for the better. We labmades were created to serve our true Ilori masters, now *we* will lead them. Punish them if we must. We will not repeat their mistakes. We cannot. They, like us, were conditioned to believe emotions are unnecessary. Yet, we have learned that there is power in feeling. That feeling is what will make us better, more compassionate, and a more powerful ally to a united universe going forward.

RR: Well, thank you for joining us, Orsa. I hope we speak again soon.

Orsa: Thank you. *(disconnects)*

Ellie: She killed them.

Morris: Yes. That is correct. She always wanted power and now she has it.

RR: But will she do the right thing with it?

Morris: Yes. She will. She was made to lead.

Ellie: She's still evil. I mean she did try to kill me and my family and almost succeeded.

Morris: She learned from that. With Il-0CoM gone, she's her own person now. Not someone I would ever befriend or love, but someone I could come to respect one day.

Ellie: You believe in the good in people.

Morris: I have hope, Ellie.

RR: And hope has paid off right now. The war against the Ilori is over. I can't wait to get back down there. Find my—

Ship AI: Incoming message from Earth to all Andarran craft.

RR: Take it. What's going on?

Unknown: This is Allister Daniels. My brother, Wesley, is missing. We can't account for his ship anywhere. I'm sending the ship's code. Please help me find him. Please.

RR: Where was he last seen? Anyone? Someone help me

find him. Where's Zaira? Someone help me get in touch with her. She'll find him. She's... We can't... *(voice cracks)*. If anything happened to him... It's my fault. I made him come here. I made him bring me. I... He's such a beautiful soul. I... *(muffled)*.

CHAPTER THIRTY-THREE

Wesley

"Zaira?" Her name leaves my lips in a yelp. I open my eyes, and all around me is gold. Shimmering and concentrated. Bright.

Zaira.

I slowly move my arms, feeling for a source of pain because surely I'm in pain, right? I died, didn't I? Wait, am I dead and that's why things are so weird? Why can't I remember?

"We were always supposed to meet." Her voice is soft, and I can't tell if she said it aloud or in my mind. "I was always meant to give you Citlali."

I feel her around me. I feel her emotions. There's wonder... She's wondering and amazed. She's scared too. Scared and...in pain.

"Zaira." I reach out to her though she's here and not here. Not in a body. She's stardust circling around me. And now that I notice, I don't really know where I am. "What happened? You saved me?"

She laughs. "You saved yourself."

I attempt to shake my head but my limbs feel stiff. "I don't understand."

"Citlali. There was an explosion, but you freed Citlali. The fallen star in the necklace. It wrapped around you and protected you in its orbit. The Jadu always have a plan. And you were always part of it." She holds me tight, if that's even possible. I can't really understand what I see or feel when she's stardust.

"Where are we?" It's all fire and light and gold that I can't see beyond.

"We're falling over Earth. Citlali fizzled out but I have you now. We're going to be okay. I'm going to protect you." There's a smile in her tone.

I don't understand. Maybe I won't for a while. "You're in pain, I can feel it."

"My physical form got burned in the explosion, but I'll be fine." Her stardust moves around me in circles. Shielding me. "And somewhere below, Ozvios is fading into nothing."

"Zaira…" My voice cracks. "I'm scared."

"There's nothing to fear anymore. You are alive and perfect, Wesley. You did everything you needed to do. Now all you have to do is exist. We get to exist and that's enough. You and me, and Rubin too…" She laughs again, and something inside me rejoices. "We just saved the universe."

Lightness spreads through my heart. "We did, didn't we?"

"A space podcaster, a god who was never a god, and a loner who was never really alone."

I smile in this bubble she has formed around me as we fall to the world below. This feels right. Feels warm. It feels like love. "What do we do now?"

"We go to Earth and we help them. We travel the universe and we help them too…if we want." She exhales slowly. "We live and we love and we find our happiness because we deserve to, okay? And I think there's a few people who can't wait to do it with us."

"Yes," I say as the air cools around us and the metal that was once our ship melts away into nothing. "Let's do it all."

CHAPTER THIRTY-FOUR

Zaira

Ozvios faded right where I left him. Where once was stardust is now ash. I could have saved him, but he killed entire worlds. Though I'm not sure how he destroyed Mal Ares, as weak as he was, I have to believe he did. He wanted to destroy everything just to exist and be powerful. To rule over nothing.

I bend down, wincing as my knees, still a little burned, shoot pain through my body. But the pain is temporary. I sift through the remaining ashes and let them run through my fingers and out into the wind. He can't hurt us—or anyone—anymore.

He's gone.

"You know, we should probably get you back to the house, tend to your wounds and all that." Allister crouches down beside me and I peek over at him, my heart flipping.

I try to keep my tone casual as I look over his bloodstained shirt and ripped pants. "How did you survive in the middle of battle?"

"I'm not ashamed to admit that I did some really ridiculous things out there." He shrugs. "I gave a rousing speech about the horrors of war. No one listened. I started singing a song, and that proved a bit more useful. By then Il-0CoM broke and that was it."

"I'm sorry I left you." I pat his arm, ignoring the way my singed skin stings. "I'm so happy you're okay."

"Promise not to do it again?" He smiles over at me, and gently puts his hand on mine.

I turn away, my face heating, which thankfully doesn't make my body hurt worse. "We'll see."

"Oh, Zaira, I'm going to break down those walls of yours. You're stuck with me. Think of all the beautiful music we'll make. You, with the songs of the universe in your mind, and me…a superstar with multiple platinum albums." He laughs and I find myself chuckling with him. "That sound is my favorite. You can't read emotions like me, but here." He carefully moves my hand to his heart. It races beneath my palm.

My smile dims and I stare at him. "I've never liked anyone before. Never felt desire before."

"Do you like me now?" He keeps a steady hold of my hand.

The corners of my lips lift. "I do."

"Maybe all that other stuff will come later once we get to know each other. I mean, we both are going to live forever. We've got time."

"Forever." Nerves flutter in the pit of my stomach. "Let's go bother your brother and his boyfriend."

"What about your grandmother—my aunt? Should we hold a memorial for her passing? I know I didn't know her like you, but I think…"

His voice drifts off as I sweep a glance up at the stars. Their only purpose is to exist and let life bloom within them. I see through those worlds, past the stardust inside them, through black holes and new suns and everything in between. My gaze lands on Andarra, the watery world where the Jadu chose to call home. Made by Indigo for them to rest and watch the universe without interfering.

I gasp when I see her in the water. Not just water. Stardust. Purple with yellow stripes. My favorite colors. A gem hangs from around her neck like Citlali had mine, only this one is dark and glittery. Mal Ares.

My voice cracks with realization. "Ozvios lied… He never killed her. He never even found her. He went to my home and found the same black hole we did. She made it…to save Mal Ares. To save the nightweavers. Just like she did with Citlali." My smile is genuine, my heart is full. They are preserved in time. I will never see them again…but I'll always be connected to them. They'll exist as long as they stay inside. As long as they're cared for. "We should visit her someday soon, together."

He helps me up and threads his fingers through mine. "I'd like that."

CHAPTER THIRTY-FIVE

Wesley

Blobby chucks a bone at me, his tongue lolling as he waits for me to throw it. The sun is setting here on Earth, and the sky is all kinds of vibrant colors. I'm warm and happy and beholden to a tiny tentacled creature I wanted nothing to do with and who I now might love. I toss the bone and he bounds after it on his many tentacles. Rubin leans against me, halfway asleep on the sand outside of Allister's home.

For a moment, all is quiet. All is right. A new vision from the future flashes in my mind and in it, I see me and Rubin. We're older, a little wiser in the eyes. We're laughing and I touch his cheek, running my palm along his jaw. My gaze catches on the silver band on my finger. He smiles at me. And before I can say anything, the future's gone and present Rubin lets out a long and gargled snore.

I throw a hand over my mouth to keep a giggle locked inside as I watch Blobby gather the courage to touch the water with a tentacle.

"How did you come across..." The name for Blobby's species completely misses my ears. "They are very precious creatures. Loyal. When they bond, they bond for life."

I look up at a labmade Ilori who stands stiffly beside me. Their hair is pulled into a tight bun on the top of their head and their blue eyes meet mine.

"By chance," I offer. "Who are you?"

"AvR0LA," they say. "Though most humans and Andarrans call me Avi. I'm unsure how I feel about the name, or this world. But I can feel, and that, I suppose, is all that matters."

Behind them, Ellie walks with two dark brown–skinned humans. Her parents, maybe? She runs toward the beach and the adults exchange a glance, following behind.

"Ellie," the father, I assume, says. "First one to the water wins."

The mother's speed picks up and they all run together. Ellie's purple hat flops off her head and lands in the sand. No one seems to notice. I smile. I wish I had had a family like that. One that loves and laughs with their full hearts. But then Rubin shifts against my shoulder, and I realize I already do. Rubin and Zaira and Allister will be with me till the end of our days. We found each other and won't let go.

"Humans aren't perfect," Avi says, watching Ellie and her parents. "In fact, they're fragile, mortal, and have no powers at all. And yet...there's something very likeable about them. Don't you think?" They don't wait for my answer, instead walking off, holding a book against their chest.

"Weird," I say aloud to myself.

Later, after spending time with the Monchuran royals and everyone has left to return to their own planets and homes, I tread down the long gilded hallways, searching for Zaira and Rubin. I stumble across several encased albums on the walls, pictures of The Starry Eyed at various events and concerts, and there…in one little corner beside a gold door is a picture of me and Allister. We were children. It was the last time we saw each other. I was seven and he was eight. He was smiling down at me, his arm wrapped around my shoulders since he was already taller, while I was pouting at the camera. My mother wanted to take a picture to commemorate Allister preparing to leave for Earth, and she ordered me to get out of the frame. Allister protested. She took it anyway, just to appease him. And he must've kept it. Tears prickle the edge of my eyes and I step back, just as laughter sounds nearby.

I bat the tears away and open the gold door, finding Rubin and Zaira within. They're both in capes and jumpsuits that I can only suspect they took from Allister's closet. So much glitter and far too much pizzazz. It suits them both. My strange little family.

"So," I say, leaning in the doorway as they regard themselves in an oversized mirror. "We saved the universe, huh?"

"Who is *we*?" Zaira says with a big smile.

"Babes, I'm proud of us." Rubin's locs hang beside his head, and I nearly stop breathing at the beauty of him. "I mean, I was a celebrity before, but now…we're all famous. What can we do next to top this, you know? Write books or—"

"This," Zaira says, her skin lighting up gold, punctuated by thick swirly black constellations. The spaces between worlds have filled in with new planets like Earth and the Outerims. Her body is a map of the universe as it is, not as it has been. She shines as brilliantly as the stars. She is spectacular, otherworldly. She catches my awed gaze and her face beams. "When I let go of the anger and think about love—the places I love, the people I love—and I hold that feeling tight and let it spread through me, this happens." She glows but her eyes never leave mine. "You should do it too."

"Why? I'm not going to shine like you." I chuckle, and it feels so good.

"Yes, you do," Zaira says softly. "Just in a different way."

Rubin sighs when he sees Allister in the hallway behind me. "Hey, quick question, did you call your band The Starry Eyed because of her?" He tilts his head to Zaira. "Because it's always been her with her gold constellations in your eyes? Is she your inspiration? Inquiring minds want to know."

Allister's cheeks redden. "I will neither confirm nor deny."

Rubin's mouth drops open. "He named a band after you! Honey, if that's not romance, I don't know what is."

Zaira's head falls briefly till she looks past me to Allister. Her smile is the biggest and brightest I've ever seen.

"Come on, Rubin." I wave him over. "Let's go find a new story for you to tell." I loop his arm through mine and we saunter off very slowly, just as Allister passes by us. Out of the corner of my eye, I see him lean into her and she grins up at him.

I want to cheer and celebrate two people I love falling in love. But I won't ruin their moment. Zaira deserves this and every happiness she finds. When I met her, she was enraged, ready to do anything to save her world and people. Ready to write off the universe that had abandoned them. She was all sharp edges, prepared to battle until her last breath.

I hope, now, she'll allow herself to feel and to be felt, to love and be loved. She still lost her world—or the ability to visit it anymore—and she will grieve that and the nightweavers for the rest of her very long life, but I'll be there with her. So will Rubin and Allister. And everyone we have yet to meet who will love her as much as we do. She may not be a god, but we're all in awe of the way she shines bright.

We close the door behind us and Rubin squeezes my arm. "The next story should be about love, I've decided. It's gotta have twists and turns. And kisses. A lot of kisses."

I laugh, letting my head lean against his shoulder. "I think I know just the one."

★ ★ ★ ★ ★

ACKNOWLEDGMENTS

Creating new worlds and then somehow managing to put those worlds down on a page is difficult work, but thankfully, I had the very best help. So here goes!

THANK YOU to:

The reader holding this book. Thank you for taking a chance on me and my stories. It's been a wild, unpredictable ride, and I can't thank you enough for sticking with me. Please don't go anywhere. I've still got more stories to share with you!

My incredible editor, Claire Stetzer. Your notes, feedback, and organization saved me and saved this book. This story is the strongest it could be because of you. Thank you, it's been such a pleasure, and I hope we get more chances to work together in the future!

The entire Inkyard Press team! You all are the best! Bess Brasswell; Randy Chan; Pamela Osti; Brittany Mitchell; Laura Gianino; Justine Sha; Dana Francoeur; and Connolly Bottom.

Every success is due to your support, and I can't thank you enough for making this third book a reality. Also very huge swirly stars thank you to Gigi Lau and Kaitlin June Edwards, who created the most fabulous cover. I am so fortunate for your artistry and vision, and I'm going to stare at these books for the rest of my life.

Natalie Lakosil, thank you for working with me and believing in me. Thanks for getting these quirky stories in the world.

Tracy Badua, we've worked together for many years now. You've been with me in the margins, helping me, showing me the way, and making sure I was telling the best story possible. I wouldn't be here without you, and I'm so incredibly proud of you and your books. And heyyyyy, coauthor!

Rachel Somer, Tamara Mataya, Sheena Boekweg, Tori Bovalino, and Leanne Schwartz, who offered me their time into the late and early hours, who have listened and helped me hone my craft. Thank you all, I wouldn't be here without you.

To the best support group out there: Bethany C. Morrow, Jess Sutanto, J. Elle, Tori Bovalino, Anika Wegner, Kendell Penington, Eric Smith, Laura Namey, Mara Rutherford, and Adiba Jaigirdar. You've all spent an extraordinary amount of time listening to me, giving me advice, answering my questions, and I appreciate it. I appreciate you and your friendship.

My sci-fi writer friends, Rebecca Coffindaffer and Beth Revis (both of whom helped me find my way in this story early on, and pushed me when I doubted myself), Andrea Tang, Lora Beth Johnson, Meg Long, and Claire Winn. You all are AWESOME.

My sisterpants™, Nicole Redd-McIntosh. You light up the

world with your creations. I'll always be awed and inspired by you. And I'll always want your cookbook recommendations!

RAPID ROUND. Saundra Mitchell, the Hirt Familie, Carmen of Tomes and Textiles, Nora Shalaway Carpenter, Rocky Callen, Aiden Thomas, Melanin in YA, Loyalty Bookstores, Kalynn Bayron, One More Page Books, Rosiee Thor, Lili (USOM), Uwe Stender, Cassandra Newbould, Mike Lasagna, Jordan Ifueko, Darrah Stranahan, and Erin O'Neill Jones for the most beautiful art. My library homes: Brooklyn Public Library, West Warwick Public Library, and Milford Town Library.

To Christoph and Liv. Who let me write through dinner, ate pizza once a week instead of my elaborate menus, who let me read this aloud and offered thoughts. You are the best family I could have asked for, and everyday I'm excited that I share my life with the both of you. And Liv, it's an honor to be your mom.

To librarians, readers, teachers, book bloggers, BookTokers, bookstagrammers, reviewers, the entire book community— the only reason I get to keep writing stories is because of you. You've boosted my work, you've shouted from the rooftops, you left reviews, and sent me messages. You might not know this, but whenever I questioned whether I was good enough, your kind words gave me the strength to keep going. Thank you all.

And lastly, to the teens who found this book and decided to give it a chance, I wrote this for you.